The Line of the Sun

The Line of the Sun

A Novel by
Judith Ortiz Cofer

THE UNIVERSITY OF GEORGIA PRESS
ATHENS AND LONDON

© 1989 by Judith Ortiz Cofer
Published by the University of Georgia Press
Athens, Georgia 30602
All rights reserved

Designed by Sandra Strother Hudson
Set in Linotron 202 Walbaum
with typositor Corvinus Medium display
The paper in this book meets the guidelines
for permanence and durability of the Committee on
Production Guidelines for Book Longevity of the
Council on Library Resources.

Printed in the United States of America

93 92 91 90 89   5 4 3 2 1

Library of Congress Cataloging in Publication Data

Ortiz Cofer, Judith, date.
The line of the sun : a novel / by Judith Ortiz Cofer.
p.   cm.
ISBN 0-8203-1106-5 (alk. paper)
I. Title.
PS3565.R7737L56 1989
813'.54—dc 19   88-22042
CIP

British Library Cataloging in Publication Data available

To John and Tanya

Acknowledgments

MANY PEOPLE SHARED their memories, their family stories, and their factual knowledge with me during the years I worked on this book. I thank them all, especially my husband, John Cofer, for his interest in the story, and for typing it chapter by chapter until it was told. I am grateful to Betty Jean Craige, who read the manuscript in progress for accuracy in the use of both my languages, and whose enthusiasm for the work never flagged. I also wish to thank Stanley Lindberg, for giving a stack of pages a "red-pencil read" that confirmed it as a novel; and Edna Acosta-Belén, who answered my questions on matters of Puerto Rican culture and literature. To Berenice Hoffman and Liz Makowski, my agent and editor, respectively, to Malcolm Call and all the talented people at the University of Georgia Press who worked to see the novel in print, my gratitude, always.

The Line of the Sun

Chapter One

THEY SAY Guzmán had been a difficult pregnancy for Mamá Cielo, who had little patience for the bouncing ball in her belly. She claimed the monkey was climbing her ribs, that she felt fingers grabbing her bladder and squeezing, so that she had to stop attending mass for the shame of urine trickling down her legs. She took to slapping her abdomen smartly as if she were killing a pesky fly. Her meek husband, Papá Pepe, worried about the unborn child but did not dare to interfere. During her pregnancies Mamá Cielo always became fiercely self-absorbed, not even letting him sleep in the same bed with her.

Many years later, after Guzmán disappeared into the New York City subway system, Papá Pepe dared to say at the dinner table that it was his wife's prenatal violence that had made Guzmán the runaway he would always be. For that remark Papá was banished permanently from her life. From that day on Mamá Cielo would never address the old man directly; instead she talked to him through an intermediary. "Ask your grandfather if he wants to eat now," she would command. "Go tell your *abuelo* that it's time for his medicine." Even if he was in the same room with her she never spoke to or touched him again.

Guzmán became her obsession—and Mamá Cielo did not spare the rod. Guzmán's sister, my mother, has scars

1

on her knees from one of her mother's unique methods of punishment. For talking with a boy in town while on an unescorted errand, the twelve-year-old girl had been made to kneel on a tin grater for an hour. She said she had difficulty washing the dry blood off it in time to grate the green bananas for making *pasteles* that night. She also remembers that when she awoke the next morning her legs were sticky with the aloe Mamá grew in her kitchen.

But Guzmán did not seem to feel pain. He had to be walked to first grade every day or he would wander off to the river, where he would catch tadpoles in the tin cup his mother had given him for milk at school; worse, he would go into people's houses uninvited, usually old or crazy people who gave him candy and money. Franco El Loco's room was one of Guzmán's favorite places. An old couple had given Franco the cellar of their house to live in after his "accident." Franco had been a normal man, a successful undertaker, until he got part of his spinal cord severed by a jealous man's machete at a dance. He was now a seventy-five-degree angle who apparently lived only to collect bright objects with which to fill his dark hovel. On the dirt walls were embedded hundreds of pieces of glass from bottles in a mosaic Guzmán found fascinating. Franco, who spoke only in mutters to himself, allowed the boy to dig the pieces out with a spoon and rearrange them by the light of a candle.

They say Guzmán's frantic childhood kept the household in fear both for the skinny, curly-headed child and for Mamá Cielo's sanity. She would swing from anguish over his recklessness to an amazonian fury that often culminated in beatings, after which she mortified herself with all-night vigils at his bedside. Once—after the belt, the grater, the hysterical threats had had no effect—she stripped him naked and hid his clothes. She locked him in

2

the house and went to sit with a sick neighbor. When she returned, she found the kitchen window wide open. Guzmán had disappeared. The search began, by now almost a rite in which all able-bodied neighbors participated. Of course they looked first in his usual haunts, but the old people had not seen him, the crazy ones were not hiding him. Night came and Mamá Cielo's hysteria rose to her throat in waves of nausea. Women came to tend her. It was, they say, like a funeral and a birth at once, with Mamá Cielo holding her great belly distended by her last pregnancy and wailing for her *niño del diablo:* Guzmán the demon child.

Papá Pepe kept vigil over his Bible. He was a spiritist in contact with various benevolent entities, and he prayed now, hands clenched over the white linen of his altar. He fell into a deep sleep and dreamt that Guzmán was digging a hole in a garden of fruit trees with a tiny gold shovel. When he awoke he said to his wife, "La Granja." Then they knew where to look.

The high school had begun an experimental farm whose territory extended to a few yards from Mamá's house. It was surrounded with barbed wire. Bananas, papayas, breadfruit, and other fruits and vegetables were grown and tended by the students. There were also animals—some milk cows, horses, and a famous mean-tempered sow. She weighed over two hundred pounds and had wantonly killed three of her litters.

Guzmán had eaten green bananas, and when they found him, he was curled into a dirty brown ball, like a fetus, in a corner of the mare's stable. Mud was caked in his hair and face, and he had vomited all over himself. In his arms he held a runty piglet. Mamá Cielo had to be restrained. The men washed the boy with buckets of water but could not pry the half-dead animal from his arms. Guzmán only repeated that its mother did not want it, that she would lie on it and kill it if they put the piglet back in the pen. It was Papá Pepe who whispered to Guzmán that he could keep the pig, that he would buy it for him. They say Guzmán soon forgot about the animal, and it was Mamá Cielo who sent a tin around the neighborhood for slop to feed it. In time the runt grew to be as large as its mother and just as mean.

To make a little extra money during the hard years, Mamá Cielo sold hot lunches to the men working in the cane fields and at the *Central,* the sugar refinery just outside town. In the mornings, on their way to work, the men dropped off their stacked tin lunchpots, into which she would pile rice and red beans topped with fried plantains or sometimes seasoned codfish. She could not deliver them all herself, so she had her oldest son help her. This was Carmelo, a slow-moving, melancholy sixteen-year-old who had—she despaired—inherited her husband's irritating love of books and solitude. Until he was blown into a thousand pieces over the Korean soil years later, Mamá Cielo tried in vain to build a fire under his plodding feet, to stir his blood with ambition. In secret, though, she admired his fine long hands, so often caught at the forbidden pleasures of strumming his father's guitar or going through the books Papá Pepe kept in a painter's shed behind the house. The thick black hair that grew into a widow's peak Carmelo had inherited from her. He was too handsome, really, cursed with the light olive skin of his father's family, skin that would keep him from doing a man's work in a cane field. Mamá Cielo had asked her son to spend his two hours of school recess delivering lunches to the cutters, and Carmelo agreed reluctantly. Those were his hours to be alone, to find a grove behind the school and dream or sleep, but it did not occur to him to say no to his mother.

4

It was Guzmán who came up with the solution. On the way to the fields one day, Carmelo had stopped to rest a little under a mango tree whose branches were so low and thick that they practically formed a little hut. There he pulled out his copy of Luis Llorens Torres's poetry and began to read the poem about Puerto Rico, "The Ugly Duckling," in which the poet called the Island the "blue swan of the Hispanic race." He had just started to read when he heard laughter beyond the tall reeds, and a familiar voice.

Carmelo walked silently to the edge of the bushes and parted them to look. To his astonishment, there was little Guzmán with a friend—both naked, sitting on their clothes Indian-style, each pointing to the other's body and giggling. The little girl was fascinating, beautiful and repulsive at the same time: Angélica, the hunchback, the poor crippled daughter of the town's most notorious whore. The child did not go to school and was very seldom seen in town. They said her mother had tried to kill herself by swallowing bleach when she was pregnant. Angélica's skin was a milky white, and the lump on her back, half as large as her body, stretched her skin like a drumhead. It was as if the blond girl were a species of snail carrying her home on her back, Carmelo thought.

"Guzmán!" Carmelo called out, pushing through the rushes. The girl scurried off on all fours, dragging her bundle of clothes behind her. Guzmán stretched up and grabbed his brother's neck, wrapping his skinny brown legs around the older boy's waist. The brothers had become close friends over the years as Carmelo fell more and more into the role of mediator between his mother's rages and his brother's propensity for trouble. Carmelo tried to pry the naked boy from his chest. "Get off of me, Guzmán. You have some explaining to do. Put your clothes on, you nasty savage." Guzmán giggled and jumped down.

5

"You won't tell her?" he said, not pleading. "We were just playing."

"You know very well that what you were doing is a sin, Guzmán. If Mamá found out she would whip you with her belt. How did you get that poor girl to come out here, anyway?" Carmelo helped the boy with the buttons of his white school shirt, now limp from sweat and dirt. He felt moved by the bony chest heaving under his hands. Guzmán's asthma was getting worse, to the point where Mamá had moved his cot to her room so she could listen to his breathing. Guzmán kept stealing away during the night to sleep with Carmelo, wrapped around him like a hyperventilating monkey.

"She's my friend. She doesn't go to school. Her mamá sleeps all day. She doesn't have anyone to play with," he said, his speech as fast as his breathing.

"Don't bring her out here any more." Carmelo knew the boy would listen to him. For years he had tried to explain to Mamá that beatings did not affect Guzmán, who forgot pain quicker than any other human being, child or adult. But Guzmán reacted to short simple commands if they made sense to him; and if they didn't violate his peculiar code of loyalty to his friends, he would obey.

"You won't tell her?"

Guzmán, Carmelo knew, was not afraid of the beating Mamá would surely give him, but of the convulsion of anger that would seize her, the silence and self-recrimination that would follow. It was hateful to all the children to watch their mother go through this familiar pattern of violence and guilt. Carmelo was amazed that even at his age Guzmán already understood this.

"I won't tell her." Carmelo drew his comb out of his pants pocket and made a few attempts at smoothing the jumble of tight curls on Guzmán's head. "Hurry to school now, boy."

"I'm not going today." Guzmán crept through the rushes back to the mango tree.

"Wait. What do you mean you're not going to school? You can't just stay out and play all day. You're already in trouble, remember? I may just change my mind and tell Mamá after all." Carmelo grabbed his brother's wrist and turned him around to face him.

"You won't tell her. You know why? I've gone to classes all week. Every other Friday, I fish." The brown eyes looking up at him were so serious, the voice so earnest, Carmelo felt like laughing. Guzmán was talking like a hardworking man justifying a day of leisure, instead of an eleven-year-old fifth grader. Suddenly both boys heard a loud barking. Two scraggly dogs were fighting over the food they had tracked to the wheelbarrow where Carmelo had left it at the mango tree. "Oh, my God. The cutters' lunches. I forgot all about them."

"Let me help you deliver them, Carmelo. I'll help you." Guzmán ran to the wheelbarrow and began to push it toward the dirt road. It was heavy with lunch pots and the muscles in his arms and neck stood out like thick wires, but he would not relinquish his hold. When the two boys got to the field, the men were already sitting in the improvised shelter they made by hanging their shirts from sticks hammered into the ground. They took to Guzmán right away. They liked the way he ran back and forth, filling their coffee cups from a thermos jar, and the way he lit their cigarettes deftly, like a miniature bartender. He listened intently to their jokes and laughed hard and loud as though he understood the sexual innuendoes and macho boasting.

7

More and more, Guzmán took over the job over Carmelo's protests. Seeing how much the boy enjoyed himself, the older boy allowed himself a break to read under the mango tree. Soon he became accustomed to the new routine and let his capable little brother deliver all the lunches while he read the forbidden books of poems, and dreamed.

Because Guzmán's skin was getting darker, and because when she felt the palms of his hands at night they were rough as old shoe leather, Mamá Cielo knew that her son was doing something she should know more about. Carmelo's hands had not become toughened or stained by work. When he held his book up to his face to read at night, she could see the perfect roundness of his nails, clean and smooth as those of a kept woman or a lazy man. From the boys' hushed conversations at night, when they thought she was asleep, Mamá Cielo suspected that whatever was going on involved them both.

So one day, after Carmelo had come home at noon for the wheelbarrow of lunches, she took the black umbrella to protect her from the sun and followed him at a distance. She watched her older son maneuver the wheelbarrow off the dirt road and into the mango-tree grove. There, sitting like a sultan's son with his white school shirt wrapped around his head, turban fashion, was Guzmán. He was gulping down an Old Colony grape soda. She watched Carmelo park the wheelbarrow under the tree: by squatting behind a clump of bamboo Mamá had a good view of the boys not twenty feet away. Guzmán threw the empty bottle in a wide arc over his head. It landed at Mamá's feet, where it shattered into purple fragments. She heard Carmelo say to Guzmán:

"I've told you not to do that, boy. You'll be the one to step on the glass, you or one of your crazy friends."

8

"I don't meet anyone here any more, Melo, it's our secret place, right?" Guzmán was apparently in a hurry to get away from his brother. He grabbed the handles of the wheelbarrow and began to push it with a great effort to the dirt road. Carmelo grabbed his elbow.

"Let go, man, the cutters are waiting. Let me go." Guzmán tried to wriggle out of his brother's grasp.

"I just want to give you your share of the money, boy," Carmelo said, digging into his pants pocket. "If you want it, that is." He held two quarters in his fingertips just out of Guzmán's reach: "But this first," he said, undoing Guzmán's head wrap. "You are going to get sun stroke if you don't protect yourself."

"Lay off, will you?" Guzmán made a pretense of trying to get away from his brother, but finally held still while Carmelo buttoned his shirt and tucked it into his khaki shorts.

"You're as bad as Mamá," Guzmán giggled as Carmelo spit into a handkerchief and wiped the purple mustache off Guzmán's upper lip.

"She's been acting peculiar lately," Carmelo said. "If she finds out that I'm letting you do my work, she'll beat us both with a broomstick, or worse. You know, Guzmán, it might be best if I took over again."

"No, man, please. What about your books? I'm doing a good job, aren't I?" Guzmán was bouncing from one foot to the other now, as he did when he was excited.

"Mamá won't find out, Carmelo, I swear. I'll even go to school every day." Guzmán was crying now. Mamá's legs had begun to cramp, so she stood up shakily and leaned on a nearby stump. She saw the two boys embrace. From the same belly, and as different as a cloud and mud puddle. She saw Carmelo, tall and skinny as a bamboo shoot, bend down to place his pale cheek against Guzmán's fuzzy head. Then Guzmán squirmed away and once again grabbed the handles of his lunch wagon. Carmelo dropped the coins into the younger boy's pocket. Mamá watched her oldest son spread a paper bag carefully under the shade of the mango tree. He then stretched out, placing his head on a rounded stump that was part of the ancient tree's roots, and, crossing his arms over his face, he turned over and closed his eyes. Mamá walked toward the dirt road. Ahead she saw the little cloud of dust being raised by Guzmán and his wheelbarrow; opening up her umbrella, Mamá Cielo prepared to follow him to the fields. She kept to the edge of the road and walked behind her son in the sweltering noonday sun. Sweat poured down her face and arms as she held her black umbrella above her head. Guzmán walked down the middle of the dirt road. A couple of times he stopped and punched out at his shadow like a boxer to stretch his muscles. A scraggly white dog came out of a thick section of cane and sniffed at the boy's hands. Guzmán said something to him, and the dog fell back a few feet and followed him.

When they were very close to the field the cutters were clearing, Mamá Cielo went around the quadrant and after depositing her shoes and umbrella by the side of the road, walked deep into the canes, stopping where the cutters had left off before their break. Behind some tall cane stalks she squatted. She could hear the group of men talking and laughing. Guzmán was greeted with shouts of welcome and affectionate pats on the shoulder and head. One of the men mentioned the name Leticia, which made Mamá Cielo start, crushing some twigs under her feet. There was a pause but he continued.

"Behind the school building," a young man with a large black mustache and a red bandanna tied around his neck said.

"I don't believe it, *hombre*," said another. "Her mother is like a hawk. She'd never let her out by herself."

"It was last Saturday. She told her mamá she was going to confession. And she did, man. She poured all her little sins right into my ear."

Mamá later said that she had come close to fainting right there when she heard her goddaughter's name passed around like a ball in a nasty game these men were playing.

The men kidded their fortunate companion and asked him for details. Mamá Cielo was horrified to see Guzmán join in their laughter, though he seemed to be absorbed in handing out each man's lunch pail, serving them with such solicitude that it made Mamá Cielo's blood boil. She had to make an effort to keep silent and watch. After the men ate, they lit cigarettes and discussed their work. Someone named Jésus had passed out on the job that morning. When they removed his shirt to let him cool off, they had seen horrible open sores all over his back. They knew at once the sores had been caused from leaks in the cylinder that he had strapped on his shoulders to manually fumigate the field the previous day. The American had introduced this economical new system. A crop-duster airplane cost a bundle to run and it wasted chemicals over unused land. Manual dusting could be done by the men themselves in shifts, and nothing was wasted.

"He was driven to the clinic by Don Juan Santacruz himself, in the company truck," said one of the cutters.

"He'll probably dock Jésus' paycheck for the gas," said the one with the red bandanna.

At that moment Guzmán walked up to them to collect the cups. Several voices insisted that he sit down in the circle with them. A little man with a nervous twitch in one side of his face which made him look like a black rabbit

11

pulled a cigarette from the pack in his shirt pocket and stuck it in Guzmán's mouth.

"All right, my little man, it's time for another lesson." Guzmán giggled and tried to pry himself free from a pair of arms that held him down from behind.

"Hey, are you *macho*, or what? Sit still," the man behind him said.

Guzmán crossed his skinny legs Indian fashion under his body and laughingly accepted the cigarette. The Black Rabbit Man lit it with his own. The boy smoked it with expertise, holding it between index and middle finger and blowing out small clouds of white smoke.

With a great effort Mamá Cielo rose from her painful squat and walked back to the road. There she realized she had left her shoes and umbrella in an unlucky position: forming a top-heavy cross.

When Mamá Cielo passed her *comadre* Julia's house and did not call out a blessing, as was customary in greeting the godmother of one's children, the old woman left her pots on low flame and followed her distraught friend home. She sat silently rocking on the front porch until Mamá Cielo indicated she was ready to talk. Mamá Cielo came out of the kitchen with two steaming cups of *café con leche*, which spilled on her trembling hands. Without hesitation Doña Julia broke off the tip of an aloe plant growing in a coffee can on the porch and, helping Mamá set down the cups, took her hands and applied the gooey secretion on the irritated skin. The children were at school, Papá Pepe at work. The house was silent. Mamá Cielo finally spoke:

"Comadre, I don't know what to do about him. He's now leading the older one to laziness and trouble."

"Guzmán?" Doña Julia really did not have to ask. Many times she had had to comfort Mamá after one of the boy's escapades. She was Carmelo's godmother and thought of him as her own son. She had been blessed with three girls herself, all safely married now. She quickly crossed herself, so as not to tempt the Devil to her house.

"What has he done now? And how is Carmelo involved? Though I must say, Cielo, you should know he always tries to protect that rascal Guzmán, even at his own expense, so don't judge him too quickly."

"I don't know about that. Not this time, comadre, listen." Mamá Cielo told her friend everything she had seen that afternoon, under the mango tree and at the cane field.

Julia said, "It's not like Carmelo to shirk his responsibilities. Guzmán is obviously under the spell of those men's vices." Julia was many years Mamá Cielo's elder and a woman respected by the community for her wisdom as a mother and wife. She had outlived her alcoholic husband. She had endured a lifetime of scrimping to raise three girls, and all this without a man to help her. Mamá felt calmer listening to her comadre's husky voice. She knew that Julia would give her good advice in this difficult situation.

"Cielo, have you taken those boys to a spiritist?" The question surprised Mamá Cielo. Julia knew that Papá was a Mesa Blanca medium. Julia herself had consulted him many times about the untranquil spirit of her dead husband, who bothered her from time to time.

"Why should I take them anywhere, comadre? Pepe would know if something was wrong." But the older woman crossed her arms over her large abdomen and shook her head.

"Not necessarily. Don't you know that a doctor is not allowed to treat the members of his own family? It is possible that your husband can see ghosts but cannot see evil in his own home."

13

"You think that one of the boys needs help?" Mamá Cielo could not say the word she feared, *possessed*. Julia sat up and slapped her thighs with both palms to emphasize how certain she was.

"Guzmán is a wild boy. He gives you no rest. Now he has our gentle Carmelo disobeying you, and God knows what else. This is a *prueba* if I ever heard of one. You're being made to pay for something, woman. Can't you see that?" Both women crossed themselves.

"You may be right, comadre. I can't control that child. When I whip him, *I* feel the pain. I haven't felt well since I got pregnant with Guzmán. I need to do something now, before he kills both of us."

"There is a woman they call La Cabra. Have you heard of her?"

"She's a witch!"

"Nonsense. That's malicious gossip." Doña Julia had Mamá Cielo under the spell of her wisdom.

"I heard she sells charms." Mamá Cielo felt a chill course down her spine.

"Herbs and medicinal potions—to cure constipation and love sickness. Nothing out of the ordinary," said Doña Julia in her best no-nonsense manner. "Now, Cielo, are you going to listen to what I have to tell you, or are we going to believe evil rumors?"

In truth, Mamá Cielo at first resisted the idea that it was a troublesome spirit that made Guzmán such a cross for her to bear. After her talk with Doña Julia she felt calmer, as one does upon reaching a decision, but she made no immediate plans to take the boy to see La Cabra. The things that were said about the woman were too disturbing. She did not punish the boys—not at first, and then not in the usual way. Instead she took Carmelo aside and explained to him that she was giving up the lunch business

14

for a while. She said that it was too exhausting to cook all morning long. She had made arrangements to have Santita, the American's housekeeper, take over for a while. She was a widow and needed the money.

"But Mamá, we do too," Carmelo protested feebly. "And besides," he added, "I was getting used to it."

Mamá Cielo fought the urge to expose him as a liar. How easily her best child had slipped into deception. Guzmán truly must have the devil on his side. "Don't concern yourself with money right now, son. I am requesting more gloves from the factory in Mayagüez to cut and embroider. We'll manage. Just concentrate on finishing your schooling so you don't have to end up in the fields. You wouldn't last a month in the sun with your thin skin."

Carmelo told Guzmán the news that night while they were in bed. Mamá Cielo had made it a point to leave her bedroom door open, and the younger boy's sobs, though stifled by a pillow and his brother's arms, were plainly audible to her.

One afternoon Doña Julia brought Mamá Cielo a basket that contained several herbs she had gone to the country to pick; among these were *yerba buena,* geranium, wild garlic, vines of passion flower, and rue. She also brought a bottle of *agua florida,* flower-scented alcohol, in which she had already mixed some greenery. Since it was Tuesday—a good day for a spiritual cleansing of the house—and since the old woman had gone through so much trouble for her sake, Mamá Cielo and her comadre spent the morning fumigating the house with a concoction of the herbs which they boiled in a can over hot coals. This allowed the steam to penetrate all the corners of the house, which they had sealed by covering windows and doors with sheets tacked up. They poured the mixture on the floors and mopped them. This would drive off evil influ-

15

ences lingering in the house. Last they sprinkled themselves and the furniture with agua florida, which would
attract the protecting spirits. Mamá dusted the painting of
Our Lady of Miracles, her patroness, and placed it on her
night table, lighting one white and one blue votive candle
in her honor. After their labor, the women sat on the porch
for a cup of coffee.

Truly, doing something physical always made Mamá
Cielo feel better. She said, "Thank you, comadre, I can
think more clearly now."

"Don't thank me yet, daughter," the old woman replied.
"Your work is not finished."

"Doña Julia, I am most grateful for your help and your
concern, but it would upset my husband if I were to do
what you have suggested."

"What do men know about a woman's problems?" Doña
Julia had risen from her rocking chair abruptly and was
gathering the remnants of her offerings in her straw basket. She was offended. "May God forgive me for telling the
truth, but I am glad my Jaime is dead."

Scandalized, Mamá crossed herself. "Let us not speak
badly of the dead," she said softly, afraid of upsetting the
old woman even more.

"It is the truth—the man was possessed by a demon. If I
had known then what I do now, I would have done something about it and saved his soul. I've been told his spirit will
not find rest. I have spent a fortune in candles and
novenas."

Mamá felt that she had somehow let this suffering
woman down. Doña Julia was at the front door when
Mamá made the decision that would bring Guzmán's
childhood to an end.

"Doña Julia, forgive an ignorant woman. Make me an
appointment with . . . La Cabra." She felt funny saying this

name, which meant "the she-goat"—an epithet more suitable for a prostitute than a medium.

"I'll go with you, Cielo. You won't regret it. This woman can work miracles."

As Carmelo had feared, Guzmán continued to be devastated by the news that he could not deliver the lunches to the cane cutters. In a few months these men had taught him much about hard work and laughter: how to swing a machete so that the cane fell gracefully as a dancer away from you, and how to roll a perfect cigarette. They had also spoken about women. Their talk had been in vague terms so that the real location of their pleasure was never mentioned, but Guzmán felt the knowledge creeping over his skin. Their words were the dowser's hazelrod pointing to an underground well in exciting circles. He had done a lot of growing that season. Tears did not come easily any more, and his body summoned him from sleep, addressing him in a language he did not quite comprehend.

Carmelo no longer spent much time with his younger brother. He had found a friend who shared his love for books—a young priest, Padre César, who had come to Salud straight from his seminary in the capital to assist the aging pastor, Don Gonzalo. Timid around people, he had come supplied with trunks full of books he had bought in San Juan and Spain. A thin, sallow youth, he had the look of one who has spent much of his life indoors. The old women loved him and sent him food at the rectory, the young women ignored him, and the men avoided him. His refined speech and the way he brought his scented handkerchief to his nose made them feel ill at ease. He got to be known around town as El Padrecito, the Little Father.

Every Sunday after mass, Carmelo and César would walk around the atrium of the church while the young priest greeted the parishioners. As was his duty, he lis-

17

tened to the old ones' complaints: aches, pains, graphic descriptions of recent surgery. He accepted envelopes with donations for the church from the well-to-do matrons, blessed babies, and generally made life a little easier for the older priest, who had heard these same complaints and blessed these matrons when they were infants. Now Don Gonzalo would rush back to his room right after his mass, supposedly to pray, but, as everyone knew, the old man took his medicinal toddy more often than recommended and slept away most of his days. Carmelo soon became César's confidant, thus gaining access to his magnificent library. Mamá Cielo did not like the idea of Carmelo spending his free hours holed up with another bookworm, but Papá Pepe intervened on his son's behalf, and, at least on Sundays, the two reclusive young men would be allowed to visit at the rectory. There they spent entire afternoons taking advantage of the privacy and peace of the young priest's rooms.

In the meantime Mamá Cielo watched Guzmán carefully. She waited for his reaction to her decision not to sell lunches. She heard the boys talking at night as usual, but their conversations were brief and lacked their former urgency. By their tone she could tell nothing was being planned. Guzmán woke her often with his pacing. One night she awoke to the creaking of the rocking chair which she kept in the porch. Not quite alert, she thought it might be the restless spirit of its former owner, her mother-in-law, a domineering woman who had never approved of Cielo's marriage to Pepe. Fortunately she had passed on not too long after their marriage. She had willed the rocking chair to Mamá Cielo and all her other furniture to her other children. Not trusting her motives even in death, Mamá Cielo had always kept the rocker out on the porch.

Listening more attentively, Mamá Cielo perceived the

rocker to be occupied by living flesh, for she could also hear the tapping of bare feet as they touched the floor in time with the rocking sound. She walked quietly to the parlor and looked through the curtains of the front window. She saw Guzmán sitting on the rocker in his white shorts. He was looking up at the sky in deep concentration. Looking at what? She knew there was a crescent moon tonight; the sky was so dark with clouds that the only way she saw her son so clearly was that her neighbor's light was on upstairs, in the attic room she sometimes rented out to single women. She looked closely at her son. The boy had put on weight. He had gotten taller. How old was he now, twelve, thirteen? Yes, Carmelo would be seventeen in July so that made Guzmán fourteen. His skin was dark as tanned leather, his hair thick and tightly curled and his thin frame showed corded muscles underneath as if his bones were tied to each other with wires.

Mamá Cielo followed Guzmán's gaze up to the lighted window. A figure moved against the backdrop of a yellow light. A woman was combing her long hair in slow motion. She would bring the brush to the top of her head and then with a graceful bending of her elbow lower it down along the length of her back to her waist. Guzmán rocked slowly, keeping time with the movement of the woman's arm. He kept his eyes fixed on the figure, his hands folded tightly over his chest as if he were praying. Mamá went back to her bed. The next day she took him to see La Cabra.

La Cabra lived in a house that sat on tall stilts on the banks of the Red River. This river was little more than a snaking track of thick mud most of the year, but during the rainy season it flooded so that a small boat, covered with a tarpaulin, was kept under her house. Here the hens made their nests and laid their eggs. La Cabra's mother had left this house to her children upon her death two years be-

19

fore. All three of them, two sons and a daughter, lived in New York City. They had moved there as teenagers and had not returned to the Island again. Doña Lupe, the old lady, received infrequent letters from her offspring, but until the day of her death she had walked daily to town to check for mail at the post office. The postman refused to deliver her mail. It meant a three-mile hike through an overgrown coffee plantation where the Taino Indians were said to have their burial grounds, and across that unpredictable Red River. It was he who first noted Doña Lupe's absence and sent the authorities to her house, where they found her dead on her hammock, a pile of old letters dating back twenty or thirty years on her lap. From these they got her children's addresses. The only one who responded was her daughter, Pura Rosa, who showed up a week after the old woman had been given Christian burial at the expense of the town. Pura Rosa produced a letter signed by her mother in which she stated that upon her death her house should be given to her children.

Rosa, as she was called until the evil tongues of Salud rechristened her La Cabra, had arrived with her eight-year-old daughter, whom she immediately enrolled in a Catholic boarding school in Mayagüez. The girl was from then on seldom seen in town with her mother. Very rapidly La Cabra established herself as the district's most sought-after medium. The women went to her to have their futures told, and for potions that she sold to cure almost any female trouble, including jealousy and infertility. She saw men too, they say, but with such discretion that few people knew until after she disappeared from Salud years later, and the legend of La Cabra grew.

The walk to La Cabra's "spiritual center," as she insisted her clients call her place, was not unpleasant when it was early in the day and it wasn't raining. Mamá Cielo prepared a thermos of coffee, and with it in a paper bag under her arm and her huge black umbrella held over her head, she and Guzmán set out for the country. When his mother got him out of bed at dawn, laying out his best clothes, Guzmán at first thought that he was being taken to the clinic for shots. But it seemed strange to him that she gave him a pair of old sandals to wear and wrapped his shoes and socks in old newspaper for him to carry. He was even more puzzled when they took the dirt road out of Salud instead of heading for the highway for the bus to Mayagüez. Mamá acted sullen, and Guzmán did not dare break the silence. Just at the crossing where roads fork toward the canefields on the left and the river on the right, Doña Julia joined them. The two women walked ahead, talking softly under Mamá Cielo's umbrella. Only once did Mamá address him. This was when he left the path for a minute to urinate behind some bushes.

"Don't get muddy," she yelled at him, making him burn with shame. Doña Julia laughed mightily, staring with pointed interest at his crotch when he emerged from the bushes.

"You don't have to worry about a mud puddle with this one yet, Cielo," she said to Mamá Cielo, who did not look at her son but kept her back to him.

The Red River was no more than a shallow stream of mud, but it was still difficult to cross. They all removed their sandals at the bank. The women lifted their dresses up to their knees as they held each other's waist for balance. Guzmán bounded across it, splashing a little muddy water on Doña Julia by accident as he passed her.

"Son of the Devil," she hissed at him.

On the other side they dried themselves with paper Mamá Cielo had in her bag and sat under a shady tree to drink the steaming hot café con leche Mamá had prepared. Guzmán excused himself and climbed the little hill covered with wild coffee-bean bushes to survey the area. He saw La Cabra's house with the white chickens scratching around the yard and the ancient boat resting on its belly under the house. Then he saw a figure rising from the river that curved around the little valley. A cement wall about four feet tall had been built to trap a pool of water. It had only three sides with the open side facing the current so that it was constantly moving water, emptying and replenishing itself though the river was low. At first he saw the head, masses of piled black hair above a pale face. He could not distinguish the features, but she seemed inordinately white to him. She must have been sitting or squatting, because abruptly she rose, uncovered to her waist. Naked, her great breasts were a surprise after the smallness and delicacy of her head and back. Guzmán closed his eyes tightly for a moment, leaning on the nearest tree. He felt dizzy and suddenly afraid, yet unable to lift his feet, as if they were stuck in thick mud. When he looked again, the woman had wrapped herself in a black towel and was walking barefoot toward the house.

The boy retraced his steps back to the tree, where the women were gathering their belongings.

"Well, there you are, boy," said Doña Julia with an annoyed tug at her dress. "We were beginning to think you were lost."

"Where are we going, Mamá?" Guzmán had to know if they were heading in the direction of the house on stilts.

"You'll see when we get there," Mamá Cielo answered, avoiding his eyes. "But I'm warning you right now, Guzmán, you are to do as I tell you. Don't speak to anyone unless I say you can. And"—here her voice softened a bit— "don't be scared, son. It's nothing to worry about. You'll understand more later."

22

"I don't know why you bother explaining anything to this one, Cielo. Look at that fresh face. He acts as if he'd invented fire."

This time Guzmán walked ahead of the women, leading them up the little path that footsteps had leveled on one side of the hill. He walked slowly and deliberately, kicking large rocks out of the women's path, gathering ripe guavas for the three of them to eat. The wild coffee beans were red, and to the boy they seemed like the eyes of many small animals peering at them from all sides. A sweet smell surrounded them and the branches of overhanging mango trees shaded them. Guzmán felt joyful, as he had among the cane cutters. A sense of expectancy put springs under his feet. He ran ahead of the women, jabbing at the shadows like a boxer. Doña Julia shook her head and made a *tsk, tsk* sound.

"It's like I told you, comadre. The boy is taken by a malicious spirit," said Julia. Mamá Cielo made the sign of the cross on her forehead.

The clearing where La Cabra's house stood was bathed in noonday sunlight when the three of them emerged from the woods. To Guzmán the square box of a house on stilts with the white boat underneath looked like a brown hen sitting on an egg. At the top of the cement stairs, standing on the pedestal, stood a woman in a white dress. Her black hair was pulled back into a tight bun at her neck. Even her sandals were white, so that her paleness was accentuated. She seemed almost a spirit, her substance lost in the folds of her nunlike dress.

"That's La Cabra?" Mamá Cielo took Doña Julia's arm.

"She likes to be called Sister Rosa, Cielo." Doña Julia nodded towards the figure who still stood motionless allowing the breeze to billow the skirt of her dress, making her look as if she were floating above them. "Only those jealous women who are afraid of her beauty and of her powers in matters of love call her the She-Goat. They have spread rumors that Rosa entertains men here. Lies . . . all lies. She is an angel of mercy."

Mamá looked around for Guzmán. The boy was already at the foot of the steps, and Sister Rosa had opened her long-sleeved arms in a dramatic gesture of welcome for him.

"Guzmán!" Mamá Cielo's call to her son echoed off the hill, "Guzmán!" off the water, "Guzmán!" off the very walls of the house. "Guzmán!" The boy kept climbing the steps to the woman in white.

"If you want to help your son," Doña Julia said, "you must not interfere. Can't you see that Sister Rosa already knows that he is the one that needs her attention? Look at how she has him in her power already. You must be patient."

"You are right, comadre. You have been so kind to us. I will do as you say. I just hope Guzmán is not up to some devilish game. He's been acting funny since we stopped for coffee."

"He seems as wild as ever to me."

Doña Julia pressed her finger to her lips as they approached the house. Sister Rosa and Guzmán had already disappeared into the dim interior. At the door the women paused. Adjusting their eyes to the sudden darkness, they saw a room bare except for several chairs arranged around a table which was covered with a red cloth and religious artifacts. On it were ceramic statuettes of saints, a mahogany wand with a gold tip, a bowl of water, and several cigars. Mamá Cielo felt a tug of fear at her heart. Papá's table was white and he kept nothing but a Bible on it when he practiced spiritism. But she had heard that this woman had learned new ways in New York, and her co-madre trusted her.

"Please come in and sit down, sisters." Sister Rosa emerged from another room separated by a black curtain from the *centro,* as she called the room where she "worked causes." The women were startled by her sudden appearance, for in the dimness the black curtains could not be easily detected. With an elegant motion of one hand she motioned them to the chairs. "Guzmán will help me prepare the room for our meeting." The women sat down, and to their amazement Guzmán knelt at their feet and removed their shoes. He placed little porcelain tubs under their feet and filled them with perfumed alcohol from a bottle labeled agua florida.

"We must make ourselves receptive to the spirits through purification," Sister Rosa said softly. She lit a cigar and started puffing on it as she closed the door. The room was practically pitch black, but, amazingly, a candle lit it-self in the middle of the altar. Sister Rosa went around the room filling it with cigar smoke. Guzmán dried the women's feet with a cloth and went behind the black cur-tains. To Mamá Cielo it seemed that he had vanished like a ghost.

"Now dip your fingertips into the bowl in front of you and rub agua florida on your temples and the backs of your necks," instructed Sister Rosa as she made strange designs with the smoke of the cigar in front of them.

"The evil influences that you may have brought in here from the world outside will pass from your fingers into the bowl," she said.

Guzmán had returned and quietly taken a seat in front of the woman. Still puffing on her cigar, Sister Rosa dipped her hands in the liquid and began to rub Guzmán's neck

25

and shoulders. With each stroke she said something unintelligible to the two women, wringing the water off her fingers back into the bowl. She massaged his arms and dipped his hands in the bowl. She made him stand by pulling him up, and she knelt behind him rubbing his body down to his ankles and repeating the motions of wringing her hands over the bowl.

"The cleansing is complete," she announced in a loud whisper with a heaving of her chest. The room was filled with cigar smoke. "We have exorcised the evil ones that cling, from our bodies and into the water. We can begin to work this cause now."

Mamá Cielo's eyes were brimming with tears brought on by the cigar smoke. She watched her son take the bowl and once again vanish behind the black curtain.

When they were all sitting around the altar, Sister Rosa produced four crystal wine glasses. By candlelight they flickered in hypnotic colors. She held each one aloft, said a few words, and filled it with a black liquid from a bottle, handing a glass to each of them. All these things she was producing from beneath the table. Mamá Cielo fought an urge to lift the red cloth and look.

"Drink this slowly and with faith, my beloved friends," Sister Rosa whispered, making a little ceremony over each glass. "It is coffee from the plants my spiritual guardians tend. They will recognize it in your bodies as they respond to my summons today."

Mamá Cielo sipped the bitter liquid and felt it burn going down her throat. There was the syrup of sugar cane in it and more.

"Perhaps the boy should not drink this," she ventured. "He has a weak stomach."

"It won't hurt him, sister." Sister Rosa's hand was on Guzmán's head. "His spirit calls to me for help. I am now his spiritual mother. Sister, if you want me to help him before it is too late, you must trust me. Drink now, and meditate. Decide now whether you can give me your total trust. If you cannot, then you must leave and may God forgive you." She stubbed out her cigar on the lap of a black Buddha statue on the altar and lit a fresh one. The air was thick and tears were running down everyone's faces. Guzmán gulped noisily. He was sobbing.

Mamá Cielo felt as if she were suffocating. She wanted to take her son by the hand and leave this smoke-filled room, but she felt weak and disoriented. The woman's words had shaken her. She had to help Guzmán and herself find peace. Sister Rosa kept rubbing the boy's shoulders and head. His eyes were closed and he was shivering. "Yes, yes," she said in a husky voice. "I feel the presence of a rebellious spirit, an untranquil spirit within this boy . . ." She puffed incessantly on the cigar as she spoke over the boy's head. He felt dizzy, as if he were about to faint. The image of a woman rising from water formed in the clouds of smoke before his eyes, and he strained toward her smoky arms.

"This spirit wants light," Sister Rosa hissed through her clenched lips. "Give me light, give me light!" she screamed, dropping the cigar from her mouth, buckling over the boy in the throes of spirit possession. Mamá Cielo made to rise, but Doña Julia's hand pulled her back. Sister Rosa was on her knees before the quietly sobbing boy.

"Do not fear me, boy," she spoke from her chest, lowering her chin and raising her arms over her head. "I am the soul of a great warrior slain by the priests, for I would not swear allegiance to the Spanish cross. I was murdered by a knife from behind so that I could not see the face of my enemy. I cannot breathe . . . I cannot breathe," the woman screamed and collapsed. Guzmán covered his face with

27

his hands and began to gasp for air. He felt one of his asthma attacks coming on. His diaphragm was constricting painfully around his lungs.

"This one is mine," Sister Rosa said rising and pointing to Guzmán. "Through his eyes I see the faces of my enemies. Through his hands I will find my revenge." At this point she made two passes with her arms over her head, drawing the spirit away from herself. She rose and drew the sobbing boy to her chest. Holding him by the waist, she took him to the door, which she threw wide open. Guzmán swallowed the fresh air in gulps. Mamá Cielo shook her head as if coming awake from a dream. She rushed out to the porch, where Sister Rosa sat on a bench with the boy, his head in her lap. He was not struggling for breath anymore. His eyes were closed and she was rubbing his temples.

"There is much more to be done to help this one, sister," she said to Mamá Cielo.

"What can I do?" Mamá Cielo wanted to get the woman's instructions and leave as soon as possible.

"First, you must believe. Do you believe?"

"Yes."

"You must light a red and a white votive candle each night to give this untranquil spirit light."

"I will do that." Mamá took Guzmán's arm and gently tried to pull him up from the woman's lap, but the boy seemed to be fast asleep. "Guzmán," she called softly, her face next to his. "Time to go home, son."

"No." Sister Rosa rocked the boy's head on her lap. "Guzmán must stay a while with me. He needs my protection from this great evil that is within him."

"What are you saying? I can't leave my son here!" Mamá rose to her feet.

"You do not see, sister," said Sister Rosa, "that you are

drawing this evil to him yourself. The spirit that has taken your son was meant for you. He is attracted by your anger and the boy's sensitivity. He is your demon!"

"No! You lie! I will not leave my son with a witch." Mamá yanked at Guzmán and the boy stood up groggily, supporting himself on Sister Rosa's shoulder.

"I want to stay here, Mamá," he said.

"You come with me." Mamá grabbed his elbow and pulled. Guzmán resisted.

"I want to stay."

She slapped the boy hard across his face. Great sobs built up within his chest, and he flailed his arms about like someone drowning. He fainted. When he awoke he found himself in the largest bed he had ever seen, his head propped up with fragrant pillows. It was night, but through the open window he saw the crescent moon and heard water gurgling on its way downstream.

GUZMÁN first saw television at La Cabra's house. It was one of the first sets in Salud, the only others belonging to the American and the priest. Reception was irregular. The only station was a government operation in the faraway capital of San Juan, and it was in English, but to Guzmán it seemed a miracle. The second night he stayed with La Cabra she turned the set on for him. It was in her bedroom, where he had awakened that morning. That first day he had felt like going home, especially since the woman had paid him very little attention except to fix him a plate of rice, beans, and fried plantains when he got so hungry he had gone in the kitchen to watch her cook.

"Are you hungry?" she had finally asked when his stomach was already learning to speak for itself.

"Yes," he said, surprised at the question. Mamá Cielo usually just set food in front of him at the right times.

"Around here you'll get only what you ask for, Guzmán. You must also help me with my work, since I live alone." She touched his arm as she spoke, and Guzmán felt the familiar weakness in his body, the tightness in his chest that her nearness provoked. Always behind his eyes was the image of a woman pale as the moon rising from the river.

"When you finish eating," she said, leaving the kitchen, "come to my room and I'll show you something."

They watched the flickering images on the television as if it were a crystal ball, with the woman explaining to Guzmán what the people said in English. When he asked her where she had learned the language, she told him about her many years in New York. She had been sent to her brother's house at age fourteen to separate her from a married man she had fallen in love with. He had promised her in secret that he would follow, as soon as he was able to get away from his clinging wife and five children. She had given birth to her daughter while she waited for him. She had grown tired of waiting for him, tired of her mother's letters which were sermons of damnation, tired of her brother's vigilance. She had taken a job at the Nabisco cookie factory, where the boss, a tall, brash man named Jackson, fell in love with her. All this had been foretold by a spiritist she had visited in the Bronx before taking the job. With her daughter, Sarita, she moved into the apartment her boss found her. She got off welfare and lived pretty well on the groceries and pocket money that Jackson gave her. At first she had stayed on at the factory, but the other women who worked with her on the line, packing assorted cookies into tins, became so hostile that finally she had to quit. She was used to making it on little money; her biggest expense was her child, who was sickly, and whose doctor bills sent Jackson into a rage. He had kids of his own, and a

30

demanding wife. Though they had great times together at first, Jackson complained that she was spending his money on someone else's brat. It always ended in shouting matches with Sarita joining in with her hysterical crying. Though she hated to do it, Rosa started looking for a job and made plans to move out on her own.

"Am I boring you, Guzmán?" She had him sit on the floor with her and rubbed his shoulders as she spoke. He did not understand everything she said, particularly since she mentioned the names of strangers as if Guzmán was supposed to know them. But the details did not matter: only her hands, the way they smelled like incense, and her voice, telling him about people and places he could only imagine.

"I like hearing you talk, Señora."

She kissed him lightly on top of his thick hair, so that he imagined her lips rather than felt them.

"Good. Call me Rosa," she said. She told him how Jackson had followed her to her brother's house and pounded on the door until a neighbor called the police; how her brother had insulted her, calling her names she could not bring herself to repeat. In despair she had written to her mother. The old lady had written back a testament of recriminations, saying Rosa could come home if she put her bastard child up for adoption. In Puerto Rico, the old woman had written, a fatherless child, particularly a girl, was spat upon. That was when Rosa met El Indio, a spiritist known throughout the city, who ran a thriving centro. She had attended a meeting where El Indio had singled her out while in a trance. He had rolled on the floor and danced, possessed by the spirit of Santa Bárbara, who he claimed was Rosa's patroness—Santa Bárbara, a bold and talkative spirit attracted to the color red and burning liquids like wine. El Indio, a mahogany-skinned man with oriental eyes, had draped his shoulders with a red cloth and skipped around the basement-apartment living room with a candle in his hand. Suddenly he had grabbed her hand and dragged her around with him until she had felt dizzy. Then holding her in his arms he had said, "Daughter, daughter, there is nothing to fear. You have found your brother and your spiritual guide. Give me your faith, promise to serve me all the days of your life, and you shall never be alone again." Well, *Madre de Dios,* she had broken down and cried. Everyone had embraced her and welcomed her as a member of the group.

El Indio had asked her to stay after the others had gone home, and over a cup of black coffee fortified with rum she had told him about her life, which at the time was nothing more than a catastrophe in progress. He had looked at her with compassion in his face, a taut oval like a walnut. He had seemed a saint to her at the time. He told her to think of him as her only family. He put her in a taxi to take her home, and paid for it out of his pocket. She had never taken a taxi before, and she felt like a queen with the back seat all to herself. In a few days she received a letter from El Indio telling her that he had found a small apartment for her in his building. She rushed over to his centro with Sarita. When she got there she found El Indio playing dominoes with several other men. He asked her to wait in the kitchen while they finished their game. Sarita had begun to cry and El Indio yelled at her to keep the kid quiet. She listened to the men laugh and curse. She found it hard to believe that El Indio, who had seemed so saintly just a few nights before, could take part in such rowdiness. But she shrugged her fears away. Men are men, and they need their diversions. She had heard this said so much in her life that it was part of her subconscious.

After what seemed like hours she heard El Indio close

the door behind the last of his guests. She heard them making plans for a party. When El Indio walked into the kitchen, Sarita was asleep in Rosa's arms. Before he sat down at the table with her he said, "It'd be a lot simpler if you didn't have that one." It seemed to her that everyone was always telling her to get rid of her child.

"You said you had a place for me," she ventured to say.

"Yes, I do, daughter. It's on the third floor of this building and the rent is cheap. The super here is my *compadre*." El Indio lit a cigar, and Sarita started whimpering in Rosa's arms. Rosa prayed to God the child would not wake up screaming and ruin her chances.

"That is good news, señor, but I don't have money. Not even a job. How will I pay rent?"

"I have that figured out, too." El Indio put his elbows on the table and drew his monkey face close to hers. The cigar smoke made her eyes water. "You'll be working for me."

"Working for you? Doing what? You mean at the centro?"

"At the centro to begin with, yes. I need an assistant. A good-looking woman like you will attract more men."

"I don't understand, señor. I am not a spiritist. I've had no training. It takes years to develop *facultades* as a medium, doesn't it?" She was feeling more confused and frightened by the minute. El Indio must have noticed her nervousness because he took her hand in both of his. He put out his cigar on the kitchen's linoleum floor.

"My child," he spoke gently, "the minute you walked into my centro I knew you had strong spiritual guides that needed to be given light. You are like me, and you were sent to me so that I could help you develop your facultades as a spiritist."

"I don't know if I can. I just don't know if I can do what

33

you are asking me to do." She was seeing her last chance to escape her brother's oppressive home and the fear of Jackson's retribution crumble before her eyes.

"I am offering you a home for yourself and your little daughter as well as the opportunity to develop your talents, and all you can do is sit there and cry all over my table. Perhaps I was misled by a demon instead of guided by a beneficent spirit. Perhaps," El Indio had gotten up and was pointing an accusing finger at her, "you are a lost soul who wants to stay lost."

"No, no, I want you to help me, that's why I'm here. Tell me what I have to do."

"You don't have to do anything for now. Just bring your things in the morning and I'll help you move in."

"That was the first step in my descent to hell, Guzmán." La Cabra turned the boy around to face her. "El Indio was an evil man, Guzmán. Although he kept his word about letting me work at the centro, he soon began sending men up to my apartment after the meetings. The meetings, you see, were a cover for his real business. He was a pimp. Do you know what a pimp is, Guzmán?"

"No, señora." The boy was getting very sleepy and he fought to keep his eyes open so as not to hurt her feelings.

"A pimp is a man who solicits desperate souls for the Devil."

"Huh?" Guzmán had long ago lost the thread of her story.

"Nothing. Nothing, my sweet Guzmán. Come, you will sleep in my bed tonight. I'm going to the river for a swim. There is a full moon. See? It's the best time to swim. There." She placed a fragrant sheet over the boy and turned off the television.

During the time Guzmán spent at La Cabra's he helped her tend her herb garden. She taught him the names of each plant and what it was used for. Black sage was boiled into a tea and taken as a purgative. Geranium, its leaves dried and burned like incense, kept mosquitoes and (she chuckled) evil spirits away. Mint was used for dispelling the devil influences that hide in the body as gas. The seeds of the papaya fruit steeped in boiling water would make your blood thick and red, rekindling waning passions. And the passionflower—a vine that wraps itself around any tree like a clinging lover, its tiny orange fruit like kisses all over the bark—was a tonic that cures hysteria, turning a harpy into a pliable angel, a scoundrel into a solicitous husband.

The boy followed her around the little plot of cultivated earth behind the house, where there was a natural grove of mango, papaya, and breadfruit trees. He helped her pull weeds, listening to her description of each plant, laughing when she did. He stopped caring about anything but the sense of ease he felt with this woman who talked almost constantly, as if she were hungry for words, as if she had been recently released from solitary confinement. They ate a papaya she had pulled from the tree, its juicy yellow meat dripping down their chins. Guzmán asked her: "Why did you want me to stay with you, Rosa?"

"I had heard about your . . . shall we call them, adventures? Your neighbor Doña Julia is a frequent visitor here and she told me about you and your mother. Did you know that old woman is trying to get a man? She's had me prepare potions and spells as if I were a sorceress. For the money, I've given her quite a few purgatives with a little rum mixed in. She says she feels younger when she takes them." They laughed at the image of Doña Julia getting a kick from Rosa's "love potions."

"What did she tell you about me?" Guzmán was curious about Doña Julia's tales. He knew the woman didn't like him.

"She said you were a wild boy who was killing his

mother with worry and frustration. She wanted me to give you a potion to dull your rebellious spirit."

Guzmán thought about all the delicious drinks she had prepared for him in the last few days. He had not felt any different except that every day he was happier.

"Have you cured me, Rosa?"

"Do you feel cured, Guzmán?"

"I'm happy here. I don't ever want to go back to Salud. I'll stay here and help you with your garden." He laid his head down on her lap. She stroked his temples.

"I like having you here, Guzmán. You remind me of myself when I was your age. So much energy, so sensitive to others. But all that changed quickly for me." She let her voice trail. Then she rose abruptly to her feet.

"Your Mamá will want you back soon. But we will be friends, all right? You can come visit me any time. Now, I have company coming tonight, and I need you to help me set a cot for you in the kitchen and do a few other things." She pulled him up to his feet.

"Who's coming to see you? Doña Julia?"

"No, darling, it's a man from town. A good friend." She detected his disappointment and quickly added: "How about a swim? Come on, I'll race you to the water." She took her dress off as she ran and tossed it into the air. It floated down onto a wild coffee-bean bush, where it fluttered in the breeze like a white flag.

That evening, after a meal they prepared together from the garden vegetables they had gathered earlier, Guzmán brushed the woman's long black hair while she painted her nails into hearts. First she put on white enamel, blew on each finger until it was dry, then she shaped a crimson heart around the edges of the nail. She powdered her face and made her skin glow like white porcelain. She splashed cologne on her shoulders and thighs, getting a little on Guzmán. The boy was fascinated with the ritual of beauty.

36

It was almost like a religious ceremony, with incense and bright colors, and the hypnotizing movements of the celebrant, all coming together to make him feel a little drunk. He wished that she was doing all this for him, but he had already received his orders for the evening. While her "company" was in the house, Guzmán was to stay in the kitchen. She had moved the television in there. He was to be quiet and keep out of sight. When he had asked her why he could not meet the visitor, Rosa had answered that the person was a very important customer of hers who did not wish the gossipy townspeople to know he was consulting a spiritist. Guzmán understood this. It was fine for women to seek guidance for themselves and their families from a spiritist, but for a man it was a little different, unless of course he was a medium himself, like Papá.

"Do you know my Papá, Rosa?" he asked following a stroke of the brush down from the crown of her head to her waist.

"I know about him, querido. He has helped many people."

"Why don't you visit him? You and he would have many things to talk about. He has books, and you could teach him about your plants."

La Cabra laughed. It was laughter like Guzmán had never heard from a woman: loud and from deep inside so that her whole body shook and he had to stop brushing her hair until she finished.

"What's funny?" he asked her, smiling widely himself, entranced by her face reflected on her dresser mirror.

"My sweet Guzmán, I don't think your Papá would approve of my methods. No, don't frown, it's not that I do anything bad . . . not really. I just make a living the only way I know how. But you see, I represent a new way. I'm not from Salud. Though I was born here, I was away for many years, and I learned new things in New York—things that your father would not understand." She turned and hugged him to her. "But we'll always be friends, won't we, my little monkey?"

His "yes" was muffled by her perfumed arms, where he wished he could remain for eternity. At that moment they heard a loud roaring like that of an engine. Guzmán started to run to the window, but the woman held him.

"It's my friend's motorcycle. He has to leave it on the other side of the river." The nights in this isolated valley were so silent that a frog hopping into the water could be heard in the house.

"Here, give me a kiss and go watch television until you get sleepy."

AT MAMÁ'S HOUSE there had been no peace since she had left Guzmán at La Cabra's. A normally reticent man, especially with his wife, Papá Pepe had denounced La Cabra as a phony who made her living from gullible women and perhaps even practiced sorcery. He and Mamá Cielo had kept the argument going for three days, to the point where Carmelo had found it necessary to intervene, playing his familiar role of mediator.

"Mamá," he had addressed his mother while she stirred a huge pot of chicken soup for dinner on the evening of the fourth day of Guzmán's absence from home. "I think you were right to take Guzmán to the lady for help. I know you were worried about his spiritual well-being."

"I wish your father would understand that, son. Since all he knows comes from books, he has no common sense. He knows nothing about handling problems in a practical way. He would like words to be food so he would never have to stop reading to eat again. Honestly, sometimes I wonder what would happen to my children and my house if I were to start reading poetry and stop cooking and cleaning . . ."

Seeing that his mother was about to begin a tirade

against his father, Carmelo interjected: "Mamá, as I said, you were right to seek help for Guzmán, but I'm a little worried about him."

This got her attention. She stopped stirring the noodles and wiped her hands on her apron.

"Why are you worried about Guzmán, son? Have you heard something?"

"It's his asthma, Mamá. You know his medicine is here and if he has an attack way out in the country . . . well, that lady may not know what to do."

"She seemed to handle him pretty well from what I could tell. But to tell you the truth, I had thought about that myself. I would have gone to get him yesterday if your father hadn't upset me so much." She looked very worried and Carmelo felt this was the time to make his move.

"I'll go get him tonight."

"Tonight?" Mamá Cielo sounded doubtful. Carmelo knew that she wasn't about to agree to his going out in the dark, and he had promised César that he would come up to the rectory that night. The young priest had sent him a note saying that he desperately needed to speak to him. Carmelo carefully framed his lie for Mamá Cielo.

"Mamá," Carmelo spoke in a dramatic, serious voice, "I wasn't going to tell you this so as not to alarm you, but I had a dream about Guzmán last night."

"A dream?" Mamá turned from the stove to look closely into her son's eyes. "What kind of dream?"

"I dreamed I saw Guzmán in a bed surrounded by people dressed in white. They were praying for him." Carmelo lowered his eyes, knowing that her fear for Guzmán would force Mamá to give him permission to go out.

Mamá crossed herself and said a quick Hail Mary under her breath. "It'll be dark soon. How are you going to find your way there?"

"Let me show you," Carmelo said, going quickly to his

39

room and coming back with a flashlight, a gift from his friend César so he could read in his bed at night.

"What is it?"

"It's a modern lantern. From New York. I did some work around the church grounds, and Father gave it to me." It was not really lying, Carmelo thought. He did not want to start her on the subject of César.

"The way people come up with miracles in Nueva York, the Lord Jesus will probably be spotted there next." Then she hastily crossed herself for her blasphemy. "Go get your brother, Carmelo. Maybe he'll have learned a few things about responsibility. That would really be a miracle—the kind you can't buy in Nueva York."

Carmelo headed for the rectory first, promising himself that he would not stay long. César, César. What had happened? At the rectory Carmelo was denied entrance by the housekeeper, Leonarda. She had never liked César, and they had caught her listening in at his door more than once during Carmelo's visits. Looking like a vulture in her black shawl, she held him back at the door.

"No visitors tonight, young man. Padre Gonzalo's orders."

"But, señora," Carmelo protested, "I have an appointment with Padre César."

"El Padrecito César cannot see anyone tonight." She grinned with a half a mouthful of black teeth. Leonarda knew more than she was saying, Carmelo was immediately certain. "No visitors," she repeated. "Padre Gonzalo's orders."

Before she slammed the heavy oak door in his face, Carmelo heard something like a woman's wail of grief. With a shock he recognized it as his friend's hysterical voice. Tomorrow morning he would try to see César after the early morning mass.

40

When Carmelo came to the hill that overlooked La Cabra's valley, he saw a brightly lit house. He paused to let his eyes adjust to the sudden brightness after his long walk in the woods. He also needed some time to dispel the confusion and anger he still felt from his visit to the rectory. Besides, what could he say to this woman, La Cabra, as an excuse for showing up unexpectedly and taking Guzmán? Now that his ears had tuned out the murmur of rainfrogs and crickets, he heard shouts. Alarmed, he stood up and leaned over the edge of the ravine. Two figures were running toward the river. One ran like a graceful animal tossing a white dress over her head; Carmelo could see now it was a woman. She looked pale as a ghost in the moonlight. At the edge of the water she stopped to pin her hair up, and she was nude. For a minute she looked like a statue of marble, like the ones Carmelo had seen in the books César lent him. The other runner was a heavy man. By the time he reached the bank the woman was already in the water. Carmelo lost sight of her dark head in the black water. The man sat down on the ground and began to strip. He was a large man with thick white hair. Carmelo recognized him at once as the American, Mr. Clement. The two people were shouting at each other in English. The woman waved to the man inviting him into the water. César had been tutoring Carmelo in English, and he was able to understand some of the phrases.

But where was his brother? Had this crazy woman done something horrible to him? Was she really a witch, as some people in town claimed, or just another whore, as she appeared to be now? Either way Guzmán was in trouble. Carmelo went the long way around the hill coming up to the house from the rear. Through what he assumed was the kitchen window he could see another kind of light, flickering on the wall. He heard several voices speaking in En-

41

glish. How could this small house hold so many people? Putting his lantern inside his belt, he climbed up one of the stilts and reached the window easily. This house had been built with floods in mind. He carefully peeked in and saw his brother sitting up on a cot watching, as if mesmerized, the moving figures on a television set. The program was in English. Carmelo was amazed to see a set way out here in the country. César and he had used the one in the rectory to practice their English. Carmelo leaped into the room. Guzmán ran at him like a battering ram and knocked him down.

"Wait, hold on, you idiot. It's me, your brother." Carmelo fell under Guzmán, who was practically sitting on his head so his voice came out muffled. Through the corner of his eye he could see the little knife in Guzmán's hand.

"No, no! Guzmán!"

As if he had just woken up Guzmán shook his head and released Carmelo from a vicelike hold. "Carmelo, is that you?"

"You were going to kill me, you savage. Mamá is right. You're hopeless. Where did you get the knife?" Carmelo rubbed his kidneys where Guzmán had kicked him in the process of bringing him down.

"What are you doing here at this hour, Carmelo? Is Mamá sick? Why did you come in through the window?"

Carmelo sat on the edge of the cot. His head was reeling. The whole world was going crazy tonight. "Look, Guzmán. Mamá wants you home. Just get your things together and let's get out of here before the lady of the house returns from her midnight swim."

Guzmán thought he was still asleep and having a nightmare. He didn't want to go home now. Rosa said they could pick wild coffee together tomorrow morning. She was going to teach him how to tell a person's future with cards.

He went to the sink and splashed water on his face. When he turned around Carmelo was still sitting on his cot looking like he was going to vomit any minute.

"I'm not going, Carmelo. Not without speaking with Rosa first."

"You are wrong little brother. You are coming home even if I have to tie you with a rope and carry you like a pig over my shoulders." Carmelo stood up with a wince of pain. Guzmán had never seen his older brother look so menacing before. The eyebrows drawn together into one black line and the eyes bright with tears of pain made him look like Mamá before one of her rages.

"But why, Carmelo? What have I done wrong?" Guzmán tried to come close to his brother but the older boy pushed him away.

"I'll let you confess what you may have done wrong to Mamá. All I know is that she wants you home. Now." They both turned to the window at the sound of laughter coming from the river.

"A friend from town is visiting her," Guzmán said.

"We are both too old for fairy tales, brother," said Carmelo. "I'll climb down first and wait for you. Think you can do it without a light? We don't want to disturb your friend and ruin her visit."

Guzmán was amazed at the sarcasm in Carmelo's voice. He had changed a lot in a few months.

"And by the way, little brother. Don't pull any tricks once I leave the room. After all, if you don't come with me tonight, Mamá will come get you herself tomorrow morning. It's your choice."

"She has been good to me, Carmelo. I should let her know I'm going."

"She's a whore, Guzmán. Do you know what a whore is, Guzmán?"

43

Guzmán went to the window and looked in the direction of the river. It was not quite a quarter moon: it looked like a face someone was covering with a hand. But there was light enough to see the pale back of a woman, a long white neck topped by a mass of black hair. Hair that sometimes fell over her shoulders and down to her waist like a heavy mourning veil.

"I'll go first, Carmelo."

The television was going off the air for the night, and the first strains of the American national anthem could be heard by the two boys as they came to the dirt path. Guzmán, barefoot, stumbled over a large rock. Carmelo turned on the lantern and saw that the large toe was bleeding.

"I'll walk ahead with the lantern, Guzmán. Did you forget your shoes?" Carmelo tied his handkerchief around the boy's toe. "Stay close," he said. When they got to the bank of the Red River, Carmelo squatted so that his brother could climb on his back. Though only a few inches shorter than he, Guzmán was skinny and light-boned. Guzmán wrapped his arms around his brother's neck and his legs around his waist. Like a two-headed giant they crossed the moving stream. Carmelo fought the pull of the soft mud on his ankles, which like an insistent mouth tried to suck him down to the bottom. Guzmán closed his eyes against the call of the water. This same river curved around the hill and came to a house where a woman swam and played in the water. If he could only slip silently from his brother's shoulders, the current moving in the direction of her valley would carry him back to her.

SALUD!

The town of Salud was the result of a miracle. It is said that four centuries ago, on the site where the church now sits, a woodcutter had been charged by a crazed bull. The horns of the animal had pierced the man on the left side, much as Christ had been wounded by a Roman lance. As a pious man, the woodcutter had taken this as a divine message: he immediately called on the Blessed Mother for assistance. The Lady appeared on the top branches of the same tree Lorenzo Aguilar, the humble woodcutter, had been about to fell with his sharp axe. It is said that both man and bull dropped to their knees at the heavenly sight. She had spoken one word, "Salud," and the wound had been healed without a trace. The bull had become as tame as a lamb. And Lorenzo Aguilar became the spiritual founder of the town of Salud. He died of pneumonia at an early age, it is said, called to heaven to take his place among the saints.

News of the miracle traveled across the Island, and soon people from all parts of Puerto Rico came to Salud to visit the Shrine to Our Lady of Salud. Many people moved to the surrounding area to be near this salubrious place, to pray for the restoration of their health, either for themselves or for a loved one. And some miraculous, or nearly miraculous, recoveries were reported in time. The hamlet's repu-

45

tation grew. Soon the bishop in San Juan, a pragmatic Spaniard who had been sent to the Island by the Crown to lead his missionary priests in the conversion of the Taino Indians, took an interest in the popular shrine. Converting Indians was a slow and dreary business, with some of the priests reporting the loss of entire flocks of newly baptized savages to disease; it was impossible to keep accurate records. Building churches was the kind of constructive enterprise His Eminence truly enjoyed. A church was concrete proof of God's presence, even among heathens. As long as there were Indians left, labor was cheap, even free. Within a decade the magnificent cathedral-like church of Our Lady of Salud was completed. Unfortunately, the bishop had gone to his reward years before—a victim of typhoid, which he had caught during a visit to a remote village—but the work continued in his name. The famous shrine attracted the best sculptors and painters of the time, for it was considered blessed work. One such painter was Don Gustavo de La Lama, who later gained fame as official court painter of the Royal Infantes. As a young man he had come to Salud to paint the renowned scene of the woodcutter, Lorenzo Aguilar, and the bull kneeling before the Lady, who is suspended above the top branches of a tree in a circle of light. The fresco is located above the main altar. To this day the faithful may look up and witness the miracle at every mass. The lovely Lady is all in blue, her lips slightly parted because she is saying, "Salud."

And so Salud grew around the church, the little houses built to face the Holy Hill, where it sits like a great white hen spreading her marble wings over the town.

Chapter Two

SMALL TOWNS are vindictive, and when it became known that El Padrecito César had been sent away to a mountain retreat for his health, a rumor began to circulate that the young priest had been caught "in flagrante" by the housekeeper, Leonarda, who had then aroused Don Gonzalo from a deep sleep. For days Leonarda was sought after by the townswomen for afternoon coffee, and even invited into the wealthier homes in town, where the old woman had never crossed the threshold except to wash floors. They interrogated her endlessly about the scandal up at the rectory, but she played the coy maiden and would only say that the little priest had too many wild friends visiting him in his room; that he would stay up till all hours reading poetry with one of them in particular; that it didn't seem natural to her for young men to spend so much time together, reading love poems to each other. And who were his special friends? They all wanted to know. One or two names would be sufficient. No names, no names, insisted Leonarda holding a porcelain coffee cup, little finger extended up to her toothless mouth. Some of her hostesses would later mark the same cup with an X and use it only when beggars or pilgrims asked for a drink at their back doors. Leonarda was soon forgotten, but it wasn't long before another name was brought up for speculation.

There was a young girl who watched the rectory door with great interest. Her name was Isabel, and she was a devout churchgoer. A bright girl, she had often lent books to and borrowed books from Carmelo. She appreciated his sensibility and his love of good literature. Before Carmelo started devoting all his free time to Padre César, she had secured permission from her father to invite Carmelo up to the house to study with her. They would have been chaperoned by her young aunt. It would have been lovely. But Carmelo had turned her down. It was young Isabel who had seen Carmelo knocking at the rectory door. From the second-story terrace of her house there was a fine view of the church and priests' rooms. She had heard the loud voices and the high-pitched wailing of the little priest. Before dawn the next day she had heard an automobile drive up to the rectory. She climbed up to the terrace in time to see boxes and suitcases being tossed hastily into the back seat of the black vehicle which looked like a hearse. Then Padre César's blond head appeared briefly through the front window as the car turned around and drove down Salud's one paved street. That day the seven o'clock mass was said by a groggy Padre Gonzalo.

Isabel met Carmelo at the post office, where he went to check the mail every morning. She was sending a letter to her married sister in New York.

"Carmelo." She waved him over to her. She had to make the conversation quick or somebody was likely to see her talking to a boy unchaperoned and tell her father.

"Isabel. How are you?" Carmelo looked around. He was uncomfortable in her presence. She could see that.

"Fine. I've missed talking with you. Since summer started I've hardly seen you."

"I've been busy. We'll talk again when school starts. Our last year of high school, can you believe it?"

"Yes, time has flown, hasn't it? But listen, Carmelo, I

have some new books my sister sent me from New York. Would you like to come over and practice English with me? Father said you could once a week." She took a chance and placed her dainty hand on his forearm.

Carmelo recoiled instinctively. Once again he looked around nervously. "I'm grateful, Isabel. But I can't. I have to help out at home. Mamá is sick again and I may have to take a job in the fields. No time for reading. You understand."

Isabel lost her color. She wanted to shout at him that she had seen him knock at the door of the rectory at hours when other boys were visiting their sweethearts, and that she had seen the silhouettes of two heads close over a book through the curtains, the lacy white curtains of El Padrecito's bedroom window. Softly she said: "Of course I understand, Carmelo." And she forced a sweet smile. "You know, you're such a good Christian boy, you may end up taking vows."

"What do you mean?" Carmelo blushed deeply.

"You know. Become a priest. Poverty, chastity, and obedience." Leaving him in a state of confusion, Isabel hurried to the street, where several of her girlfriends waited for her in a giggling group.

CARMELO and his brother Guzmán were thrust together in the months that followed César's hasty departure. Mamá discovered she was pregnant again just when Guzmán turned fifteen. She turned inward and spent much of her time in solitary tasks like tending her chickens and gardening. She left the care and feeding of the family up to her fourteen-year-old daughter Ramona and advised the boys to find jobs for the summer. Papá Pepe was once again complaining of insomnia and headaches, which Mamá attributed to all the books he read.

Once when the two brothers had walked up to town to

pick up Ramona after an evening mass, not long after Guzmán had been fetched from the country, they saw La Cabra entering the domino hall. This was a bar where men drank rum and played games for money. Very few women went into the place. Guzmán hardly recognized her. She looked so different in a tight red dress, with high heel shoes and her hair piled high. Several men leaned out of other curbside establishments and whistled, calling out *piropos*, those exalted compliments bordering on hysteria that a beautiful woman elicits. Guzmán ran to her calling her name, "Rosa, Rosa."

The men took up the chant. "Rosa, Rosa, Rosita," they sang out. The woman ducked into the domino hall and Guzmán followed. Carmelo called his brother, and the men, many of them drunk, added "Guzmán, Guzmán" to their chant.

"Rosa," Guzmán caught up with the woman at the bar. "Why do you run away from me?"

"Isn't this one a little too young for you, Cabra?" One of the men from the game table turned around to the bar.

"Hey, if she's giving free lessons, I could use a few myself." Another man with a red bandanna around his neck who was wrinkled like a monkey shouted out, "I hear she learned a lot of tricks in Nueva York."

Guzmán tried to speak again but the woman turned to the bartender: "You allow minors in this place?" she asked, turning completely away from him. She sat on a stool and the man placed a drink in front of her without asking her what she wanted.

Guzmán made his way back across the room to the door. The man with the red bandanna yelled out, "Better luck next time, kid. Don't forget your wallet next time." Carmelo was waiting for him outside the door. When they found their sister, mass had been over for a while, but instead of walking around the atrium with her girlfriends as she usually did, Ramona was sitting in the darkened church.

"What's wrong, Ramonita?" Carmelo asked, seeing that the girl had been crying into her handkerchief.

"I can't tell you."

Guzmán pulled her up from the pew where she was crumpled. "Did somebody get fresh with you? There are a lot of drunks in town tonight." He felt like hitting somebody. Why had Rosa ignored him?

"You're hurting me, Guzmán. Let go."

"Ramona, tell us why you're crying." Carmelo took the handkerchief from her hands and wiped her eyes gently. The weariness of having the responsibility of the household now that Mamá was "indisposed" was telling on her.

"It was awful, Carmelo. It was Isabel . . . you know her."

"We go to school together. What about her?" Carmelo felt a sense of dread at the mention of the girl's name.

"She wouldn't really explain, but it had to do with you," Ramona said. "When I went up to her and my other friends after mass to ask them about the sewing group we were supposed to organize—you know, to make bandages for the soldiers, it's a school project—well, they stopped talking; then Isabel said something really peculiar."

"What did she say, Ramona?" Carmelo felt a wave of nausea building up to his throat.

"She said that since now you didn't have anybody to read love poems with, maybe you could join the sewing circle too." Ramona was in tears again.

Guzmán spit on the ground and said, "Bitches." This upset Ramona even more, since they were still standing on sacred ground.

"Let's go home. Mamá is not feeling well. She may need you, Ramona." Carmelo led them out.

51

"But what did Isabel mean, Carmelo?" Ramona asked. "I thought you two liked each other."

"Don't worry about this, Ramona. And don't say anything about it to Mamá. Isabel and I have had a misunderstanding, that's all."

But the town was small enough in those days to concern itself with small matters. They say Carmelo could not walk down the street without some shiftless person calling out to him that his trousers were too tight in the crotch or that his cologne could be smelled for miles and that if he didn't take care dogs would confuse him for a bitch in heat. Once a man dropped a nickel in a juke box as the two brothers were passing by a store and called out to Carmelo that the song was for him. It was a love song popular then about a man who had joined the priesthood when the woman he loved left him for another. Guzmán had torn himself away from his brother's grasp and grabbed the man by the throat. It took two men with Carmelo's help to pry him loose. They say that to the day he died the man wore a necklace of half-moon nailprints, compliments of my wild uncle.

In 1951 Carmelo lied about his age and joined the army. It had been a terrible year for the family. Another child had been born to Mamá Cielo, a terrible ordeal that kept her in a sickbed for weeks leaving Ramona, at fourteen, in charge of the household. Papá Pepe held two jobs, one painting houses and the other at night, keeping the books at the sugar refinery. The children looked after one another the best they could, but not always did they remember to attend school, not always did they come home when they were supposed to. Mamá Cielo sank deeper into a dark hole she had discovered inside her after Luz, the new baby girl, was born.

On the morning that Carmelo was to catch a ride in the cane truck that would take him as far as Mayagüez, where he would take a bus to San Juan, Mamá Cielo called him to her side.

"Son," she said, "you should not leave my house." Her long black hair was spread out over the pillow behind her, and her thin face had a sickly green sheen. To Carmelo she looked like a woman drowning in a black pool of water. This was the image he held behind his eyes when a year and three months later he was blasted into a thousand pieces over the soil of Korea.

"I have to go, Mamá." Carmelo kissed her limp hand. "Another year and they would have called me in anyway. This way I will be able to help you, and not by getting my skin burned in the cane fields as you are always saying." He had turned his face away from her because he didn't want her to see him crying. When he turned back around he saw that she had raised herself up on her elbows. She looked like a skinny brown bird poised for flight.

"Mamá, what are you doing?" Carmelo tried to gently push her back into the pillows.

"No," she said gasping with the effort of swinging her legs over the side of the high poster bed. "I will make you breakfast before you go. Go get your sister so she can help me dress. And tell Guzmán to see about some fresh eggs." She looked up at her son, his pretty face dark with concern.

"Carmelo."

"Yes, Mamá."

"Without you around to help me keep up with Guzmán, he will kill himself one of these days."

"Guzmán will survive, Mamá." Carmelo kissed his

53

mother on her clammy forehead and went to get the children together for breakfast.

They say Mamá cried all she was going to cry for her oldest child that day that he left her house; that she did not cry when she got the telegram calling him a good soldier who had given his life for his country. Beloved son.

There was a large photograph of Uncle Carmelo in his uniform in Mamá Cielo's bedroom. It was the kind popular in the fifties, where a photo was blown up and painted over in pastel colors. His cheeks were chubby and pink, and he had a thin mustache over a sensuous mouth partially opened in a smile. He was wearing his cap at an angle. Many years later I asked Mamá, "Is that your son who was killed in the war?"

She did not reply at once. She looked at the oval, ornately framed picture as if she were trying to find a familiar landmark in that too-rosy face.

"The mustache doesn't suit him," she said, "and he looks like he has learned to drink." Then she remembered it was me she was talking to: "Yes, *niña*, that is a picture of your Uncle Carmelo."

After Carmelo's death, Guzmán had found himself a paying job with the cutters, as an errand boy between the office in the refinery and the field. It was then that he met Rafael, the foreman's son. The foreman was Don Juan Santacruz, a man with a history and a violent temper. He was a blond, muscular man whose father had come to Puerto Rico from Catalonia, Spain, as a special agent for the Spanish Crown and had remained to found a fortune in land and a dynasty of sons who feuded endlessly over their inheritance. They say Don Juan had maimed one of his brothers in a machete fight and had been disowned by his father. No one really knows how it happened, or even if it really did. When Guzmán met him, he and his wife and their four children had already been in Salud for several years. Don Juan made friends with no one, spoke only to the American when he was called up to the Big House, and had a reputation as a man who could hold his cups and who was easily aroused to anger.

Rafael and his brothers and sisters were known as the "Sad Angels." Fair-skinned and blond, they stood out everywhere they went in Salud. They were seen only in the company of one of their parents—the boys dragging behind their father, carrying his lunch or his machete, or going into the store while their mother waited outside: a shy, tragic-looking woman who miscarried every other child, so that out of numerous pregnancies she had salvaged only four children.

When Rafael was seventeen years old, his father told him he had a job for him. His wife objected because Rafael was in high school and at the top of his class. Don Juan said it was time for his son to grow up and start contributing to the house. There were tears and violence, which drove Don Juan to his rum. The house was locked up all the next day and the people who passed by worried that there had been a tragedy. When the first blond head appeared at the door of the cottage, two things had been promised: that Rafael would work the fields, and that the next time Don Juan hit his wife Rafael would kill the old man.

ONE DAY Guzmán was washing himself at the bend of the little creek that runs behind the cane field. It was dusk and he had worked hard delivering paychecks to the cutters from the office. He had gotten two dollars in tips and as he stripped, he heard the coins jingling in his pants pockets and felt good. He was still scrawny, but he didn't care about his size. There was a current running through wires under his skin that made him feel he could jump higher than any other boy, maybe fly. He ran the three miles from the Central to the field several times every day, and still, when he went to bed at night, he had to hold on to the sides for fear that he would spring up and go right through the ceiling. Every morning he leaped into the day like a diver jumping off the highest cliff.

With a "whoop!" Guzmán dived into the deepest part of the water and collided head on with another body. If he had not felt flesh he would have called it a ghost: a pale, naked boy with blood streaming down his face from a cut above his eye where Guzmán's sharp elbow had landed like a tomahawk. Blinded, the blond boy struck out at his attacker, screaming "Who are you?" at the top of his lungs. Guzmán dived into the water and came up behind the injured boy, pinning his arms back.

"Hey, calm down. It was an accident." He was having trouble keeping the other from kicking him in the groin.

"Who is it, and why did you jump on me?"

"I'm Guzmán. It was an accident. I jumped in and there you were. Are you going to hit me if I let you loose?"

He freed the other who immediately swam to the bank and wiped his face with a shirt.

Guzmán followed him. "Are you all right?"

"I'll live, I guess," Rafael replied. He had seen this skinny kid Guzmán before, hanging around the Central office. Rafael's father called him "the mutt" because if he wasn't sleeping in the shade, he was trotting back and forth between the office and the field.

Over Rafael's protests, Guzmán ripped into strips his own shirt and bandaged the young man's head.

"Aren't you the errand boy at the Central?" Rafael asked.

56

He would always find it difficult to make friends, his atten-tion during childhood having been directed to the survival of his family.

"That's me," said Guzmán, pumping Rafael's hand with energy. "and you're the boss's son?"

"I'm Rafael Santacruz. I work in the fields," Rafael said.

"Don Juan's son," Guzmán said. "Why didn't your old man get you a job in the office? You're not going to last long in the fields." Guzmán was looking at Rafael's skin on his neck and shoulders which were irritated and peeling from the sun.

"What do you mean?" Rafael felt insulted by Guzmán's remark. He knew the other cutters resented him for being the boss's son, and to gain their respect he had been cut-ting in the hardest areas, often working through his lunch break. It was true that he still vomited from the exertion and the heat, but he was getting used to it.

"I didn't mean to offend you, man. I just meant that you're fair as a gringo. My brother was almost as white as you, and my mother never let him go to the fields. He's dead. He was killed in Korea."

Guzmán didn't know why he confided this to Rafael. He had not talked to anyone about Carmelo, and it had been nearly half a year since they got the telegram. Not enough pieces of his brother could be found to send home. They did send his books and his dogtags. Mamá Cielo had burned the books, many of them inscribed by Carmelo's friend César. Rafael and Guzmán dressed in silence.

"I heard about your brother. We went to the mass that was said for him. Your mother is a strong woman. I didn't see her cry. My mother is the opposite. She cries for every-body and everything."

Guzmán had not seen his mother cry, either. Since the new baby was born, pretty Luz, Mamá Cielo had lost some

57

of herself. There had been so much blood that Guzmán and Ramona had had to carry it out for the midwife in pans. Mamá Cielo did not get up from her bed for weeks. And after the telegraph boy had parked his bicycle outside the house, she had fallen almost completely into silence. Papá Pepe had also withdrawn into his own world: he would spend entire nights sitting at his Mesa Blanca altar trying to communicate with Carmelo's spirit.

"Hey, where are you going now?" Rafael brought Guzmán back from his thoughts.

"I was going to town. But that was before I met you by accident. Look at my best shirt." Guzmán pointed at the bloody rag Rafael had removed from his wound. It was only a surface cut and had quickly stopped bleeding.

"Come home with me. My mother will find you another shirt to wear, then maybe we can do something together," said Rafael.

"I don't know, man. Your father might not like me coming to your house." Guzmán had once seen Don Juan Santacruz in one of his violent rages. He had decided long ago to stay out of his path.

"It's my father's drinking and dominoes night, Guzmán," said Rafael. "We won't be seeing him at home until tomorrow morning."

"What about your mother?"

"Mamá is safest when the old man is not around. She's so busy with the children, she won't even notice there is an extra person in the house. Come on."

THE SANTACRUZ FAMILY lived in the caretaker's cottage at the gates of the American's estate. It was not a large house, but it was one of the better homes in Salud, with indoor plumbing and mosquito screens on the windows and doors. It had been built to the American's specifications along with the Big House. Once indoors, Guzmán saw that it was also well furnished with beautiful mahogany furniture, but that it all seemed out of place. The sofa was facing away from the center of the room, one chair was turned on its side, and over one lovely cut glass lamp there were several diapers hanging. One by one, blond heads peeked out from behind curtains and furniture.

"You'll have to forgive my brothers and sisters, Guzmán. We get few visitors, and they are very shy." A little girl about eight years old came out of one of the rooms carrying a teapot. Surprised to see a stranger in the room, she stumbled over a shoe in her path and dropped the teapot. It broke on the tile floor, spilling the hot liquid. The little girl looked up, terrified. She knelt on the floor, and her shoulders began shaking with silent sobs.

"What happened?" a woman's weak voice called from within the room.

"Nothing, Mamá, just a little accident. I'll take care of it."

Rafael knelt down next to his sister and raised her face with his fingers. "It's only me, Inés. Don't worry. Nobody is going to hurt you." The little girl finally looked up, but Guzmán saw that she was nearly paralyzed with fear. He had seen rabbits and pigs about to be slaughtered with the same look in their eyes.

Rafael helped his sister pick up the pieces and clean up. In the meantime, Guzmán had met the other children: another boy about ten years old, and the baby who crawled up to Guzmán and raised herself on his knee. She was close to his idea of an angel, with lovely brown eyes and a halo of soft yellow hair.

"How old is she?" Guzmán asked Rafael, who had just emerged from his mother's room.

"Eighteen months."

"Your parents must be crazy about her. She's beautiful."

Guzmán saw that the little girl was raising her arms to him, and he picked her up. He had not given his new sister much of his time yet. He resolved to do so. How trusting little children were.

"My father hasn't even registered her."

"What?" Guzmán was shocked. "You mean he hasn't signed her birth certificate? Why?"

"Maybe I shouldn't be telling you this, but I'm going to kill that son of a great bitch one of these days."

Guzmán saw the furious light in Rafael's eyes that he had glimpsed at the creek.

"You don't have to say anything, man. We've all got problems. Can you get me that shirt now?" Guzmán felt a sudden urge to leave this house.

"I'll get you one. Mamá is not feeling well. And no wonder: you know what that old bastard told her tonight before he left to get stinking drunk?"

"Rafael. You don't have to say anything."

"He's given the baby away. Just like that. He gave her away."

"What are you talking about?"

"My father, he gave Josefa to the American."

"That's crazy, Rafael. You can't just give a child away to a stranger just like that."

"If you knew my father, you'd know that it *is* possible. He told Mamá that since Mrs. Clement is barren and we depend on Mr. Clement for food and shelter, he had agreed to give them Josefa."

"I don't believe it." Guzmán put the child gently down and she wobbled unsteadily away on chubby legs toward her brother, who was reading quietly in a corner of the room. Inés kept coming in and out of her mother's room carrying steaming pans of water and towels.

"Is she any better?" Rafael asked.

60

"She's still bleeding, and I'm scared."

"Don't worry Inés. You know this happens to Mamá often. She's got weak insides." Rafael turned to Guzmán, who did not know what to say.

"I'll get you one of my shirts, but you'll have to go on without me. I'm going to stick around here in case Mamá gets worse. Sometimes the bleeding stops after a while but she's upset tonight, so I don't know."

"I understand, man."

Rafael brought out a fancy *guayabera,* white with blue embroidery.

"I can't take this. I won't even borrow it. With my luck it'll get stained."

"Keep it. Mamá makes them herself from material left over from the sewing she does for Mrs. Clement. I've got more fancy shirts than reasons to wear them."

It was during the carnival week for Our Lady of Salud that Guzmán saw Rosa again. During the nine days of religious services in honor of the town's patroness, a carnival set up its rides in the ball park and its games right in the street in front of the church. Christmas lights were strung between the houses and the church, turning the streets into a fantasy land of music and color. Pilgrims from all over the Island came to visit the shrine, and many of them stayed for the celebration. For nine nights Salud transformed itself from a drab, dusty hamlet into a colorful carnival, seducing the faithful like the hag in the fairy tale who turns into a beautiful woman just long enough to trick a prince into making love to her.

Guzmán had asked Rafael to meet him on the church steps. Since there are two hundred steps carved into the hill where the church sits, it's possible to choose a vantage point where one can observe the festival. Sitting there in his black shirt and his white pants pressed to perfection by Mamá Cielo, Guzmán looked like a lover waiting impatiently for his girl. His nervous gestures were symptoms of impatience—but for what, he did not know yet. He was sixteen years old and tired of school, tired of life at home, where his parents were still in deep mourning for Carmelo. It wasn't a good time for his sister Ramona, either. Mamá Cielo was keeping her busy with the baby and the other duties she claimed Ramona must assume. The poor girl was finding it difficult to keep up with her school work after staying awake nights with the baby, who had turned out to be a restless child.

Guzmán tried to help Ramona, but he was restless himself. More and more, he spent time at work at the Central, or with his friend Rafael. Rafael was completely different from Guzmán, and not just physically. He was easily the most intelligent person Guzmán had ever met. Just like his brother Carmelo, Rafael read every chance he got, but it wasn't poetry. Rafael read science. He dreamed of being a doctor someday. He showed Guzmán books he had ordered from the U.S. with plastic pages showing the insides of human beings. Guzmán, though he didn't say so, thought the blue, pink, and red innards that Rafael looked at with wonder and amazement were no different from the quivering masses of dead dogs often seen on roads where trucks ran over them. Rafael's plans were to graduate from high school in a year and join the navy. The U.S. government would then pay for his university studies. "If you come out of it alive," Guzmán had almost said, but Rafael's dream was too important to disturb with the thought of an improbable death in combat.

RAFAEL was nearly a half hour late. Guzmán scanned the crowded street for his friend's easy-to-spot blond head. It

62

was then that he saw Rosa. It was her familiar back, the pale shoulders, long neck, and mass of black hair; but when the woman turned around he saw that she was wearing a veil. She was dressed like a gypsy in a scarlet dress with a black apron. It was customary for the carnival people to wear costumes. The costumes served a double purpose: identifying the carnival people to the public as they wandered through the crowds enticing people to the games and tents, and, since they traveled from town to town, it made it hard for anyone to trace them should they run afoul of the law. The more Guzmán observed the gypsy standing in front of a bright green tent with white letters on its side that read TAROT, the more he felt that it was Rosa. It had been nearly two years since he had seen her. He had felt humiliated by her rejection, yet he dreamed about her constantly. Ever since he spent that week with her, all other women seemed coarse to him. All the girls he knew seemed like tadpoles in comparison with the radiant mermaid of his memory. Many times he had taken the road out of Salud, but only once had he dared to come near her house. The valley itself seemed an earthly paradise to him, and he often thought about what it would be like to live there with her. On a day when he was supposed to be in school, he had walked to the Red River. There he had floated in the clear water. It being the rainy season, the water was at its fullest, a true flowing river, not a swollen creek like the last time he had seen it as he crossed it on Carmelo's shoulders. After a while he had climbed up to the hill overlooking her house. He had felt exhilarated with his daring but also afraid of her reaction when he descended on her unexpectedly. He had not made it to her door. From where he stood he had seen two figures working in the garden. The other person with Rosa had been a child, a little girl. Wearing a straw hat, so that

Guzmán could not see her face, she had pulled weeds while the woman patted the earth, securing her little plants with long pale hands—magical hands that smelled like the herbs she tended, cooked with, healed with. Guzmán had heard thunder in the distance. The two figures had risen from their knees and looked up at the sky. There would be rain soon.

By the time he got home he was drenched. For the pleasure of seeing her from a distance, Guzmán paid with two weeks of high fever and racking coughs which left his chest sore and his body exhausted.

IT WAS SHE. It had to be she. Forgetting Rafael and everything else in his life, Guzmán climbed down the steps and made his way to the green tent. The gypsy was inside with a customer. Guzmán felt as if his bones were liquefying. From within came a familiar voice that said, "The Queen of Coins is a lucky sign." Guzmán leaned against a post trying to will himself strong and calm.

When the flaps opened and the man whose fortune included unexpected money walked away, blending into the currents of people that filled the street like so many iridescent fish, Guzmán entered the dimness of the tent. Rosa gasped with the fierceness of his embrace. She silently tried to push him away. There were people outside, all around the tent, unaware of the struggle within. In whispers she promised him a meeting, soon, at her house, if he would only let her go. But the hunger he had felt for her all this time, his need to hear Rosa's voice, to feel her hands on his body comforting and healing him, overwhelmed Guzmán. With bewildered anxiety he held her, burying his face in her neck, in her hair that smelled of wild flowers and incense. The strength in his arms and the legs that caught her own like pincers belied the slenderness of Guzmán's body.

64

"Not here. Not here." She kept pleading but he had her on the straw that covered the tent floor. Now he crouched over her, and her whole body exhaled a lament as she softened to his touch. She guided him into her, and with the vague smell of fresh straw in his nostrils Guzmán sank into the perfect darkness of her body. She moved under him like the river's current and drew him forth with a muffled cry deep in her embrace. Undone, he wanted to be cradled in her arms and sleep. She touched his face.

"I want to be with you, Rosa," he said to her, still on his knees while she picked the straw from his clothes and hair. She did not try to talk him out of it but kissed him full on the mouth.

She said, "I will be back home on Sunday."

They heard footsteps coming closer to the tent, a voice called out: "Hey, fortune teller, are you open for business?"

Guzmán and Rosa held each other in a silent embrace and then he came out into the brightly lit carnival scene and looked up at the church steps. He saw Rafael standing under a light, looking more than ever like an angel in his white trousers and guayabera, his yellow hair illuminated by the streetlights. Guzmán ran up to meet him two steps at a time.

"Been waiting long, friend?"

"No, I just got here. There was some trouble at home with the old man, and I had to wait until he fell asleep in a drunken stupor."

"Let's go try our luck at the bingo table, man. I feel lucky tonight," said Guzmán.

THEY TRIED all the games of chance that lined the street. Rafael had good aim and won a rag clown by bursting three balloons in a row with darts. He and Guzmán tried the horse races where twelve mechanical horses jerkily made their way to the finish line. Guzmán's number came in third, and he was presented with a plastic cigarette case. It was gaudy with rhinestones. They used their last nickels to ride the ferris wheel. Going slowly around, they got a panoramic view of the carnival eclipsing the countryside and even the church, a massive white structure sitting on its hill like a reproving matron, dim and dowdy. Stalled for a moment at the top of the ferris wheel while other people got on, Guzmán spotted the little green tent; a candle had been lit within, for he could make out the flickering silhouettes of two people facing each other over a table; Rosa was divining someone else's future with her cards.

"Have you had your hand read yet?"

"What?" Rafael's voice had startled Guzmán.

"The fortune teller, man. I'm asking you whether you've been to her yet," Rafael said.

"Yes, why, have you?" Guzmán felt exposed. Had Rafael seen him going into Rosa's tent?

"No. I wouldn't waste my money. But I know you are a true believer," said Rafael, and he winked at Guzmán.

Guzmán had told Rafael about his visit to Rosa's valley. Not everything. No one would ever understand everything, but he explained enough to defend Rosa's reputation to his friend, who, like many people in town, thought of Rosa as a woman who lived a questionable life. There had been a lot of loose talk about her in the last year. If he hadn't craved even the mention of her name, he would have deplored it, or even tried to defend her as he had just now with Rafael. Not that anyone would listen to him.

At nine the church bells began to toll announcing the first mass of novena to Our Lady of Salud. Within minutes the rides were shut down and all music stopped. Canopies were locked over the games and exhibits. The agreement from time immemorial between the church and the carnival people was that they could operate until it was time

66

for mass. If the people were not distracted and already in town for the carnival they would come to church. The novenas were always well attended, and the collection basket filled with coins that had gone in and out of different pockets for other reasons earlier in the evening.

Rafael suggested that they go to the mass. Guzmán protested, but, still feeling expansive, he finally agreed. When they entered they looked for a pew in the back of the nave. In the very last row nearest the door Guzmán saw Ramona. She was wearing a long white mantilla and had the sleeping baby Luz in her arms. He kept his eyes on them until the service was over, then he rushed to their side.

"Ramona, what are you doing here?" Guzmán was surprised to see his sister in town. With Mamá Cielo's demands on her time, the poor girl had not even attended church very much lately.

Ramona did not answer him right away. She was looking past him to Rafael. Rafael was sitting in a pew across the way. Shyly he looked back at Ramona.

"At school they used to call him the Archangel Rafael," she whispered to Guzmán.

"Ramona," Guzmán insisted, slightly peeved at his sister's behavior, "can you please tell me what you are doing here this late at night with Luz? Shouldn't she be in bed?"

"I came with Doña Julia, Guzmán. You don't have to worry. Luz was very restless tonight so Mamá told me to bring her too. She's sleeping now. Like an angel." Ramona had not taken her eyes off Rafael. To Guzmán his sister was acting "boba," retarded or something.

"Where is the old hag?" he asked.

"What?"

"Doña Julia. Your chaperone, where is she? If Mamá only knew what a poor job she's doing of keeping an eye on you."

"Don't be so offensive in God's house, Guzmán. Doña

67

Julia knew I'd be perfectly safe here while she went to have her fortune told."

"Just make sure you stay right here. Do you understand, Ramona? I'll walk you home."

"Will Rafael come with us?" Ramona asked while she replaced the rubber nipple in her sister's mouth from where it had slipped. She looked like the painting of a young madonna and child on the church wall. Guzmán felt a wave of tenderness for her. Ramona had been deprived of almost all pleasure because their parents would not lift the blanket of mourning that had fallen over their house after Carmelo's death.

"You think two brave men will be enough to defend the lovely Doña Julia?" Guzmán asked sarcastically.

Ramona smiled but her eyes were not focused on him. He went to sit next to Rafael.

"You know my sister Ramona?" Guzmán asked his friend who was sitting stiffly facing the front of the church.

"I used to see her at school. I spoke to her once in town but I heard your Mamá punished her for it so I never stopped her again. We were just discussing schoolwork, you know? Your mother is a strict woman, Guzmán."

"Ramona is a good girl. We don't want her to get into any trouble," Guzmán said, surprising himself at the seriousness of his tone.

"I know that, Guzmán, I feel the same way about my sisters."

Doña Julia returned looking like an ominous bird in her black shawl and mantilla. In her hand she had a little bottle filled with a greenish liquid which she tried to conceal when she saw Guzmán and Rafael flanking Ramona outside of church.

"What's the devil's son doing in God's house?" she said to Guzmán.

68

"I'm going to walk my sister home, Doña Julia. That is, if you're quite through shopping for potions tonight."

"Ramona is safer with me than with you two hoodlums. And by the way, wasn't it you coming out of the gypsy's tent a while ago? Getting curious about your future, boy? Well, you don't need to be. You have no future."

Guzmán decided to ignore the old woman's taunts. He fell a few steps behind the women and offered Rafael a cigarette.

"No, thanks." Rafael kept his eyes fixed on Ramona, who walked slowly with the heavy burden of her little sister in her arms.

They soon left the festival grounds, taking the dirt road to Mamá's house. It was a cool night and not yet ten o'clock. Guzmán did not want to go home, but he knew he could not go back to town. Doña Julia had seen him coming out of Rosa's tent. He could not risk others seeing him with Rosa. As they approached the house, they could make out Mamá Cielo sitting in a hammock on her porch. Guzmán kissed his sister on top of the head and told her to go on with Doña Julia. The old woman grumbled under her breath the whole way and would surely cause trouble for him with Mamá.

"Where are you going, Guzmán?" Ramona seemed reluctant to part with them.

"We're going back to town." Guzmán felt the current of attraction like a dust devil stirring between Rafael and Ramona. "Tell Mamá I'll be home late. Tell her not to wait up."

Rafael suddenly placed the rag clown he had won on the sleeping baby in Ramona's arms. The girl smiled at him and slowly walked away. She was still wearing her white mantilla over her long black hair. In the deepening night she looked lovely and fragile.

Rafael said suddenly, as if just awakening, "I can't go back to town, Guzmán. There is something I have to do tonight."

"That was just an excuse I gave my sister, man. I don't have any plans."

"If that's the case, maybe you'll want to come on a secret expedition with me."

Guzmán looked at his friend in surprise. Rafael was one of the most honest people he knew. Guzmán had never been able to convince him to participate in anything that had to do with risk.

"What kind of secret expedition, brother? No matter what it is, count me in. But tell me quick."

"A visit to the American's house."

"Are you crazy, Rafael? You know they have killer dogs there. I've heard he even has a guard on duty round the clock. We might get shot, did you think of that?"

"Well, if you don't want to go with me . . ." Rafael said in his soft voice, "I don't blame you, but I'm going . . . I have to."

"I'm not going to let you go alone. We'll die together." Guzmán laughed. He felt excited with the idea of the adventure already. "But why do you have to go? Is the American holding your old man for ransom or something?"

"If he were, that would solve everyone's problems. No, my old man is sick. His liver is giving up on him finally."

"Sorry to hear that, man."

"Don't be," Rafael said with the usual bitterness his voice took on when speaking of his father. "Mamá is finally sleeping nights."

"Then why the sudden urge to visit the Big House?"

"It's my little sister, Josefa, remember her? You saw her at my house. The baby."

"That's right. Your old man gave her away. I see. You want to make sure they're treating her well."

"Seeing Ramona with the baby reminded me. No one at home has been allowed to even mention Josefa. It's like we never had her. You understand?"

"What are we waiting for?" Guzmán was already focusing his eyes on the distant light on the hill.

To get to the Big House they had to pass Rafael's cottage. Rafael silently approached the window to his parents' room. The loud groans of Don Juan in his sickbed could be heard through the open window. There were light footsteps and a woman's soft murmurings.

"She takes care of him like a child night and day," Rafael whispered to Guzmán. "And she's ill herself."

"What's wrong with him?" asked Guzmán.

"The old man's sins have finally caught up with him. It's the liver and the stomach mostly. He throws up everything he eats. But he still sends me out for rum. Can you believe it?"

"Do you hate him that much, Rafael?"

"I don't wish he were dead, if that's what you mean. Mamá loves him. He works like a horse. It's his drinking I can't stand. It makes him act like a madman."

Guzmán put his hand on his friend's shoulder. "Maybe the pain he's going through will teach him a lesson."

"The American, Mr. Clement, sent his own doctor to see him this week. He told us unless the old man is sent to a sanatorium and kept off liquor, he'll be dead within a year."

"What does your father say to that?"

"He won't go."

There was a muffled scream from within the room and the sound of footsteps running.

"Is there anything we can do?" Guzmán asked, alarmed.

"No, that's how they'll spend the night. Let's go up to the Big House now. I promised Mamá I'd have news of little Josefa for her."

So as not to stir the dogs, Rafael led Guzmán up a dirt path used by the workers rather than the well-lit paved driveway up to the Big House. The place was bright with lights. Even from the far side of the lawn they could detect several people moving behind the drapes. It was obvious that Mr. and Mrs. Clement were entertaining guests. They went around to the back of the house, where if they happened to be seen it would be by the cook, Santa, or one of the other servants in the kitchen. Cautiously they approached the large window, from where they could see through the kitchen door into the dining room. The maid was setting up a long table with gleaming white dishes and silverware. There were two long candles at either end. A crystal chandelier was suspended over the table. Guzmán had never seen anything like it. He felt an urge to climb in through the window to take a closer look at the intricate tiers of crystal that glittered like diamonds.

"Stay down, Guzmán. I think they're about to go in for dinner," Rafael whispered.

At that moment the maid rang a little gold bell and threw wide open the double doors that connected the dining room to the parlor. A dozen or so elegantly dressed people walked in, all talking in subdued tones. When Rafael and Guzmán got closer to the window, very close in fact, because several of the chairs had their backs directly in front of the window, they realized the people were speaking in English.

"Do you understand, Rafael?"

"Yes, a little. Quiet now."

When everyone was seated, the same maid rolled in a

beautifully carved mahogany high chair and set it near the head of the table beside the one empty chair. A tall, thin woman with a tiara in her gray hair came in the room carrying a chubby blond child. The child was dressed in an ornately ruffled green velvet gown and she seemed irritable. She was trying to get at the woman's tiara with her chubby hands.

As the woman entered, everyone rose to their feet. She said something, smiling widely. At the same time she held the child up like a trophy in front of her. Everyone applauded. The baby grabbed the woman's tiara and yanked. For a moment there was confusion as several of the other women rushed forward to disentangle the baby from the jewelry. The maid rushed to take the child and nodded when the tall woman leaned forward to tell her something.

As the guests returned to their chairs the boys had a good view of the child being wheeled into the kitchen in her mahogany high chair, still screaming.

"What did the woman say, Rafael?"

"She said, 'I want you all to meet my daughter, Josephine.'"

It was that night, while walking back to Rafael's house, that Guzmán told his friend that he had decided to live with Rosa. Rafael was shocked at the plan.

"Your mother won't allow it, Guzmán," he said. "Besides that, it'll cause a scandal, the woman is twice your age, and what about school?" In his excitement Rafael had spoken out loud, and in the distance the boys heard the barking of dogs. They started running toward Rafael's house. A light still shone in his parents' bedroom. Panting, they reached the far edge of the yard. There they rested in silence for a few minutes.

73

"I'm telling you, Guzmán, moving in with that woman will only bring trouble for everyone."

"Please don't refer to her as *that* woman, Rafael. Her name is Rosa." Guzmán was feeling a determination building up within himself. Why shouldn't he and Rosa be together? He was a man. He felt what men felt, he did what men did. Hadn't Carmelo been just a year older than he was when he went off to Korea?

"Mamá will just have to understand. I don't need school any more. Rosa needs me at her place, she needs a man to help her out."

"I think you're making a mistake, friend. You'll see fireworks when you tell your parents." Rafael was concerned about Guzmán's impulsive decision, but he kept glancing at the window where he could see his mother bending over the sickbed. The old man was getting worse. Surgery was absolutely necessary, the doctor had warned them, but Don Juan was being stubborn about it. Money was getting scarce, and his mother kept looking to Rafael for support more and more. He couldn't concentrate on school and take care of the family too. Rafael looked at Guzmán. Only his dark, heavily lashed eyes were like his sister Ramona's. Ramona was dark-skinned, but her hair was long and silky. Guzmán could pass for an Indian with his red complexion and lanky body. But it was his wildness, too, that made him so different from the elegant, shy Ramona. She had looked so lovely in church with the chubby infant in her arms. There was noise from the house, a deep groan. Rafael got to his feet.

"Can I help with anything?" Guzmán asked.

"No, I'll go in. It's always worse at night. Just take my advice and forget about that . . . Rosa. You don't want more trouble in your family."

"Rafael." Guzmán placed his hand on Rafael's shoulder.

74

"Yes?" The screams continued and Rafael was anxious to go in.

"Promise me you won't tell anyone about my plan."

"I'll try to keep that promise, Guzmán. Good night."

THAT SUNDAY, without seeking anyone's advice, Guzmán took a few of his things and appeared at Rosa's door. She did not act surprised to see him. She allowed him to circle her waist with his rough laborer's hands and when he embraced her she could feel the anxiety of his desire for her. She tasted her own need in his mouth.

WHEN GUZMÁN did not come home that first night, Mamá sat in her hammock and waited up for him; by dawn she was dressed to go out, and by midmorning she had visited every place she thought he could be. Doña Julia, sensing disaster, came to the house early. It was her idea to call on the priest. Don Gonzalo, tired of the passions of youth and their consequences, put the matter in the hands of the Ladies' Civic Council and Holy Rosary Society. The group was made up of young and energetic married women, who did everything from decorating the church with flowers to embroidering his vestments. It was, they say, the beginning of the last witch hunt in Salud.

Chapter Three

THE PRESIDENT of the Holy Rosary Society was Doña Martina Modesto, the plump young wife of the town of Salud's only lawyer. Married only five years to the town's most eligible bachelor (now its most zealously guarded husband), Doña Tina had once served Don Modesto as his very able secretary. She had since assumed her rightful position as queen of Salud society, a situation that by its nature demanded that she and her ladies be the watchful guardians of the moral status of the town. With the church as her center of operations and Don Gonzalo so dependent on their assistance, Doña Tina and her contingent of devout followers had no problem enforcing their rules of conduct. It was Doña Tina who first heard the story of young Guzmán's abduction by La Cabra from Doña Julia's own lips in the presence of Padre Gonzalo, who had invited them both to the rectory. The priest willingly turned over the discussion to Doña Julia. In fact, he secretly resented the whole episode with its prurient connotations and, worse, the effects that he perceived it would have among the women. Behind his watery eyes Padre Gonzalo imagined a muddy pond into which a stone would be cast; would there be ripples or would it sink unnoticed to the bottom? He yawned behind a blue-veined hand, turning the motion into a sign of the cross when the two women entered the room. Almost time for his afternoon nap.

"Your blessing, Padre." It was Doña Tina who spoke first. She had not acknowledged Doña Julia yet, though the old woman had caught up with her at the door of the rectory. Doña Tina had had to quicken her pace to an almost unseemly trot earlier when she had caught sight of the old woman in her perennial half-mourning gray dress. More like a sack really. A sack of potatoes. Ever since she had invited the disgusting creature over for coffee at the start of the Guzmán–La Cabra affair, the poor woman had tried pathetically to get close to her. She'd even gone as far as to harass one of the Holy Rosary Society members for a recommendation to join their organization. Doña Tina despised pushy people, especially old people who did not act dignified. "Thank you," she said in response to Padre Gonzalo's lethargic gesture, which managed to include a motion for them to take a seat. The ridiculous old woman actually genuflected when she crossed in front of the priest.

There was an uncomfortable little pause as both women waited in respectful silence for the old priest to open the discussion. Padre Gonzalo, in the meantime, had taken mental leave of the room. In lieu of the nap he yearned for, he was practicing a new talent he had recently discovered in himself: telepathy. He could, he believed, transfer his thoughts through concentration to his housekeeper, although it didn't seem to work with anyone else. He had been successful in summoning the faithful old servant on three separate occasions in the previous week. Each time she had claimed she heard him call out her name. Padre Gonzalo was hoping he could make her come in with an urgent message for him. Anything to take him away from the unpleasant business at hand.

"Padre Gonzalo." It was Doña Tina who finally found it necessary to bring the priest out of his trance. Though she said his name gently, Doña Tina found herself wondering whether Don Gonzalo had passed his years of usefulness. Perhaps it was time for a replacement. Then she remembered the trouble she and her friends had had to go through to get the bishop in San Juan to recall that nasty little seminarian, Padrecito César, not too long ago. And Padre Gonzalo was easy to take care of.

"Padre, you sent for me. A matter of some urgency, you said. I'm here to do all I can to help." Doña Tina, after making sure she had the old man's attention, modestly lowered her eyes and waited for the priest to speak.

"Don Gonzalo summoned me too, Señora," Doña Julia piped up, leaving the old priest looking like he had just swallowed a fly, for he had been about to say something. Something now forever lost. Just as well. "We need your help in bringing to justice that *puta*, La Cabra . . ."

In her haste to get out of her chair, Doña Tina dropped the missal she had so carefully set down on her ample lap only a second earlier. Don Gonzalo swallowed noisily. All this because of the word for whore, *puta*, one of the harshest sounds in the Spanish language. Like the expulsion of spit. Doña Julia had forgotten herself in her excitement. She had forgotten her audience.

"Padre, why is this woman here? I won't stay . . ." Doña Tina was livid with anger.

"Doña Julia, please mind what you say. We understand how upset you must be. However, from now on you will please refer to the woman we are discussing by her Christian name."

"I'm sorry, Padre. Doña Tina, forgive me. It's just that La . . . , I mean Rosa, has hurt some people I love. My comadre, Doña Cielo, and her son Guzmán."

"Please sit down, Doña Tina. That's it." Don Gonzalo reconciled himself to the fact that he would have to stay for the duration. These two women together in the same room

78

were an explosive combination. Both egotistical. He wasn't blind to people's sins—not yet. "Doña Julia, please tell Doña Tina what you told me about young Guzmán's involvement with this woman Rosa."

"Yes, Padre. It's awful how she has ruined the life of an honest family. She's a witch, I tell you. And worse . . ."

"Doña Julia," Don Gonzalo's voice expressed all the weariness he felt, "please just tell Doña Tina the plain and simple truth about this matter. It is grave, as you say, but we need facts before we can take action."

Doña Tina was by now on the edge of her seat. This was going to be interesting. La Cabra had been on her list for a long time. A whore masquerading as a spiritist healer. But the woman had always covered her tracks so well. She urged Doña Julia on. You had to give the old woman credit. She had a finger on everything: "Please, Doña Julia, take your time and tell me everything you know about this evil woman . . . Rosa?" And she gave Doña Julia her most ingratiating smile. Don Gonzalo groaned a little in his chair.

"Well, Señora, it's like this. My comadre, Cielo, has always suffered because of her wild younger son, Guzmán. The boy is possessed. There is no other explanation. She took him to doctors and hospitals, here and there, and nothing helped. He just got wilder. I could tell you stories that would curl all the hair on your body . . . oh, pardon. I mean that boy has no respect for anyone—not even her who bore him. Anyway, a few years ago Cielo got so desperate that she decided to take him to Sister Rosa—that's how this woman likes to be called—for a spiritual reading. Of course, as her comadre I took an interest in the terrible situation. I warned her that this woman had a bad reputation. But you know how it is in these family affairs: the heart takes control and there is no persuading anyone once they've made up their minds to do something, no

79

matter how foolish. Well, Doña Tina, I felt like the only thing I could do was accompany my comadre and her son to La Ca . . . I mean, Pura Rosa's center."

"Pura Rosa!" Doña Tina was fascinated. Don Gonzalo had folded his hands on his lap in the attitude of the forbearing confessor.

"That's what her mother named her, poor woman." Doña Julia was speaking more confidently now. She had that snob Tina lapping it up. Doña Julia was determined to keep her control on this. It wasn't going to be Tina's show. "She can't be resting very peacefully after giving birth to a viper." Both women smiled knowingly at one another.

"Doña Julia, why don't you let the dead rest in peace?"

"I'm sorry, Padre. May I continue?"

"Please do, Doña Julia." Doña Tina placed her missal on the end table and settled back comfortably in Padre Gonzalo's padded mahogany armchair. A rich woman had willed all the furniture in the rectory. Padre Gonzalo hoped it had bought the old sinner a little grace, though he doubted it.

And so two hours passed while Doña Julia recounted the story, as she knew it, of Guzmán's stay at La Cabra's. Her godson Carmelo, now a saint in heaven after being blown to pieces on the foreign soil of Korea, having to go and rescue Guzmán from the woman. Mamá Cielo's strange silence about the matter. Her breakdown from the grief of having lost her best son in a war, and not even a big enough piece left of him to send home in an envelope. The awful things that were said about Carmelo and Padrecito César—oh, excuse me, Padre Gonzalo; all lies, of course, but painful for a mother to hear. Poor woman, poor martyred mother. And now, Guzmán had been taken away from her by that woman again. They say the two of them

80

live in that house by the Red River. A woman old enough to be his mother. And so on and so on.

Doña Julia had embroidered the story like a pattern of vines on a pillowcase; the threads were tangled underneath, but on the surface a complex design was becoming clear and evident to Doña Tina. When Doña Julia finished her story or could not talk anymore because the excitement and the effort had worn her out, the women walked softly out of the rectory parlor so as not to awaken Don Gonzalo. At the front door Doña Tina directed the other woman to meet her at Doña Cielo's house the next morning. She would have a plan by then.

"Will you call a meeting of the Rosary Society, Doña Tina?"

"I may." Doña Tina paused, seeing clearly how this old conniver was manipulating her. "I will, that is; why don't you drop by my house tonight, dear Doña Julia, about seven?"

"I'll be there a little earlier than seven so we can talk."

"No need, Doña Julia, no need. We've talked enough. Good-bye."

Doña Tina rushed off, her taffeta dress and silk stockings making a rustling sound like the wind on the palm trees. Doña Julia pulled down her cotton frock over her drumlike abdomen. The rough gray cloth was limp from her sweat. She had worked hard this afternoon. Doña Leonarda, the housekeeper, came out from behind the staircase. She smiled toothlessly at Doña Julia.

"Julia, how about some coffee in the kitchen?" she said.

MAMÁ CIELO had summoned Rafael to her house. He had been expecting to hear from Guzmán's family, and frankly he wanted an excuse to catch a glimpse of Ramona, whose madonna face had stayed in his mind since he had seen her at the church. She had quit school to help her family through these hard times after Carmelo's death in Korea. And now Guzmán was bringing them more heartache. His own family revolved around Don Juan's suffering. The old man was still resisting going to the hospital, so the American's doctor who came from San Juan periodically to check the baby, Josefa, would drop by and look at Don Juan. He predicted things would only get worse. Rafael sat down on the porch steps and waited in respectful silence. Her mother was dressing to receive him, Ramona informed him shyly from the doorway.

"Are you busy, Ramona?"

"There is always something to do around here, why?" She smiled and it transformed her. She was always so serious, always the little mother with a child by the hand. But today she looked like what she was, a fifteen-year-old girl. Her skin was lighter than Guzmán's: a café-con-leche color. And her brown eyes were almond shaped and smiled when she did. Rafael thought she was a little too thin. He pitied her for the burden she had had to assume so early. Both of them were bearing the heavy cross of family problems.

"Where is your little sister?" Rafael was trying desperately to think of ways to keep Ramona from leaving.

"Sleeping." She came a little closer and stood above him. Their eyes met for a moment and she started to turn away.

"Ramona, don't go. Please, sit down next to me." He took her thin wrist gently and tried to pull her down. She was trembling.

"No, no. Mamá will be furious. I'm not supposed to talk to men." *Men.* Rafael liked the fact that she thought of him as a man. He let go of her wrist and stood up to face her.

82

"Ramona," he said, "we have to talk. Soon." She lifted her face and let him look full into her eyes. They were clear and innocent as a child's, but he could sense her readiness to accept him. "I'll be back for you." He wasn't quite sure why he made that promise to this woman-child he had spoken to only a few times, but he was to keep his word.

Ramona and Rafael were to be man and wife not a full year after they faced each other on Mamá Cielo's porch.

MAMÁ CIELO asked only one question of Rafael: "Is my son with the whore?" Though he felt ashamed at the reproof in her voice, Rafael could see how much this woman suffered, and he pitied her. He recognized in her lined face and weary eyes his own mother's pain. Instead of answering, he offered to bring Guzmán home. "Do you think my son will listen to you when he does not obey his own parents?" Doña Cielo said. But she fixed him with a hopeful look. "Will you go today?"

"Yes, señora. I will go now." But just as Rafael was getting up to leave, Doña Julia burst in.

"Cielo, Cielo." She was shouting in her excitement. "Doña Tina is on her way here." She saw Rafael and stopped abruptly.

"What is this *Angel Triste* doing here, Cielo? I've seen him conspiring with your son many times. Is he sniffing around for your daughter now, too?"

They all heard Ramona's gasp from the kitchen door where she had been silently watching Rafael. The old woman's words, so crass and brutal, hurt her. With a great effort Mamá Cielo rose from her chair.

"Doña Julia. Comadre. Please don't judge this young man too harshly. He has offered to help me find my son." Her voice was weak and even Doña Julia felt a small sense

83

of compassion for this woman visited all at once with death and betrayal from her children. She took her friend by the arm and led her back to her sofa.

"Cielo, you cannot expect help from the young ones. They will be faithful only to each other. Listen to me. Doña Tina has been sent to help you by Padre Gonzalo. Last night we had a meeting at her house."

"We." Doña Cielo was now following her friend's words. Why had Doña Julia brought outsiders into this family problem?

"The Holy Rosary Society. They are fine ladies. But I'll let Doña Tina tell you what we've decided to do about that whore who stole your son."

"Doña Julia! I did not ask you to speak to anyone about this." Mamá Cielo came close to tears of shame, but she saw Doña Tina's plump, overdressed figure crossing her front yard and held back her tears. This society gossip must not see her weakness.

Rafael, in the meantime, had inched his way toward the kitchen. Aware of Doña Cielo's distress, he had motioned to her behind Doña Julia's back. He would go see Guzmán. In the kitchen he found Ramona sitting at the table. Tears were streaming down her face. He stroked her lustrous black hair. "Is your father at the Central office?" Ramona nodded yes. "I'll send him home. And don't worry, some- day we'll both be far away from all this." She took his hand and brought it to her damp cheek. So many promises he had to keep; Rafael felt the words were like stones in a sack he had to carry.

Doña Tina sat down without being asked. She was in- congruously dressed in red, though she knew that Mamá Cielo was still in full mourning. Out of respect for this sad home, she should have worn a dark color.

"Doña Cielo, I would like for you to tell me everything

84

you know about this woman Rosa. The society has decided, with Don Gonzalo's blessing, of course, to do something permanent about this disgraceful woman who is
endangering so many souls in our town of Salud . . ." She
paused to take a breath before continuing her prepared
speech, but Mamá Cielo rose slowly from the sofa.

"Doña Tina. With your permission I will take my leave. I
am ill. I'm certain that Doña Julia will tell you anything
you need to know about my family, for she is my comadre
and has been my neighbor for twenty years." She looked
defiantly at the intruder and continued. "As to the woman,
do what you will. My son will return home, and I will deal
with him."

"Cielo!" Doña Julia was shocked at her comadre's curt
dismissal. Doña Cielo walked slowly into her bedroom and
closed the door. In all her life she had never insulted a
visitor in her house, but when she collapsed on the bed,
she saw only the faces of her sons in her mind's eye. Carmelo—handsome and sensitive, forced to leave his home
because of the evil minds that could only see that he was
different from the other young men—killed in another
man's war. She felt in her heart that people like Doña Tina
had killed Carmelo. And Guzmán, blown about like a leaf
by the winds of his passions. She would lose him too. After
a while there was a soft knock at her door, and she feared
Julia had been bold enough to follow her. She would sever
all ties with the conniving old woman whom she had mis-
taken for a friend. Papá Pepe walked shyly to Mamá Cielo's
bed and sat down on the edge. No words were exchanged.
They were both too full of grief and too tired. He took her
limp, warm hand in his. It was the first time they had
touched since she had banished him from her bed a second time, after her belated last pregnancy. He was not a
strong person. The death of Carmelo had dimmed his life

light, and he worked like an automaton these days, without joy, and he said little. Mamá Cielo gathered the last little bit of energy and made a decision. "Pepe, we cannot fight Guzmán any longer. We have to let him go." The old man simply nodded.

THE ONLY THING Rafael could think of to do was to reach La Cabra's valley before the Rosary Society women did. In order to do that he would have to enlist Mr. Clement's help. Mr. Clement owned several motorcycles, which he had shown off to Rafael more than once. Rafael believed the man liked him because, as Mrs. Clement was barren, he had no sons. Of course, now they had a daughter, Rafael's own little sister, Josefa. The man would not refuse his request. Rafael walked quickly up the hill toward the Big House. He decided to be bold and take the paved driveway leading to the front gate. Workers always approached the house from the rear. When he came to the front door, Rafael took a minute to wipe the sweat from his face with the clean handkerchief his mother always put in his trousers. He ran his fingers through his fine blond hair. People were always telling him he looked like a gringo. He rang the doorbell, and Santa, the housekeeper-cook, opened the door. She seemed surprised to see him there; then with a look of pity she asked, "Is Don Juan . . . I mean, did your father . . .?

"No, Doña Santa. My father is still very ill but he's not dead." Rafael suddenly remembered the chaos in his own home. He had to get Guzmán quickly and return to his own duties. "I need to see Mr. Clement," he continued. "It's very important. Is he home?"

"Yes." Doña Santa gave him a look that said *It better be important.* "Wait in here." She motioned him into the foyer. Rafael looked around him. All things sparkled in this house, from the polished mahogany furniture to the great tiered chandelier which he could see at the far end of the house in the dining room. He heard footsteps and the booming voice of Mr. Clement directing Doña Santa in his heavily accented Spanish to go to his wife at once. Then he saw Rafael. He addressed him in English. He had once told him that if he learned English well enough, he would take him to the U.S. with him on business trips. Of course Rafael's father had encouraged him to do so. It seemed as if Don Juan were anxious to give all his children away to the American. Rafael's own ambition lay elsewhere, but learning English was part of his plan. So he had taught himself through books and practiced it whenever possible.

"Come into my office and sit. Santa will bring us something cool to drink in a minute." Mr. Clement ushered Rafael into a small room off the foyer. It had a desk and an easy chair. "Make yourself comfortable, son, and tell me what's on your mind."

Rafael nodded his thanks and sat down, though somewhat stiffly. "Mr. Clement. I'm sorry to bother you in the middle of a work day . . ."

"Don't apologize, boy, I was here anyway. I don't stay out in the midday sun. Only mad dogs and Englishmen do." And he laughed. Rafael did not understand the meaning of the man's words, but he smiled politely.

"Yes, sir. I need a favor." Now that he was about to say what he needed, he felt foolish. What if the man got angry at his request? As it was, his family depended on the American for their very survival. Don Juan was getting disability pay, and Rafael was still working in the fields when he wasn't in school.

"Well?" It was obvious Mr. Clement was getting a little impatient with the boy's hesitation.

"I need to borrow one of your motorcycles," he blurted out.

"My motorcycle?" Mr. Clement exclaimed in his thunderous voice. The man was over six feet tall and built solid over heavy bones. But his skin was pink as a newborn baby's. There were many jokes made about this contrast. When he looked up at the face of the man now standing right in front of him, Rafael saw that he was surprised at his request but not angry.

"My friend Guzmán is in trouble. I need to bring him home before there is more trouble."

"Guzmán." The American pronounced it "Gooseman." "Is that the boy who runs errands at the refinery?"

"Yes, sir, that is Guzmán. He's a good person, but many people do not understand him."

"What's happened to him? Is he in trouble with the law?"

"Not exactly. He's in trouble with his mother and with the ladies of the Holy Rosary Society."

"That's even worse, son." Mr. Clement smiled widely. "It must be woman trouble then. Am I right?"

"It's very complicated, sir. Everyone thinks he's been bewitched by the one they call La Cabra. Only I know that he went to her house because he wanted to."

"Jesus! He's mixed up with her? I've known Rosa for a long time and I always thought she was a practical businesswoman. She ought to know better than to rob the cradle in this tight-assed town."

Rafael remained silent. The man seemed to be talking to himself rather than to him. But he knew he'd get what he came for.

"Go to the shed and have José give you the keys to the Rough-Rider. That's the one I always take to the valley." He winked at Rafael.

"Thank you, Mr. Clement. I'll bring it back tonight."

"No problem, son. How's your old man?"

"Not well."

"That's too bad. He's a good worker when he's not drinking."

Rafael could see that Mr. Clement was distracted. His visit was over. The man walked him to the front door. They shook hands. "Take care," Mr. Clement said, "and let this be a lesson to you; you play, you pay. Yes siree, that's the way it goes."

While Rafael rode the dirt roads to La Cabra's valley, two of Doña Tina's ladies were selected to deliver the society's ultimatum to the woman. Doña Tina had not spared her resources to find a final solution to the problem. She had discovered La Cabra's weak spot in her daughter, who was at a Catholic boarding school in the city. Yes, Sarita was to be her trump card.

ON ARRIVING at the bank of the Red River, where he had to leave his motorcycle, Rafael took a minute to take in the beauty of the place. He could see why Guzmán would risk so much to live here with the woman he had chosen to love. The river, now slightly swollen with the daily rain-shower, made a pleasant noise, like the murmuring of a woman. Even the old house looked clean and shiny, glazed with rainwater under the late afternoon sun. In a few weeks the river would flood as it did every year, and the two lovers could be as safe as if they were in a castle surrounded by a moat. They could use the boat to cross the river, but unless someone was foolish enough to carry a boat on his back down the hill from town, he could not get to them. Rafael imagined himself as their Cupid, secretly bringing them supplies and leaving them on the river-bank. But, of course, that was not to be. None of it was possible. The world was not made for romance. That was mainly found in novels. Survival was the most important thing. He was drawn out of his reverie by Guzmán's excited voice as he ran into the river completely dressed except for shoes and splashed to his friend. Guzmán threw his arms around Rafael in a suffocating and drenching embrace.

"Rafael, I'm so glad you're here. To tell you the truth, hermano, I was beginning to miss the company of my friends. How are you? Do you bring me news of my family? Bad news, I'll wager. Mamá Cielo must be steaming . . ."

"Guzmán, listen to me." Rafael had to interrupt his friend's excited barrage of words by grabbing Guzmán's shoulders and facing him.

"There is trouble, friend." Rafael made his words sound grave so Guzmán would understand the need to make haste. "Let us sit down somewhere, and I'll tell you what's happened."

"Is Mamá sick again?" Guzmán took off his shirt and sat on a large, smooth rock at the edge of the river. He seemed grown up to Rafael. Though on the surface he was still the same thin, wiry boy of a few weeks ago, there was something calm in his voice. His usually nervous mannerisms were apparently under control. Guzmán seemed to be more like a man in control of his body and his mind. "Has she been asking for me?"

"Guzmán, your mother wants you to return home, but it's not because she's ill. She is the same as when you left her. Still sick at heart with your brother's death . . ."

"And my sister Ramona is working like a slave to keep the house and take care of the baby."

"That's right. She's fine, though. She's healthy and strong." Rafael felt himself burning a little at the thought of Ramona. Guzmán noticed the blood rushing to his friend's face and politely looked away toward the house. He detected movement behind the thin white curtains of her room. She was watching him.

"You said there was trouble," said Guzmán.

Rafael leaned on the trunk of the flanboyán tree behind the rock where Guzmán sat. Its thick branches loaded down with the sweet-smelling orange flowers cast a cool shade over him. "It's an incredible place. This valley has everything," said Rafael, momentarily distracted from his mission. This was the beauty of the Island all concentrated into a few acres with river, valley, hill, and turquoise-blue sky.

"Everything. Yes." Guzmán's bitter-sounding voice brought Rafael back to the cruel message he had to deliver.

"Guzmán, the church women have decided to run your friend Rosa out of town. They are probably on their way here now. Your mother wants you home. I think she's right."

Guzmán stood carefully on the slippery side of the rock and looked down on his friend. "The bitches," he said, narrowing his eyes and spitting out the words. "They are all jealous of Rosa. Jealous because Rosa dares to live her life exactly as she wants to. What are they going to do to her? Burn her at the stake? I don't think even the mighty Doña Martina can do things like that these days." Guzmán jumped down from the rock and squatted at the edge of the water. He looked at his reflection. Rafael came up behind him. Guzmán saw him in the water and stuck his finger into the double portrait and stirred light into dark.

"Listen to me, Guzmán. They won't hurt Rosa that way, but they are powerful women. They usually get what they want. Rosa can take care of herself, but if they find you here, they can make it seem like a crime since you're under eighteen. Then they'll have something legal on her. They could send her to jail, you understand?"

"I can't leave her here, man. I can't leave her to face

91

those vultures alone." Guzmán was practically shouting now. Rosa appeared at the top of the front steps. Her hair was down over her shoulders and she wore a loose shift of light blue cotton. She was barefoot. Both boys rose to their feet as if she were royalty. She looked young and soft. Rafael could not believe the transformation, for he had only seen her in town in her tight dresses and painted face. Both Rosa and Guzmán had changed. They had both traveled toward each other: she was younger, Guzmán older.

"Come to the house, Rafael. Let's have some café con leche. It's about that time of the day." Guzmán's voice was still strained, and he kept his eyes fixed on the woman. She was a vision with her bare arms by her sides, motionless, eyes calmly fixed toward the river. She could have been an apparition if it weren't still daytime.

"No. I have to return this thing to Mr. Clement," said Rafael, pointing to the large black motorcycle parked well away from the riverbank. "And I have to get back to my house. Anything can happen with my old man as sick as he is, and the kids need me . . . you know."

"She's a beauty." Guzmán glanced at the motorcycle, but he did not move. Not too long ago, he would have done anything to get close to such a machine. "I understand, amigo, you go back to your family. And thanks for coming over."

"Will you go back home, Guzmán? Your mother will be waiting for me to tell her."

"I don't know, Rafael."

Guzmán looked more serious and thoughtful than Rafael had ever seen him. He decided not to pressure his friend any more. A man has a right to decide whether he wants to be saved.

"All right, Guzmán. But if you want to come to my house

instead of your mother's, you'll find the key to the back door under an orange flower pot. I'll tell my mother."

"We'll talk again soon." Guzmán extended his hand to his friend. As he rode up the hillside, Rafael looked down on the valley. He saw the man and the woman sitting together on the large rock by the river.

Rosa sent Guzmán home. She knew the only way to save him from the vindictiveness of Salud's church matrons was to channel their anger in her direction. It wasn't an easy parting, but Guzmán had been restless in the last few days. He missed his friends, and Rosa knew, in her mother's heart, that Guzmán worried about his family. He left in anger and with tears; he walked off shouting promises of love for her and revenge for the town; he walked slowly away from her house; but he left her, nevertheless, he left her.

Rosa prepared herself for the coming of her enemies by listing in her mind all the fears such women might have. She recalled the potions she had brewed for many who sent their servants to Rosa with money. Colored water mixed with a little white rum and a few words on a piece of paper. Place the talisman under your husband's pillow, sprinkle this liquid on his food and bathwater, light so many candles; that will make him stop looking at your younger sister, his secretary, or other women in general. Or sometimes, the other way around. That will ensure he never looks at his own wife with desire again. How many times had she crossed her own clients, making the same preparations for wife and mistress. It was their own insecurity about men that made these women hate her so strongly. They wanted to punish Rosa for their own evil natures. Rosa saw, in their persecution of her, her own mother. So moral, so bound by rules, that she would cast her own child into chaos for the sake of propriety.

SHE WOULD BE READY for them when they arrived. She knew it would be her last battle in this town. But there were other places to practice her craft. Her bags were packed. She would take a few days off and visit Sarita. Though Rosa allowed herself no grief, leaving her valley would be a great, wrenching loss. Here she had come to make peace with the ghost of her mother. She had finally made the house she grew up in her own. Though an outcast from Salud society, she had loved the ancient little town, never expecting the affection to be returned.

Above all she had found one person who loved her without qualification: Guzmán, the wild boy, the complex child who was loved by his mother with a passionate fierceness. Yet Mamá Cielo's inability to convey this love to Guzmán with the words and the closeness that he longed for had created a deep chasm between them. The mother's desperate search for a way to her son's heart had brought them to Rosa's house. But instead of mediating, the medium had fallen under the boy's spell.

Rosa knew the labels the world put on her relationship with Guzmán. She was nearly twice his age, but he was not an ordinary boy of sixteen; and he hadn't been an ordinary boy of twelve or thirteen when she first met him. He had been born hungry for love, eager for new experiences, and totally committed to his own peculiar code of honor. She had taught him to unravel the threads of his emotions and express them one by one. He was avid for knowledge of the world around him, so she had taught him how nature, like love, can both heal and deceive.

Guzmán was gone now, and in spite of his promises to come looking for her when all this trouble was over, Rosa knew their paths were not likely to cross again any time soon. He was still a boy in that respect; he firmly believed that love and determination could conquer any obstacles. Not true. But one could choose to go down in flames when the obstacles were overwhelming. One could give the enemy something to remember.

Rosa had been sitting on her front doorstep looking over her garden, the river, and beyond. She would miss these few acres of generous earth. She stood up with purpose and went into the kitchen. There she filled several pots with water and set them on the stove to boil. She had decided to prepare for battle by taking a ritual bath. The recipe for it had been given to her by El Indio. That bastard who helped ruin her life so many years ago had taught her a thing or two about herbal medicine. Nothing could restore a weary body and a depressed state of mind to vigor faster than a hot herbal bath. While the water boiled, Rosa went out her back door to her herb garden, where she gathered in a basket the leaves of black sage, ginger, lemon grass, wild coffee, and balsam. Then she went to the riverbank where the tall tree grew and picked a few leaves from the flanboyán tree. She took the basket of leaves into the kitchen and sprinkled them into the boiling water. From outside her kitchen door she brought in a small whiskey barrel of rainwater which she would use to rinse herself.

She checked the time. Though this part she felt was nothing more than superstition and ritual, Rosa followed recipes carefully. El Indio had said that a ritual bath should be taken at twelve noon exactly and that one should face east while taking the bath. Rosa knew that the magical part of magic or sacred ceremonies lay in doing things precisely. She dragged the large wooden tub into the middle of the kitchen floor and poured the aromatic liquid into it. Merely from inhaling the aromas of all this she had produced, created, and grown with her own hands gave her a feeling of strength. She let the black kimono she had on slip to the floor and stepped into the tub. Her white breasts rose above the dark water like little islands. Rosa allowed herself to absorb strength through her pores from the river water. She breathed in the essence of the Island. In later years, in colder climates, she would recall her days in the valley through her senses, the smells of certain herbs and flowers, rainwater.

After her bath she dressed in her flowing white dress, the one she wore for spiritist meetings. Then she made her house ready by burning frankincense in every room. Every surface she wiped with a cloth dampened in agua florida, though she knew it would not keep any evil spirits away. In fact, glancing out of her front door she made out two brightly colored figures at the summit of the last hill before the river. Two women—one in yellow, the other in royal blue—she could see now that they had paused to look down at her house. In fifteen minutes they would be at the river's edge.

Rosa set a large black candle in the center of her medium's table. She had made it herself of paraffin treated with a harmless but intoxicating formula made from weeds she grew herself. She would light it in fifteen minutes. She pulled her mother's old rocking chair to the window and waited. The two women were moving very slowly toward the river. The river was still slightly swollen, but muddier. They would have to cross it on foot. If they wanted to get to her—and Rosa knew they did—they would have to get their feet wet. A wonderful calm descended on her. She would not win, the town was too much for her to fight, but she had made them come to her and she would make certain that her name would be remembered in Salud.

Now she could see the women much more clearly. Hand in hand they were half sliding down the hill. It was Doña Tina herself—what a prize—and her second in command, the sycophantic Doña Corina, the lame one. She knew about them both, their good points and their bad, from their husbands, who had both frequented her valley in earlier days. Rosa kept her eyes on the rise and fall of the two figures descending the muddy hill. They were like bouncing, bright balloons, so incongruous in the rural landscape of her valley.

Though Rosa had willed herself calm, her thoughts were racing to the future. She would have to leave her place here, there was no doubt in her mind about this. She wasn't clear where she would go, but it did not matter. Rosa had saved enough money in the last few years so that at least financially she wouldn't have to worry for a while. Maybe, she thought, this was the time to change her life. This business of spiritism was exhausting her. She did it well, she was as sure of that as she was of her beauty and her power over men. It had been a challenge to guess the inner thoughts of people, to estimate their most personal needs, then to tell them what they wanted to hear. Rosa recognized this ability in herself but could not name it. In other circumstances, in another era, in a different place, Rosa might have become a student of psychology, a physician, a healer; but as she contemplated her exile, Rosa was, to herself as well as to others, no more than a cunning fortuneteller and a whore.

She thought of Sarita, now ten years old. A lovely child, though often ill. The best times had been when the girl was very young and Rosa felt safe in bringing her home for short visits to garden together. She would watch the little hands patting the earth around a seed ever so gently. Sarita did everything slowly and gracefully. The nuns had

97

taught her patience and the value of silence, so even as a very young child she would do everything with such deliberation that Rosa often had to resist prodding her to hurry or to run and yell without reason as most children do. She said nothing, however, because she wanted Sarita to grow up according to her own nature's demands. She was obedient and bright, and her teachers claimed that Sarita was more pious than other children, too. On one of her visits to the school, Rosa had been led on tiptoe to the chapel where she saw Sarita on her knees before the statue of the Holy Mother. Her eyes were raised to the statue's face and tears were streaming down her flushed cheeks. It had frightened Rosa. She had wanted to run to her daughter and ask her why she was crying, but the Reverend Mother had held her elbow firmly. Sarita, she had explained, was simply expressing her deep devotion to the Virgin. Tears were not unusual. Rosa had to accept this explanation, and she did not ask her daughter why she cried.

As Sarita grew older, Rosa became afraid that the girl would guess the truth about her life if she brought her to the valley; so, instead, Rosa picked her up once a month at the convent and they took weekend trips around the Island. The girl was a model companion. She smiled, asked no questions, accepted Rosa's gifts with modesty, and never failed to thank her and ask for her blessing when they returned to the school. Fearing to shake their fragile relationship, Rosa never pressed for any more from her daughter. But it broke her heart to know that the girl did not love her.

WHEN Doña Tina and Doña Corina reached the bank of the Red River, Rosa went around the house closing windows and doors. She lit the candle she had prepared and sat by the door to wait. She felt strong with resolution. She let the anger build within her, and she felt it flowing through her veins like a warm liqueur. She watched Doña Tina lean heavily on her companion while she removed her white sandals. She did not return the favor, and Doña Corina with her short left leg had a time taking off her shoes. She hopped like a little brown monkey and even fell on the muddy dirt once, but Doña Tina did not look back. She waded into the river water, lifting the skirt of her fine dress high over her substantial thighs. Rosa could see the pale skin where the sun had never visited. And the shadowy region beyond the lace-encased fortress the old lawyer had paid so dearly for. The woman should not be underestimated. Scurrying to Doña Tina's side, Doña Corina looked like a skinny boy with breasts. She had no hips, no flesh on her legs or arms, but her bodice swelled mightily where it was supposed to. Rosa knew about Corina's burden: money but no beauty, husband but neither love nor children; and her greatest cross, the lameness that made her an object of pity to both the high and the low in Salud. Tina had found her most loyal follower in Corina, who needed purpose more than anything else in her sad life.

It was a comic sight to see these two crossing her river like flies on spilled honey. Their feet were sucked down by the mud, and a distinct little plop could be heard each time they took a step. They would be very tired by the time they reached her front door.

When Doña Tina had climbed the steps to Rosa's door with the laboring Corina behind her, she found the door closed. She knocked hard but received no answer. On trying the knob, she found that the door opened easily into a darkened room thick with smoke from the single source of light, the candle on the table. Corina emitted a gasp of fear and grabbed Tina's arm. Tina shook her off almost violently. *"Brujería,"* she spit out, "cheap sorcery, carnival tricks." She looked around the room.

"Cabra," Doña Tina called out in a voice too loud for the

small, closed-in room. Her voice bounced back in echo, startling both women. "I know you're here. Come out and face us. Or are you afraid of what two decent women have to say to you?"

Suddenly both women perceived the white figure facing them from her rocking chair across the room. Had she been there all along? Had their eyes failed to see her until they became accustomed to the dark?

"Tell me, sister." Rosa's voice was hardly more than a murmur, yet they heard her clearly. "Do decent women always enter a private home without invitation or permission? Never mind, the needy are always welcome at my Center. Please come sit here next to me."

Doña Tina, angered by Rosa's calm words, crossed the room and threw her Bible and purse down on the chair Rosa had indicated. "This is not a social visit, Cabra, and this is not the Center, as you call it. This is a whore's house . . ."

Tina would have continued except that Rosa raised one pale hand in front of Tina's face. "Please call me Rosa. La Cabra is an ugly name only the vulgar-minded use when referring to me. I am going to make us a refreshing drink. Please, Doña Corina, come join us. You must be very tired after your journey."

"Listen to me." Doña Tina had sunk into a chair near the table. She seemed to be having difficulty breathing. "Listen, Puta, we have come in the name of Padre Gonzalo . . ."

"Soon, Doña Tina, we will talk soon." Rosa walked through the black curtain into her kitchen. She heard Corina urging Tina to leave, and she heard Tina's curse. She would not retreat. The whore would be taught a lesson that day. She commanded Doña Corina to open a window. Though the woman scurried to obey, the windows had been barred and locked and there was no other opening

100

for fresh air save the front door. But to even step outside now, all three knew, would be to admit weakness. Rosa listened and waited. She heard her daughter's name mentioned. This made her afraid for the first time. What did Sarita have to do with their plans?

What had she planned to do with these two women? She wanted them at her mercy. She wanted them weak and afraid. She didn't care what they had in mind for her. The most they could do, or so she had thought until now, was run her out of Salud. She had reconciled herself to that. But what did Tina know about Sarita? Holy Mother, what were they thinking of doing? Were they planning to tell the child that her mother was the woman known as La Cabra in Salud? From the front room there came the sound of giggles. Rosa peeked through the part in the black curtains and saw Doña Tina trying to control a fit of laughter. Her face was in a lace handkerchief, and tears were streaming down her cheeks. Doña Corina was fully in the midst of a fit of hysterical cackling. Both women were doubled over in their chairs. Rosa stood and watched them for a few moments longer; then she filled two tiny wine cups with a dark liquid from a glass decanter. She placed the cups on a tray and took it in. She had no difficulty convincing the two choking women to drink.

When Tina looked up at Rosa, her eyes were brilliant with hatred, yet she could not stop giggling. "Your witch's tricks will not save you." Doña Tina gasped in between hiccuping bursts of laughter. "You're an evil woman, Cabra, a whore and a deceiver. The worst part . . ." Doña Tina held her stomach and tried desperately to control her quivering face. "The worst part is that the innocent child you brought into the world . . ." But she could not continue. The incongruous laughter of the two women filled the room with ominous echoes.

"I want to go home. I want to go." It was Doña Corina wailing.

"Are you afraid?" Rosa asked.

"Yes," said Doña Corina.

"Not afraid," gasped Doña Tina. "Are you poisoning us? You won't get away with it . . . you won't." Doña Tina started to walk unsteadily toward the door.

"Sit down." Rosa pulled the other woman down hard by the arm into the chair. "You are not being poisoned. You're just a little drunk, that's all. I just wanted to give you a taste of your own bitter medicine. Especially you, Tina, the almighty Doña Tina. Queen of Salud. I just wanted you to see what it is like when someone else holds you in her power. Just a taste of what it is like to be a victim. Now, we can talk. Relax, your dizziness will pass. In fact, if you don't fight it, you will soon begin to feel some very pleasant sensations."

"What, what . . ." Doña Tina began, but Rosa ignored her. She blew out the candle on the table. Doña Corina was curled into a bony bundle in her chair and was snoring softly. In the almost complete darkness of the room, Rosa faced her opponent.

"Tina, look at me. You feel weak as a newborn kitten, don't you? I can see that you do. Don't bother to deny it. I could kill you right now. Both of you. Throw you in the river, then disappear forever. I am a witch, as you suspect—if a witch is a woman who knows how to stay alive in a snakes' nest like this town. You and your society friends are the snakes, you know. I don't need to poison you. You are poisoned already. Your own misery is enough revenge for me." Rosa saw that Doña Tina was struggling to keep her eyes open. She shook her by the shoulders.

"You won't kill us, whore." Doña Tina spoke as if from a

drunken stupor, slurring her words. "You can't hurt us because we know where your girl is."

"Sarita?" Rosa dug her fingers into the plump flesh of Doña Tina's arm. "I swear if you hurt her . . ."

"You hurt her by giving birth to her, viper." Tina spit at Rosa.

Little by little and after pouring a scalding cup of black coffee down Doña Tina's throat Rosa got the whole story. It seemed that Doña Tina had already visited the convent school where Sarita lived and had met the girl. So far, she had said nothing to her about Rosa—only that she knew her in Salud. They had even attended mass together a few times during the last week. Rosa's heart sank at this. She had never been able to fake an interest in religion, though she knew it meant so much to her daughter. She pressed Rosa for more information. Why and when had she been seeing Sarita? What gave her the right? Doña Tina regained the power of speech long enough to tell Rosa how Don Gonzalo, on learning about Sarita, had been outraged at the scandalous behavior of the mother. He himself had called the mother superior at the convent, and they had both come to the conclusion that the child must be taken into church custody. This was the point when the priest had asked Doña Tina to visit the child to help pave the way for separation.

"How dare you. You righteous bitch. How dare you try to take my little girl away from me? I won't let you." Rosa was in a rage. She wanted to pummel this mound of flesh before her into senselessness. But she knew she had lost. The gates to the school would be barred. The courts would not listen to a woman with her reputation. Sarita!

Doña Tina lifted her drugged eyes to Rosa and made a surprising statement. "I will take care of her as if she were

my own. I promise you. Leave town. Go away forever."
This was too much of an effort and Doña Tina slid heavily
down from her chair into a heap on the floor.

Rosa looked upon her vanquished enemies strewn upon
the floor, but she felt only the sharp edge of a blade cutting
her heart out. She was the one defeated. In minutes she
had gathered what she would take on her trip without destination. She left the door wide open so the women would
awaken to fresh air many hours hence at dawn in La
Cabra's valley.

Chapter Four

COMING HOME was for Guzmán a painful thing. Mamá Cielo treated him like a leper whom she pitied more than hated. In her dark-ringed eyes he could see the sleepless nights and the pain her sons had brought her, one by scattering the precious life she had given him across the unimaginable landscape of a foreign land, the other by shaming the family in taking up with a whore. Guzmán looked at her distant face, the hands shrinking from his touch even as she placed the food in front of him, and he almost yearned for the former violence of their relationship. Rage was at least a sign of life; here there was nothing but ashes.

In the days that followed his departure from La Cabra's valley, Guzmán spent much time alone. To avoid the eyes of the curious, for he knew he was the object of scandal in Salud, he learned to see in the dark. At two or three in the morning he would rise from his bed at Mamá's and walk the deserted streets of the town. This way he learned the nighttime secrets of Salud: the widow's sigh, the lover's words of parting, the stifled fear of little children left alone in the dark. Those who caught a glimpse of the lanky young man in his black shirt and pants would probably only see the brilliant white of his eyes taking in the last act of the daily human drama. Learning. Learning how to be alone. If people saw his form moving past their windows, they would likely just cross themselves, and look away. The devil seeks the attention of the sleepless.

It was a long good-bye he was saying to his hometown, though at first Guzmán did not think of it as such. He yearned for Rosa, yet he did not want to be smothered in her fragrant arms forever. He wanted to live with her, but he also wanted to be free. This could not ever happen in Salud. He had heard from Rafael, who had received reluctant permission from Papá Pepe to visit Ramona, that Rosa had left town. Installments on what had transpired on the Rosary Society's last visit to La Cabra's valley were still making their way down the gossip channels.

Guzmán's heart leapt at the thought of meeting her in some faraway place, maybe even America, and traveling with her to all the places she had described to him. When Guzmán thought of America, which to him meant New York, he saw a great city, larger than the largest one he had ever seen on the Island, with ornate, tall structures and wide streets all in white with *nieve, nieve.* In Spanish the word sounded exotic because so little spoken. It called forth pure breezes and crystalline lakes, and cleanliness not possible where people sweat all the time. Guzmán walked at night when it was cool and made a mental record of his birthplace, memorizing the places and people whose memory would later sustain him in his exile.

THE NEIGHBORHOOD where Guzmán lived was called El Polvorín, that is, the Dustdevil. The houses had been built on a craggy hillside. Yards were of packed, black dirt, and not too many inches below was bedrock. In the dry seasons dust devils whipped through, covering everything with sticky soot, *polvo.* It was the practice of the women of El Polvorín to sprinkle their front yards with a watering can to settle the dust, and then to sweep it down in circles. This was done early in the morning, before the sun got hot, and in the gray mist of dawn, they looked like ghostdancers making magic circles with their brooms.

Papá Pepe had been the first to build his sky-blue house in El Polvorín. It was a choice location at the very top of the hill. His backyard extended down to the Granja, the high school's experimental farm. And so the family always had a view of abundance and fertility from the bedroom windows and the kitchen. Banana plants and coconut palms shaded the breeding pens of sows and cattle. Across from Mamá's house lived Doña Lula, a harborer of whores but an impeccable housekeeper. She had an attic room that she rented to women who lived alone. Mamá kept her family and herself at a polite distance from Doña Lula's always freshly painted door and kept a watchful eye on the little stairway at the back of her neighbor's house, which led to the attic room where lights were kept burning late into the night and curtains drawn until noon.

One night, Guzmán watched for the woman who was now renting the attic room. He sat in the shadows of Mamá's porch one night and waited. He smelled her perfume first, strong and reminiscent of dying roses. She was neither young nor old. Guzmán saw a plumpish figure wearing a black evening dress sparkling with sequins. As she passed by the porch he saw her face in the moonlight. She looked tired. Her red mouth was pursed with the effort of climbing the hill of El Polvorín, and her black eye makeup was streaked with sweat. Except for her party clothes, she could have been a farmer's woman coming in from a long night caring for a sick cow or working in a flooded field. When she got nearer to Doña Lula's house, the woman raised her eyes to her room, where a yellow light still burned. She sighed. That little attic room, which Guzmán imagined must be as white and spotless as the rest of Doña Lula's property, would be a sanctuary to this woman and others like her, a shelter from the passions that ruled their lives.

For once he wondered what made this woman, what made the others who had stayed in Doña Lula's attic room, choose the night life over marriage and respectability. He watched the woman climb up to her room, and he saw the shadows move as she changed clothing, then opened the window wide, and finally turned off the yellow light. Could it be for the right to own her time? No one waited up for this woman. No one asked her for explanations. She did not rise as Mamá Cielo did, as all the married women in town did, at five in the morning to cook for the day, to sweep their yards, to iron in the smoldering heat, and then at night to wait for sons or husbands, and if they were still desired as women, to continue giving of themselves. The childbearing that sapped their strength did not end until nature or husband checked their impulses. Mamá Cielo herself, for instance, with a son already dead, another ready to leave her nest, and a daughter approaching marriageable age, had a new baby. There was no *amén* for women. No end for their prayers. He had heard Mamá Cielo say this.

Guzmán left his hiding place in the shadows of Mamá Cielo's porch and walked slowly down the hill. Doña Julia's house next door had been silent this week. After the witch hunt instigated by the old woman and the society's visit to Rosa's valley, Doña Julia had decided to visit her oldest married daughter in San Juan. What bitterness that heart harbored! Guzmán had early learned to hate Doña Julia for her life-denying tendencies: her malicious gossip, her abusive treatment of him. Now, as he looked upon her neglected house, so badly in need of a carpenter and a painter, Guzmán still did not forgive Doña Julia for the suffering she had helped to bring upon Mamá Cielo, but he did allow himself to try to imagine the woman as a young girl, a new wife suddenly burdened with a drunkard for a husband, then early widowhood and daughters to raise. Could she have seen in Guzmán the side she had never allowed herself to explore? Now that he thought of it, Guzmán had never seen Doña Julia in other than mourning clothes. She was mourning all of her life—not for her husband, who had released her with his death, but for her own dead heart.

In a packed-dirt cellar under the house of two very old people lived Franco el Loco—the one who had been nearly cut in half by a jealous man but instead had been left at a seventy-five-degree angle, the one who still collected bottles to make jeweled fragments for his dirt walls. In the sun that persevered through the one smeared window of his cellar, the glass sparkled like the dragon hoard of a child's imagination. As a little boy Guzmán had added constellations to Franco's universe. How many times had he hidden in this dirt-and-diamond refuge no one else but a madman or a child could find comforting? And how many times had Mamá Cielo brought down every saint in her God's well-populated heaven, imploring him not to go into Franco's private ward, where the contagious germ of violence probably still thrived in the pores of one who had so intimately been touched by it? Not that she lacked pity—Guzmán knew she contributed to Franco's maintenance in discreet ways—but she also crossed herself when she walked past his door.

On his nocturnal wanderings Guzmán often paused to listen to the man's soft mutterings, which were so continuous that others ignored the sound as they would someone's breathing. What Guzmán learned was that Franco's time had stopped like a dropped clock at the hour of his tragedy. His mind replayed the courting of the woman. Forever black-haired, forever making her curls dance with a Spanish fan she used to summon Franco across the room. And they danced to the same tune, one made popular by Daniel Santos, the balladeer whose passionate lyrics spoke of the torments and delights of love. No true *macho* could allow his woman to dance to such a song with another man. Hypnotized by the black lace fan summoning him across the waxed dance floor, the strands of glossy black hair rising and falling to the gentle breeze stirred by that tireless hand, Franco had walked across the last dance floor of his life. He took the woman into his arms. He was straight and proud then, and a good dancer. Guzmán heard Franco mutter, *"Bailaremos, bailaremos hasta que el gallo cante."* He wanted to dance until the cock crowed at dawn. Sometimes there was a startled look on Franco's face but no words. Was this the point in the story where the machete struck him on the back, felling him like a green stalk of sugar cane? There were no more words after "we shall dance." Franco danced in the arms of a black-haired beauty. He stopped only when a bright bit of glass or a discarded bottle caught his eye. He put it in his pocket so that later, when he sat out a dance, he could continue building a cathedral window in his hovel.

Though Franco's door was locked from the outside, as the town's authority demanded of Franco's keeper, for the citizens' peace of mind at night, Guzmán came close to the cellar and looked in through the grimy, sealed window. He saw Franco sitting on a crate in front of his glass wall, looking intently at a sunburst pattern of beer-bottle glass by the light of an oil lamp. What did he see there? Grizzled and bent, wearing a piece of rope to hold his baggy pants and a threadbare guayabera some other man had worn the life out of, he should have looked like a crippled beggar, but to Guzmán the bent figure peering intently at his own creation looked wiser than any priest or teacher he had ever known. If he had believed that it would have made any difference to Franco, Guzmán would have smashed the padlock and thrown the cellar door open. But Franco would have simply looked through the disturbance with his inward eyes and turned back to his glass. At least there was no suffering that Guzmán could detect in the man. As far as he could tell, Daniel Santos sang for Franco and Franco danced his last dance, hour after hour, day after day.

A light came on in the house above Franco's, and Guzmán hurried away from the cellar, fearing he had disturbed the old people. There were still others whose memory he would take with him, so that in the cold rooms he would occupy for many years the remembrance of these lives would eventually guide him back to his birthplace like a beacon in a foggy night. This he knew: he loved this place that did not love him. And he knew that he would leave it and come back.

IN THE NEXT HOUSE, where the hill of El Polvorín began its rocky descent to the paved street, lived the scorned wife, Melina. Her husband, Luis, had come back from Korea with sergeant's stripes and bachelor vices. That first year Melina lost their first child and her last chance at one, for Luis took up with the fifteen-year-old daughter of the *patrona* of the domino hall, a woman too busy to care much about the morals of her daughter. In fact, she allowed the couple to move into her own house in exchange for Luis's services as manager of her establishment. Guzmán heard all this both at home from his mother and sister and on the streets. The story took different overtones depending where it was heard. From his family he heard condemnations for the man who would treat his faithful wife in such a despicable way. From the men at the domino hall he heard of Melina's independent ways, acquired while Luis was away; how she refused to accept his authority in the home, to the point of continuing with classes she was taking at a school in Mayagüez even though he was home now and there was no need to waste her time with such foolish pastimes. One rumor had it that she had gotten furious at the discovery of her pregnancy and had taken something to abort the child.

Though the affair stirred up Salud, it did not reach the major proportions of the recent scandal over Rosa and himself. A scorned wife was not a rare phenomenon. Melina herself was tightlipped and proud. She did not violate any of the town's conventions openly, but wrought a different life for herself out of the granite walls that separated her from the things she really wanted. In the next generation she would be addressed as Doña Melina, the teacher and later the first woman superintendent of schools. And no one but the very old would remember her as the scorned wife. In fact, though they lived in the same town, her husband with his illegitimate brood would never be associated with the severe and learned Doña Melina. Walking past Melina's house that night, Guzmán remembered briefly what Mamá had said about this woman. He balanced this in his mind with the rumor of her abortion, and felt neither pity nor admiration for her.

In the big house facing the street lived the Saturninos, a family consisting of an aging matriarch and her unmarried sons and daughters. It was said that the old woman held her brood to her like a spider holds its prey in the sticky threads of its web. Guzmán knew there were a couple of sons and a couple of daughters, but he was not able to attach a name to a face, since in his mind the Saturninos

112

were all pale, dessicated-looking people. The men had been educated in the city, and they worked there. They came and went silently. They did not associate with the other men in the town, staying within the walls of their old house doing God only knew what when they were not at their mysterious jobs in the city. Recently Guzmán had taken notice of one of the women, the one with eyes like charcoal smudges on a pale face. Many times had he seen her doing tasks around the big house with an unnatural slowness and concentration. She would sweep her front porch for what seemed like hours. Her eyes would scan the street while she worked, as if she were expecting someone. People talked about that one. Scornfully, they would call her "La Señorita Saturnino," though she was well into her thirties and past the time when "Miss" was the proper title for her. She was thin as the shadow of a palm tree, and there was a steel rod in her, for even as she performed the menial tasks her mother could have hired a maid to do (everyone knew the old man had left them well provided for), she did them unbendingly. She carried herself like an offended duchess. Rosario was her name. Guzmán remembered hearing something said about Rosario's suitors being turned away at her mother's command by her stern brothers until either her time passed or no man was left who would knock at the Saturninos' door, which remained closed so much of the time.

Rosario's haunted eyes had met Guzmán's in recent days. Perhaps she had heard about him and La Cabra. Rosa and Rosario seemed to be about the same age. Rosario was out of doors more than the other shadow-dwelling Saturninos. She was to be seen lately watering a small garden behind the house, now almost gone to wild from previous neglect. She had even persuaded a tiny orchid to take root in a pot which she hung on the lowest branch of an ancient

113

shade tree. As she worked with her flowers where she thought no one could see her, she allowed her body to emerge from the lethargy, the state of suspension that she kept it in around everyone else. Once Guzmán had been trespassing on the Saturninos' property, stealing some of the guavas that grew in profusion in the thickly vegetated acre of land behind their house. Unpicked, the fruit would ripen and fall on the ground, where the flies and worms feasted on its sweetness. It was early in the morning, and he was just coming home from his night wanderings. The whole town was enveloped in predawn mist. It was a good time for ghosts and apparitions. Rosario had emerged from her house through the kitchen door. Tall and pale, floating, it seemed to Guzmán, in a long white robe, Rosario came straight toward him but did not seem to see him. He was in the shadows behind the tree where her orchid hung. Guzmán felt a little chill of fear. What if she were a madwoman? Was she hiding a knife in the folds of her robe? He saw the glint of metal as she approached the tree where he hid holding his breath. From the pocket of her voluminous robe Rosario brought forth a pair of clippers. With the elegance of a ballerina she reached for the white orchid now at the peak of its bloom. Delicately, she cut an open flower. Guzmán watched, fascinated, as the woman brought the open face of the dew-moistened flower to her cheek and pressed it to her skin like a kiss. His heart beating wildly, Guzmán saw the miracle of beauty pass briefly over this sad woman. He fought the urge to step out from his hiding place and tell her that she looked more beautiful than the painting of the Virgin at the church. But he knew he would do nothing but frighten her or, worse, humiliate her by his presence. And he could never explain why she seemed beautiful to him, since all the world could see that she was a plain spinster with thin, graying hair and no flesh to round out any of the sharp angles of her body. As she walked slowly back into the house, the orchid in her hand, Guzmán could see that he had almost made a tragic mistake, the kind one can make only in the confusion of the twilight hours when the devil transforms the world for the fools who leave their beds to wander while God sleeps.

This night he walked quietly past the dark house where everyone slept alone. It was an old house, badly in need of paint and repair but still elegant. The windows on either side were in the French style. They were long as doors and latticed. Guzmán's alert ears heard a faint creaking sound as he approached one such window. Instinctively he stepped back against the wall. Ever so slowly the leaves of the window parted to reveal a pale, thin hand. He recognized it as the hand that had held an orchid. Long white fingers were now working carefully to open wider the leaves of a window that was resisting from lack of use. At first Guzmán thought she had perhaps seen his shadow and thought him a burglar. But in that case she would have roused others, or thrown the window open hastily. But the aim of those elegant hands was to make way without waking anyone. Was she escaping her mother's house, or eloping at this late date? Guzmán glanced about for another man's form lurking in the dark, but saw nothing. Feeling daring, he approached the window, almost at ground level, which was slowly revealing the tall slender form of Rosario.

Rosario stood framed by the latticed leaves of the window in her white robe and looked down at Guzmán. Her hair was piled high on her head, and the way she held herself reminded Guzmán of the portraits of Spanish ladies he had seen in his school books. Though he felt a strong compulsion to run toward the street not a hundred yards away,

115

he stayed rooted under her gaze. She had commanding eyes, this Rosario, deep as wells. It was plain to see that she came from an aristocratic Spanish line with little if any Indian blood in it. Guzmán's own heritage included plenty of Taino Indian, which colored his skin copper and made ovals of his dark eyes. Rosario's eyes were round lamps beckoning him, no, ordering him to come closer. He did. She placed a cool hand on his cheek.

"What is it, señorita, are you ill? Can I do something . . ." Nervous as he was, Guzmán would have continued jabbering, but the woman placed her fingers over his mouth. Still without saying a word she stepped back into the darkness of what he supposed was her bedroom and stood there as if waiting for him. Guzmán groaned softly. She wanted him to go into her bedroom. Through the window. His brain was booming out orders for his legs to run toward the street, to continue his night's journey, but that other center of his being, the one that made him him and not another, told him to take one giant step up into the unknown. He had always wondered what lay beyond the four walls of this old house haunted by its own lonely inhabitants. Rosario's hand felt cool and soft on his skin. Rosa's hands and skin had always felt warm as the Caribbean sun. To his mind came the image of Rosa in the river, in bed, in her garden. She was so totally alive. He had promised her they'd be together someday, away from Salud, and he meant to fulfill that promise. This woman now standing before him was to Rosa what the moon was to the sun, a pale reflection; even her body seemed made of beams of light rather than flesh, but she was placing herself before him this night and if Guzmán had not climbed up into her room he would not have been Guzmán, but another.

And so he placed one foot firmly on the window ledge and pulled himself up. The rotting wood gave way and with a loud crash he fell back, bringing part of the wooden

116

frame with him. Immediately, lights came on, and, lying on his back, stunned, he heard alarmed voices calling each other's names. As he rose up, Guzmán saw the old woman, Rosario's mother, making her way past the terrified daughter toward the window. Though skeletal and a foot shorter than the younger woman, she pushed her daughter hard enough to make her fall against the wall. A crucifix of heavy wood fell down and opened a gash on Rosario's forehead. It all happened very quickly. Guzmán was able to recover his wits and start running, but not before the old woman caught sight of him and shaking her fist called him a devil and a *perdido*, a damned or lost soul.

At his worst times in his future Guzmán would remember the prophetic word. He would recall the curse and the evil omen of the cross wounding the woman whom he had managed to bring down without ever touching her, for the gossip mongers in Salud would soil Rosario's reputation with their venomous tongues and she would end up a complete recluse. This he did not know for certain until much later, but the morning would bring him misfortune enough. Guzmán ran for his life. He ran past the elementary school and the baseball park and the darkened stalks of the vegetable peddlers toward the only lighted place in town, the domino hall. This night there was a cockfight in the lean-to behind the establishment, and the excited voices of the men reached his ears with insistence. Just outside the place he stood and dusted his clothes. He wiped his sweaty face with the clean white handkerchief Mamá Cielo never failed to place in his pants pocket. He took a deep breath and smelled the strong, syrupy mixture of rum, man sweat, and blood wafting out from the half-open door. There must have been a fight earlier; the concrete steps were still wet from when they had been washed clean of blood. Someone always had a

117

blade or machete ready. At least once a month there was a serious injury from a gambling fight, yet hardly ever did anyone complain to the authorities. Gambling was a man's personal business, and the ensuing fights were matters of honor between two men. It was best not to get involved or take sides. It was enough to rush the injured party to his home or, if he was badly cut, to the public clinic, where a sleepy nurse would at least keep the man from bleeding to death until the doctor came in the morning.

Guzmán allowed himself to wonder for one brief moment if the Saturninos would wait until the morning to call on Mamá Cielo or whether they were there at that very minute. He imagined them as Death and Company walking up the hill of El Polvorín toward his house like a funeral procession. His funeral.

The door to the domino hall opened and Luis, the adulterer, poked his head out.

"Who goes there?" he asked, using a phrase he had picked up in the army.

"It's Guzmán, Don Luis, what is happening tonight?"

"Good action tonight, Guzmán. But it's in or out. We're about to close the door and move the party to the back. Are you coming?"

Guzmán slid past Luis and into the hall where some men were leaning on the pool table and crouching on the cement floor waiting for the cockfight to be announced. Adjusting his eyes to the sudden brightness of the room, Guzmán noticed a familiar blond head leaning over a huddled form in a corner. Could it be Rafael? What would he be doing in a place like this at this hour? He had missed his friend in the past few weeks. But, in fact, he had been avoiding him since Rafael had asked for permission to visit his sister Ramona. He didn't want Rafael's reputation to be touched by the gossip that had followed the incident with

118

Rosa. But he had heard that things had gotten worse at home for Rafael, with his old man committing slow suicide, drinking himself into a stupor, in his own sick bed.

Guzmán approached his friend. "Rafael?" The other turned to face him startled. It was Rafael, and judging by the dark circles under his eyes and his pallor he must have been going through hell. Guzmán tried to make his voice sound casually friendly in spite of his concern: "How is it with you, man? Haven't seen you for a while." He put his hand on Rafael's shoulder to assure him that nothing had changed between them.

BUT BEFORE Rafael could greet his friend, someone slumped on the floor grabbed Rafael's arm and tried to pull himself up. "Help me, boy." The voice was familiar to Guzmán, but the yellow corpse in man's clothes couldn't be Don Juan Santacruz! "Help me up, can't you hear?" Because he had strained to shout at his son, Don Juan went into a paroxysm of coughing, doubling over with the effort. Rafael held him up like a child. Guzmán came up to help but was afraid to touch the old man for fear of offending him.

"Get my handkerchief from my back pocket, will you Guzmán?" Rafael was displaying amazing composure, considering the fact that everyone in the room was staring at the trio.

All conversation had ceased. Guzmán did as his friend requested, then went over and put a coin in the juke box. A loud mambo came on. "Now you have something to listen to," he said to the room in general.

Shamefacedly, some of the men took up their pool playing and drinking, turning their backs to the struggling old man in the back and the son gently wiping the blood from the cadaverous face. Guzmán stood by with a cup of water

119

he had gone behind the counter to get. Under other circumstances the patrona or Luis would have chopped his hands off for going into forbidden territory. Because the owners of this place had to be everywhere at once, all business in their absence was strictly on the honor system. And no one went near the cash box. Since it was the only men's club in town, everyone was interested in preserving it, and until Guzmán got his famous cup of water all the customers had treated the area as a mined field. Rafael took the cup and brought it to his father's lips. But the old man spit it out.

"What is this? You dare to give me piss to drink, you bastard son of a priest? Bring me a real drink."

Guzmán turned his head away so as not to shame Rafael. Luckily, the music drowned out the old man's weak voice and no one else could hear him cursing his own son.

Rafael sat the old man down against the wall and walked over to Guzmán, who had retreated a few paces.

"Let's get him the rum," Rafael said.

"You can't mean it, man. He should be in a hospital."

"He's dying, Guzmán. Mr. Clement's doctor said he's bleeding internally—it's just a matter of days."

"Then what the hell are you doing here? He should be at home in bed."

"That's the problem, friend. My mother has been taking care of him day and night all these months. She's exhausted. Now that he's asking for rum every minute that he's conscious, she's almost hysterical with worry. I've done all I can, and the others too. We just give him what he wants." Rafael shook his head. "Today he heard men talking on their way from the fields about the cockfight tonight. He woke up screaming for me—said he was going to win big money. Nothing would pacify him, so here we are."

Shaking his head in disbelief, Guzmán brought Rafael

120

up on his own misfortunes. But Don Juan was waving his cane in impatience for his rum. Guzmán poured some of the amber liquid into a paper cup and handed it to Rafael, speaking in a low voice all the time about the trouble he was in, about his dream of escaping to New York. Rafael kept his eye on the corner where Don Juan was obviously becoming more agitated. He handed Guzmán a crumpled dollar bill and Guzmán gave him change out of the cigar box.

Suddenly there was the loud noise of an overturned chair. Don Juan had collapsed during his struggle to get up to yell at his son. Everyone stood frozen. No one dared to approach him. Rafael ran to his father. Luis, watching everything from his post at the back door, called out: "Everyone to the back. Everyone to the back."

In the center of the lean-to's dirt floor had been concocted a pit of sorts with tin drums serving as a ring wall. Men sat on the drums or leaned on them, their voices echoing off the metal. Guzmán and Rafael waited outside the pit area until the crowd of men cleared the doorway. Then Rafael lifted Don Juan unsteadily to his feet.

"I want to place a bet. Hurry! Hurry!" the old man prompted his son, even as his legs failed to support him and he had to be practically carried in. In the meantime Guzmán had disappeared into the kitchen and had talked Luis into letting him have a folding chair for Don Juan. After they sat him down on it facing the pit, the two young men stood on either side like bodyguards to a decrepit chieftain, ready to support him with their bodies if the old man should start to slip down. But Don Juan was more alert than Rafael had seen him in weeks. He was flushed, and though he visibly shook from the pain that must have been gnawing at his ulcerated organs, he held himself erect, eyes on the pit.

The handlers had been summoned formally into the

center by Luis, who obviously loved the role of master of ceremonies. He introduced each handler and gave the information on each of the cocks. This one, the white, a year old, five pounds, winner of three matches. The other a red, older than the white by six months and heavier by a pound, but blind in one eye, so that evened it out. The men in the audience found that they could drown Luis out by beating on the drums. Someone with an ear for music began a jungle beat and the others followed. Soon the drumbeat and the shouts became a deafening wall of noise. In the middle of this frenzy, the handlers acted like priests dispensing a sacrament of blood. They displayed their animals to the crowd by holding them aloft, then brought them to the circle of officials for a final inspection. After completing the circuit, the handlers took their positions at either end and placed the gaffs over the birds' spurs.

At this point Luis raised his hand for silence, and his assistants went around collecting the bets.

Everyone knew where the money would go once it had been taken up: to the patrona, Doña Amparo, whose chair had been set up in the doorway so that no one could come in or leave without her knowledge.

Doña Amparo was a large brown woman, with a mixture of black and Indian blood which gave her skin the dark copper color of earth after a rain. She had been a great beauty in her youth, they say, and though her ebony eyes and sensuous mouth had now receded into the flesh of her cheeks, they were still souvenirs of a once intriguing face. Her hair, never cut, was rolled into a doughnut at the nape of her neck, and she wore a loose Mexican dress of parrot green with red flowers embroidered at the bodice. Unlike other women of her age, she never wore dark colors, preferring to send off for imported costumes from a mailorder magazine. One night she might be seen wearing a

Hawaiian print muumuu, and another a fringed skirt of American Indian design. This night, sitting in her chair with her fat, strong arms crossed in front of her chest, Doña Amparo looked like a pagan idol, the goddess of fertility and plenitude.

Doña Amparo owned the domino hall but also her own house in El Polvorín and other undisclosed property as well. No one was sure how much she was worth, but as a shrewd businesswoman, Doña Amparo was both respected and resented by many people in Salud. Widowed three times, Doña Amparo had been left a little richer each time by her short-lived husbands, and she had invested her inheritances well. Little by little she had managed to put the powerful people of Salud in her debt, thus buying security for herself and her domino hall. Though the men often got rowdy at her place, there was never any problem with the law. That was why she had added the attraction of cockfighting, a sport that triggered bloodlust and violence even in the most peace-loving men. She had seen it happen. Like sex, cockfighting was an activity that made men less cautious as spenders; it made them drink more of her beer and rum. If there was a fight, and if she had to intercede on a man's behalf to keep him from being thrown in the Salud jail (or worse, from trouble with his wife), well then, that man was in Doña Amparo's debt forever. Indebtedness, in Doña Amparo's mind, was as good as a blank check. She collected gratitude like bank drafts which she filed away in her sharp mind for the day when she would need to cash them in.

Not all the favors Doña Amparo did for people were based on business concerns. Many unfortunate women had received donations of money and food in times of need or tragedy—always anonymously, so that the good women would not feel humiliated at accepting charity from Doña

Amparo's questionably acquired bounty. The gifts were accepted, nevertheless, and Providence was given credit. This did not bother Doña Amparo. She had chosen power over respectability and had never regretted the choice. She also knew that in order to compete in a man's world of property ownership, she had to make others dependent on her in as many ways as possible. She did this by providing the men of Salud with a place where they could play their games, see their women, drink, and even sometimes, yes, spill a little blood. This too was a need with some men. As she grew in size and in the knowledge of men's minds, Doña Amparo had discovered that her presence, her great bulk, made the men feel protected and secure even as they pursued their dangerous vices. She was a mother watching her sometimes wayward sons at play. She used this gift of insight to her advantage, so that each of her customers felt free to confide in her and ask her for favors.

This was why she sat in the doorway this night. In her parrot-green dress, with her arms folded over her ample breasts, she watched the handlers with the roosters in their hands doing a slow dance around the pit. The birds were straining to get at each other. The men beat on the tin drums, their faces red with the effort, breathing sweat in the stifling body heat of the small place jammed to the limit. When Doña Amparo felt that the excitement had reached its peak, she looked at Luis, who had been keeping his eyes on her. He shouted for the birds to be set free: *Suéltenlos!*

Though there was blood spilled almost immediately, for the roosters attacked each other fiercely with their beaks and their metal spurs, Doña Amparo kept her eyes on the old man and the two boys. Don Juan Santacruz was dying. She could see that each breath cost him days of life. She had known Juan in the prime of his life. She had seen him

124

lose a month's earnings at dice, cards, dominoes, anything that he could bet on. She had been witness to his dangerous rages; and once, many, many years ago, she had been the object of his lust. The man had lived by his passions, and only his animal strength kept him alive now, for to the whole world he already looked like a corpse. Yet he was flush with the blood contest just like the other men. As red-soaked feathers flew over the sand pit, he too strained forward to see more clearly how the white bird had pierced his opponent's remaining good eye, blinding the red rooster completely.

Perhaps because that was all it knew how to do, the older rooster continued to strike out in all directions like a machine gone haywire, jabbing with beak and spurs at the thick darkness that now enveloped him, battling without purpose, but fiercely. The white rooster evaded the attacks of his blind opponent, and concentrated his beak stabbing on the red rooster's head and breast. The men were going wild over the bloody battle, and Luis kept his eyes on the patrona, waiting for her to give him the signal to end the fight before the white killed the red. But Doña Amparo had decided that the young rooster should have a complete victory, and she let the massacre go on until there was no movement from the blind animal. The white, his feathers streaked pink with blood, circled the carcass, stabbing at it mechanically like a hen picking the ground for a worm. When she finally raised her eyes to Luis, the handlers were already claiming their property. She could see that the handler of the red was raising hell at Luis for allowing the bird to be so thoroughly butchered. A crowd formed around the handler of the victorious rooster. There would be drinking to celebrate the victory, and there would be drinking to forget the loss, and there would be drinking to discuss the bout in detail, and to relive the bloodiest episodes; and over a drink they would make plans for the next cockfight. In her deliberate way, Doña Amparo rose from her chair. One of Luis's assistants rushed to move it out of the way and to clear the doorway so that the customers could start filing back to the store and order their drinks.

Doña Amparo had instructed Luis carefully on how to pay out the bets and how to divide the profits with the handlers. What even Luis didn't know was that the red rooster actually belonged to her. He was at this very moment probably wondering how she could have allowed the handler to suffer such a complete loss. Luis would be a little disgusted with her, and he would take the tale to Doña Amparo's daughter, who would report every word to her mother, knowing full well that everything she had, including Luis, had been acquired with her mother's money or through her influence.

What her illegitimate son-in-law thought of her didn't matter much to Doña Amparo as long as he served her. She had allowed Luis to move in with her daughter, not just to satisfy her useless daughter's whim, but because she needed a man she could trust to handle certain aspects of her business for her. Luis had been in the army. He was strong and smart enough, but he had a few weaknesses that only "La Patrona," as he called Doña Amparo, understood. The only thing that had at first bothered Doña Amparo was the hardship that Luis's desertion might cause Melina, his wife. As time passed and she saw Melina bettering herself through a city education and growing more and more independent, Doña Amparo congratulated herself secretly for the way things had turned out for all concerned: her daughter had a man and a couple of kids to keep her busy and out of trouble; Melina was making something of herself after getting rid of an encumbrance of a husband without having to go through the scandal of a divorce; and she, Doña Amparo, had a valuable male as-sistant, one who was bound to her by so many strings of debts and favors that she could count on his complete loy-alty, for she had the power to destroy him and he knew it.

On her way to hand Luis the money, Doña Amparo had stopped to say a few words to many of her customers whose lives she kept up with, advising them on problems ranging from women to employment. Though she seemed to be giving each her undivided attention, her mind was on Don Juan and the two young men. From across the pit she saw that the old man was doubled over, apparently in great pain. She saw the blond young man wiping Don Juan's face with a handkerchief and the dark boy, Guzmán, standing behind the father and son, looking pug-nacious as usual. He had a face that dared people. Doña Amparo had to smile to herself at the tug her womb gave as she gazed on the wiry young man whose skin was a lighter shade than hers, but whose dark flashing eyes and fierce stance reminded her of herself at an earlier time. Guzmán was the image of the son she would never have. She could have conquered the world with such a son.

Don Juan was in a very bad way. Guzmán was wonder-ing how he and Rafael were going to get him home unless he found someone to drive them there in a car. When he saw Doña Amparo walking toward them in her slow, ma-jestic way, Guzmán knew the solution to their predica-ment would soon be in her capable hands. Like almost every male in the neighborhood, Guzmán trusted Doña Amparo.

She addressed the sick man formally, being careful not to injure his pride.

"Don Juan, my house is honored with your presence tonight. Will you and your company join me for a drink in the back?"

127

Don Juan lifted his head and shoulders with an obvious effort. His whole body shook as if he were freezing, but sweat poured down his drawn face. "Amparo," he gasped, hardly above a whisper. "You look good, Amparo. Like a spring day." He began to cough violently.

"You were always a poet, Juan." Doña Amparo took the old man gently by the arm and signaled with her hand behind his back for Rafael and Guzmán to follow.

She took them to a small room in back of the domino hall which had a large poster bed on one side and a formica table with four chairs on the other. This was her office, and since her business hours were unusual, she often slept there too. Guzmán wondered if this room had also been where she did business in her youth. He had heard that she had been a beauty.

Though Don Juan protested feebly, she led him to the bed. There she propped him up against some pillows.

"Which of you two boys knows how to mix a Cuba Libre?" Though she addressed both of them, she looked directly at Guzmán.

"How many?" Guzmán asked.

"How many people do you see here?"

"Not for me, thank you," said Rafael, wearily. He was tired to the bone and he wanted to take his father home, but did not want to offend Doña Amparo. "I don't drink, señora."

"Don Juan's son doesn't drink." Doña Amparo stated this without sarcasm. She smiled at Rafael. "Bring our blond friend an Old Colony grape soda, Guzmán."

No sooner had Guzmán left the room than Luis poked his head in the door. "Did you give that boy permission to get into the liquor, Patrona?"

"Luis, how many times have I told you I want you to

128

knock before coming in this room? Yes, I gave him permission to serve drinks. What's the problem?"

"Well, it seems you could tell me who is allowed to go behind the counter. The men are making comments. It could cause trouble."

"You get paid for keeping our customers happy, Luis. That's your job. Telling me what to do isn't. You're smart. If anyone asks tell them the boy is trying out for a job. Do I have to do all your thinking for you?"

Luis was obviously angry, but trying to control himself: "I guess you know what you're doing."

"I always do, Luis. I always do. Now go take care of our customers." The man turned to leave the room, but Doña Amparo was not finished. "And Luis," she said softly, "next time, don't forget to knock."

Rafael was astonished. He had never heard a woman speak like Doña Amparo had to a man. In his house his mother whispered like a nun when Don Juan was around. He knew their marriage was an unhappy and cruel union, but he had assumed that women were to their husbands and all men as children were to their parents and all adults.

Guzmán came in with the drinks on a tray, and he handed them all around with a professional air. He had obviously enjoyed the sense of being in charge behind the counter. It was as if you had the power to dispense pleasure. Everyone wanted your attention—and paid you for it.

Doña Amparo sat at the edge of the bed next to Don Juan. The mattress sagged under her weight, but the old man seemed to find her nearness comforting. She brought the drink to his lips with her own hands and let him sip it.

Rafael was beginning to feel uncomfortable. If his mother found out where Don Juan was, she would feel humiliated. His father should not be in the bed of another woman, even in his condition. It was almost morning. He approached the bed where Doña Amparo was leaning over his father, who was apparently whispering something to her. He saw that Guzmán stood drinking by the door, looking alert and ready for anything else this strange night might bring. Exhausted beyond words, Rafael wondered what Guzmán drew on for his energy. At the foot of the bed, Rafael stopped to listen to his father.

"This is my last night of life, Amparo. I wanted to feel the blood in my veins one last time."

"What are you talking about, Juan? I expect you here again for my next cockfight. You won tonight. You have to give the house a chance to recover its losses."

"That blind rooster, Amparo."

"He was mine." She smiled down at Don Juan like the moon on a dark night.

The old man actually made a sound like a chuckle, but began to cough immediately. "You are a winner, Amparo." He gasped for breath. "I wish I could have gone out like him." He was making sounds like a drowning man.

Rafael thought to himself: "You are like that old red rooster, old man. Leading a life of blind violence, making everyone think you are brave, when in fact you just despise yourself so much that you are looking for someone to kill you off so that you can have it said that you died like a man."

"He sounds bad. Shouldn't I get him home?" said Rafael.

"I'll have Luis drive you." Doña Amparo rose heavily from the bed, which groaned deep in its springs.

Rafael put his arms around his father's frail shoulders and raised him to a sitting position on the bed.

"Can't you leave me alone, boy?" Pink spittle dribbled down the side of the old man's mouth, and Rafael wiped it off with his handkerchief. When Luis came in with the car keys, Guzmán helped his friend carry Don Juan to the car. After they arrived at the house where the woman waited in a rocking chair, the old man was put in his bed. Then Luis dropped Guzmán off in front of the Saturninos' house.

It was just dawn, and in El Polvorín the houses were coming alive with the sounds of women setting pots of water to boil for coffee and getting their brooms and sprinkling cans ready. While their children were getting ready for school and their husbands for work, they would sweep clean their dirt yards, taming the pervasive dust with water so that it would not get into their houses and on the laundry they would be hanging on the lines strung from tree to tree. Approaching Mamá Cielo's house, he saw that none of the normal activities were going on there. Instead, there was the ominous sign of a closed door, a door that was always thrown open at the break of each day, except in times of family tragedy, or death. Though Guzmán wanted to hurry, his feet would not obey. He knew that he would have to knock before he entered his own home.

Chapter Five

THE SATURNINO MATRIARCH had turned Guzmán's name in to the police. She had claimed that she had caught him in the act of climbing through her daughter's bedroom window to steal her jewelry. She showed the police evidence of his forced entry in the broken window frame. She wanted him arrested.

As Guzmán entered the house, Mamá Cielo arose slowly from the rocking chair where she had been waiting for him. She had been awakened in the middle of the night by the Saturnino men, she told him in a furious whisper.

"I was not going to steal anything, Mamá." Guzmán knew this explanation would not suffice.

"Then what, in the name of heaven, were you doing at that house last night?" She had come closer to Guzmán and in her voice he detected a hint of the hysteria he had gotten to know so well during his childhood. "Answer me." Mamá Cielo grabbed his arm and shook him.

"Nothing. I was just passing by on my way to town."

"Liar." She slapped him hard across his face. "Were you after that poor woman Rosario? *Hijo del diablo.* Haven't you shamed your family enough with that whore you ran away with? You left your Christian home to live with a prostitute. You bring filth in your hands, everything you touch is filth."

"Mamá." He tried to back away, but she was digging her fingernails into the flesh of his arm.

"You have been drinking liquor. I smell it on your breath. At what whore's house did you spend the night? Do you know that your father is at the police station now trying to undo what you have done? Cursed was the day you came out of my belly." Her voice was piercing in her anger, and in the bedroom the baby started to cry. Ramona rushed out from the kitchen to tend to her. Guzmán saw the fear in his sister's eyes. He knew that he could not tell the truth and defend himself to his mother or anyone else. What would happen to Rosario if he confessed that she had practically invited him into her room? She could not escape the evil tongues of Salud as Rosa had, and as he would when it all became too unbearable. The only thing to do was for him to leave Mamá's house immediately. But he would not turn himself in to the police, either. He was no martyr willing to lose his freedom for a crime he did not commit.

He yanked his arm free of Mamá Cielo's grasp and ran toward the Granja. There, in that thickly vegetated expanse of land, he would be able to hide for a while until he thought things out. As he ran he heard Mamá's voice cursing him.

That day Guzmán ate bananas that grew abundantly on plants that were man-tall but weighed down with great stalks. They looked like *campesinos* carrying heavy loads on their shoulders. There were also guavas just beginning to ripen. Their soft pink pulp was sweet and delicious. In the shade of the fruit trees Guzmán felt totally free. This land was so abundant. In a few acres grew mangoes, bananas, plantains, breadfruit, avocadoes, tamarinds, and roots such as the yucca that could be cooked and eaten like

133

potatoes. He could easily imagine how the original inhabitants of the Island, the Taino Indians, had led an easy life in an earthly paradise, subsisting on what the earth produced without too much effort, and on what the sea gave them. Even their dwellings were constructed from the trees and palm fronds that were so abundant. Of course, the Spaniards with their gold lust, their fire weapons, and their diseases had changed the Indians' ideal life within a couple of generations. In fact, Guzmán had heard Papá Pepe say that he had seen one of the last *caciques* when he was a child. The Indian had passed through town, proudly riding his horse on his way to the mountains. His color was a deep bronze and his long hair ebony black. In one ear he wore a gold earring. Though he knew that in his veins ran some Taino blood, Guzmán had never met a full-blooded Indian. It was said that they had vanished into the mountains after the massacres, after the slave labor and plagues brought by the white men had decimated their tribes.

Years later Guzmán would say that on that day and night he spent in the thick vegetation of La Granja, his thoughts of himself as a fugitive had given him an idea of the meaning of freedom which until that point in his life he had simply accepted. Not to be able to walk where he pleased and not to be able to wander freely would always be to him the most odious of punishments.

After taking a walk to make certain that no one was around, Guzmán found a good spot to take a nap. It was a little elevation in a grove of coconut palms. From there he had a clear view of the Granja. Actually, he was on the border of the school's experimental farm and the no-man's-land where vegetation was allowed to grow freely as a natural boundary. By climbing up a palm tree he could look down upon the school and the main road beyond. On the other side was the hill of El Polvorín and Mamá Cielo's house. He guessed she probably knew where he was, but it would take days and many people to find someone who did not want to be found here because there were so many natural hiding places. As a child, he had many times sought surcease from Mamá's rages under the embankment bridge that went over a little creek near the road, or in the school's barn, where he had taken naps and kept warm in the stall with the milk cow, who was so docile she rarely seemed to notice the skinny brown child using her as a pillow.

On the soft, mossy grass Guzmán slept, and perhaps it was here that he had the dream that made him an exile from Mamá Cielo's house for so many years. In his dream Guzmán saw himself standing at a pool formed from the streams of water that fell from a craggy mountainside. In the shallow water knelt an old Indian man. He was worshipping at the *chorros,* the streams of water like small waterfalls found on some mountainsides. He was facing away from Guzmán, but in his dream Guzmán knew that this was no enemy. In a strange tongue the Indian prayed to his gods and Guzmán waited. Then the old Indian looked at Guzmán and without a word rose to his feet. He was the color of leather and not too tall. His hair, streaked with gray, fell like a turbulent waterfall over his shoulders. His eyes, hooded with wrinkles, were Papá Pepe's eyes, or the eyes of all wise men. He wore one gold earring. The only clothing he wore was a cloth around his waist, like sackcloth, with a rope. The old Indian, still silent, led Guzmán deep into the forest.

They were on a high mountain, Guzmán knew. He could see plunging depths all around him and the deep green vegetation was covered with the mist of low clouds. As he followed the Indian, Guzmán felt the clammy kiss of wet grass on his feet and legs, and the drenched branches

135

slapped his arms. He was hungry, tired, and chilled to the bone, but he knew that he must follow this old man.

Eventually they came to the opening of a cave. At its mouth Guzmán felt the warm exhalation of a fire within. They entered, and Guzmán found himself facing a young Indian girl who had appeared before him as his eyes were adjusting to the dimness of the cavern. She was standing in the very spot where Guzmán had last seen the old man, but the old Indian was gone. Without a word the girl turned and moved calmly into the interior, so Guzmán followed his new guide as he had the old man. They were going through labyrinthine passages toward the source of warmth and light that Guzmán could feel intensifying on his skin. Far ahead of them was a pinpoint of light that flickered invitingly. For what seemed like an eternity she led him deep into caverns where the roots of trees dangled above them like the feet of hanged men and water dripped down, making deeper and deeper puddles so that at one point they were swimming in muddy water, always following that point of light. Tired beyond hope and gasping for breath, Guzmán embraced the Indian girl, seeing her face for the first time. She locked her arms like a vice around his neck and pulled him deep into the muck, where she held him until the thick mire filled his mouth and he could not breathe or scream.

Guzmán fought his way back to consciousness, and when he opened his eyes it was late afternoon. His clothes were drenched with sweat, and since he had been sleeping face down, his nostrils were filled with the pungent smell of moist earth and grass. Though it was late in the day the sun had burned the sky bright orange. It was humid and hot and every living thing was seeking shelter. For the first time in his life Guzmán thought of the purifying nature of winter—how for once he would like to look at the ground and not see it move with life. At that moment a fat green iguana crossed right in front of him and in a slithering fury pounced on a grasshopper and was gone. Guzmán shook the clinging leaves from his arms and looked about him for food.

ON THAT SAME DAY, about the time the cock crowed, Don Juan cut the veins on his thin wrists with a shaving razor he kept on the night table next to a Bible. Apparently he bled quietly for hours in his own bed. The feather mattress absorbed what life he had left coursing through his veins. Rafael was to mention years later that when he had carried that mattress out of the house he had felt the weight of a lifetime of sins on his back, measured in equal portions of alcohol and blood. He had let it dry in the sun, then he had burned it. The casket in which Don Juan was buried weighed almost nothing; it took only two men, one at either end, to carry it.

It was in Doña Amparo's store, later that day, that Rafael saw Guzmán, who had been driven there by hunger and nightmares under the cold and distant stars. Doña Amparo had taken him in, fed him and given him clean clothes that belonged to Luis. Guzmán accepted everything with the uneasy feeling that an account was being kept by the expansive woman for everything that passed from her hands into his. Guzmán was behind the counter helping Luis stack bottles when Rafael came in to buy foodstuffs for the wake. It would last all day and night, and the shifts of people who would come to pray for Don Juan's soul had to be fed.

"*Hermano,* what are you doing here so early?" Guzmán tried to sound enthusiastic even though he was worried about his arrest, which he believed would happen that day. He had told Doña Amparo about it and she said he was to stay at the store for that day, that she would talk to the police chief about the mistake they had made with Guzmán. In the meantime he could help at the store during the day and serve drinks at night when it became the domino hall. Frightened of the possibility of jail, Guzmán had agreed to everything. Doña Amparo had told him not to discuss any of it with anyone. This was why Guzmán felt embarrassed when he saw Rafael. He would not be able to discuss this difficult situation with his best friend. At that point he had not heard of Don Juan's suicide.

"He's finally dead, Guzmán." Rafael smiled ironically, which only made his careworn face look tragic.

Guzmán rushed around the counter. "Your father, Rafael? He looked very sick at the cockfight, man, but I didn't think . . . What was it, a heart attack?"

"He cut his wrists," Rafael said simply, with no emotion in his voice. "He cut his wrists with the same blade I used to shave him the night before."

Guzmán felt almost dizzy with the tragic turns the world was taking. "How is your mother taking it?"

Rafael shrugged: "She found him this morning, practically floating in his own blood. She came into my room and woke me up early this morning before the children were up. I took the mattress out behind the house. We laid him on the floor and cleaned him up before we called the people from the funeral parlor. They'll return him this afternoon in a casket."

Rafael had said all this in an awful calm monotone. Guzmán felt closer to tears at that moment than he had when Mamá Cielo had slapped him and cursed the day of his birth.

"I want to go with you, man, but I am in a sinking ship myself. Have you heard? Mamá is furious with me. I can't go back home, and I may be in jail by the end of the day."

Guzmán and Rafael, the fair and the dark children of misfortune, looked at each other in silence. They were brothers, and they were men at a crossroads in lives that would diverge and come together again like tributaries of a river. Each had to go his own way.

They say Don Juan's funeral procession was a pageant of fools, paupers, and princes. Perhaps as final payment for the child Josefa, the American donated a mahogany casket with brass handles, the best Salud had to offer. The cutters were given the afternoon off to attend the services. The train that pulled up that day brought not only the usual mail and salesmen but an elegant blond woman and two men dressed like lawyers in black suits. They arrived at the last minute, when the priest was intoning a few carefully chosen and noncommittal words about the deceased, who everyone knew should not be buried on sacred ground, for he was a suicide. Officially, Padre Gonzalo had been informed that Don Juan had died suddenly after a long and painful illness. Padre Gonzalo knew the truth, but of course the thought of disputing the point with the grieving widow wearied him. He was too old and the weight of sins and suffering weighed him down. Sometimes he felt like a beast of burden laden for a journey that had no landmarks and a vague destination. He sighed heavily now in the afternoon heat. The arrival of the well-dressed strangers had caused a stir in the crowd. They had an excuse not to listen to him.

The woman and her companions made their way to the widow's side. Doña Amelia Santacruz seemed to know them, for she bowed her head a little but shrank closer to her oldest son as if afraid. Rafael saw the resemblance of the two men to his father, and the woman had the blond hair and fair skin of the Santacruzes, but her features were delicate like those of Josefa, his little sister. It was easy to see that hard work had not marred her beauty. She had none of the marks of poverty. The rich relatives. It had to be the family Don Juan had forbidden his wife and children to discuss. But like everyone else in Salud, Rafael had heard that his father had been the black sheep of an aristocratic Spanish family of landowners.

Around the square hole of earth that was about to take in the remains of a wasted life were gathered the ragged and the mighty of Salud. The cutters looked like true sons of the earth, burned to a tough and dark leather in their white peasant pants and guayaberas. They were the men whom Don Juan had overseen for almost twenty years. He had claimed the job with his bravado and his natural air of being lord and master. The oldest among the cutters could remember Don Juan astride a white horse riding the perimeter of the fields like a conquistador. There were stories of his murderous rages, but the men also knew that only Don Juan could mediate with the American for them. Mr. Clement treated Don Juan as his equal. If the cutters could get Don Juan to listen to their complaints, they also had the American's ear. All the cutters, except for the younger ones, felt a sense of loss for a protector, even though Don Juan had exacted a high price in the quotas he had demanded of them. Some of the men were relieved at the overseer's death, though of course they did not show it at the funeral. They hoped the next boss would be from among their ranks—a peasant like them with sun-toughened skin and sympathy for their hard times.

Mr. Clement, his wife, and little Josefa with her nurse arrived by car at the graveyard. They stood under large umbrellas to protect them from the burning sun. Incongruously, both husband and wife were dressed in white linen. Mrs. Clement had refused to wear the traditional black, even when her maid had gasped her disapproval as she laid out her mistress's chosen dress. Mr. Clement wore his usual outfit of pleated linen pants and a shirt so light his pink nipples showed through. They did not stay long, for little Josefa, spotting her family, had begun a loud wailing. It was too much for Doña Amelia, who half collapsed in Rafael's arms.

Don Gonzalo rushed through the service speaking in Latin, which was just as well, for in his haste he blessed the bride and groom, and catching his error only added to his confusion. He ended by making a sign of the cross over the coffin as it was being lowered into the ground while he recited the story of the farmer Cincinnatus, who later became ruler of the Roman Republic, a primer lesson in Latin he had learned half a century ago in the courtyard of his seminary in Spain. These days it was much easier to remember a day fifty years ago than what had transpired in the last hour.

The earth was packed like a decayed tooth over Don Juan's grave. All the mourners, as well as the ones who came for the morbid thrill of contemplating their own mortality, walked away from the cemetery in small, dark groups.

The elegant woman and the two black-suited men were the brothers and sisters Don Juan had never mentioned to anyone in Salud, except perhaps to his wife, who practiced silence and solitude as if she had taken a vow. Rafael sat with his mother and their guests in the living room of the cottage, on which had been imposed for once the tidiness and formality of mourning. The younger children were with neighbors. The woman, Rebeca Santacruz was her name, introduced her brothers, Bernardo and Jorge, who shook hands formally with Rafael and bowed their heads slightly to Doña Amelia. Rafael noticed the family resemblance between himself and both the brothers, both fair-skinned and blond. But they were muscular, well-fleshed men. He was too skinny and had grown to his adult height at five seven.

They drank the sweet café con leche that the widow had prepared and through the condolences and pleasantries studied one another. There was no catching up on Santacruz family news, nor any offers to come live at the Santacruz hacienda in Lajas, a town only a couple of hours away by train. In fact, La Señorita Rebeca had obviously been chosen to speak a brief message, and the men seemed to be under an edict of silence. Rafael noted how the younger one, Bernardo, looked at him with generous eyes. They were eerily like Don Juan's eyes, but the good will that could be read in his uncle's gaze Rafael had never seen in his own father's.

"We understand your circumstances," Rebeca stated in her rich, low voice. Her Spanish was accented with Castilian. She had apparently been educated in Spain. All her c's sounded like z's. To Rafael she looked like a noblewoman, an aristocrat right out of the historical novels he loved to read. His imagination soared with the possibilities connected with the discovery of these relatives. "Don Juan Santacruz, my father, has asked us to inform you that a small pension has been allocated for you and your family. This will be mailed to you in monthly stipends until all of your children by . . . Juan . . . by our deceased brother Juan will have reached the age of eighteen." Rebeca paused after what sounded like a statement she had memorized. Rafael understood at once that his mother was not considered a Santacruz and that this gesture was more charity than family loyalty. "Do you need anything at the present moment?" asked the haughty woman.

"Señorita, I am grateful for your visit and your family's assistance. I . . . make a little money myself cutting gloves, and Rafael is already working at the Central. It is not necessary that your father trouble himself." Doña Amelia spoke in a low voice, eyes downcast, but the dignity of her refusal astonished Rafael, who was used to her humble acceptance of all things pressed upon her, good or bad.

The señorita sighed audibly and looked about her as if she had just noticed the plainness of her surroundings: bare walls, nice furniture that was obviously not respected by its owners, for it bore the nicks and cracks of hard and constant abuse.

The younger brother spoke up. "Señora," he addressed Doña Amelia respectfully. "This money that you will receive belonged to Juan. It was the part of his inheritance that he was not awarded on his twenty-first birthday. It is an investment that has been accruing interest for some time. Now it belongs to his children. Do you understand?" For a few minutes he explained the nature of the investment. Rafael wondered in his mind how his father could have risen from the same source as this gentleman who was obviously concerned with the fate of a woman and children he had never met before.

The older brother, Jorge, had said nothing to this point, apparently being as reserved as Don Juan had been, but then he spoke up: "Perhaps we should make clear to these people that the money cannot be used in any other way than as stated by our dear departed mother's will. It was to go to Juan and after his death, to his children. In case of the demise of all Juan's descendants it was to be given in perpetuity to the Catholic church. It is up to you, Señora, to decide whether the priests or your children shall benefit from this pension, which I assure you will not go beyond clothing them and feeding them adequately. My mother was generous but not extravagant."

With a few more words of formal courtesy on the part of

the Santacruz family representatives and of humble gratitude on his mother's part, Rafael saw the matter closed. He
had remained silent but expectant, waiting for one of his
uncles to speak to him. He never got his wish. Their business completed, the señorita led them in taking their
leave. The men shook hands with him. Don Bernardo put
his left hand on Rafael's shoulder for a moment but neither
of them spoke. In minutes they were on the road, Don
Jorge holding a white parasol over his sister's golden
head. Rafael watched them until they disappeared around
the bend that led to the railroad station. Though he knew
where they lived and could imagine the elegant life they
probably led, Rafael would never look them up or even
speak about them much to his own children in the future.
It was his one gesture of respect to his father's memory.
Don Juan had been cast out, and with him his seed. Rafael
belonged to the branch of the pariah.

Rafael, freed from the burden of providing for his family,
made the decision to join the navy and marry Ramona. In
their wedding photograph they look like children playing
at dressing up. He was wearing an oversized white dinner
jacket, padded at the shoulders and almost to his knees in
length over black trousers. Ramona's dress was borrowed
from an older cousin. It was satin, straight and simply cut.
It fell over her thin hips with graceful elegance. Her crown
of flowers sat slightly askew on her abundant hair which
she'd had cut and permed for the occasion. They stood
stiffly side by side, a teenage couple slightly embarrassed
by their bold act.

The wedding took place a few months after Guzmán had
left the Island. On the day of Don Juan's funeral Guzmán
found out that the charges the Saturninos had made
against him to the police had been dropped because the
old lady could not prove that anything had been stolen,

and Rosario refused to talk to anyone. In fact, the younger woman had secluded herself permanently in the house and was rarely seen any more by anyone outside her family.

Doña Amparo had offered Guzmán a job in her domino hall as Luis's assistant, and Guzmán had considered accepting it until the lottery came to Salud. He had filled out a coupon in *El Diario,* the newspaper that announced the dates and locations for the lottery. He was expecting an answer any day. Papá Pepe had come to see him at the store. They had a long talk in the back, where Guzmán had made a little room for himself in the lean-to that was used as a cockfighting pit. Doña Amparo had given him an army cot. Don Pepe and Guzmán sat on this cot late in the afternoon one day. The old man spoke first.

"Son, I see only hardship where you are planning to go. Don't leave the Island."

"Papá, how did you know?" Guzmán was surprised that his father knew his plans to go to New York. He had told only Rafael.

"I saw you here," the old man pointed to his temple, "and you were cold and hungry among strangers. You should come home, son."

"Mamá Cielo . . . she was angrier than I have seen her since I was a child. I cannot go back home. I am a man now . . ."

The father interrupted him gently by putting his hands on his son's shoulders. "Guzmán, your mother loves you more than any of our other children. But she hates your wildness and fears for you. She will be a very old woman before she understands your nature, son. But I want you to know this, and never tell her I spoke of it: every day she gets down on her knees and prays for you. I have heard her. And when your name is mentioned she listens carefully and stores it all in her heart, for she knows she can never bring herself to ask about you. It is her pride and your pride that make you seem like enemies to each other."

Guzmán had never heard his timid father speak this way about his wife or even this much about anything. Papá's nose was always buried in a book when he was not working at the Central, and often his own children forgot his existence, always depending on their mother to make decisions. Guzmán saw his dead brother Carmelo's connection to this gentle, wise old man, but not his own. He could never sit back and read books while there was a world to discover.

"Papá, I have signed up for the lottery. The man who runs it will be in Salud in a few weeks, and I am sure I will be leaving the Island for America soon after that."

"The lottery. That is the drawing the government has devised for choosing laborers. They say some come back rich and others do not return at all. Son, you are too young for this lottery. It is an unknown. It has never been done here in Salud, and all we hear are stories."

"I am nearly eighteen, Papá. I wrote in the application that I am of age. They pay your airline ticket. It says that there will be at least twenty names drawn in each town, so I will be among friends." Seeing that his father was still unconvinced, Guzmán added: "I will not return home, Papá, even if I don't get to go to Nueva York. I cannot. You understand?"

No more words were spoken, but they embraced. Papá Pepe brought Guzmán a suitcase with Guzmán's clothes a few days later. They had all been washed and ironed by Mamá Cielo.

Because Doña Amparo did not know of Guzmán's plans to leave his job, she took a personal interest in him. In the

146

evenings when she stayed in her room in the back of the store, she would call him in to share a meal with her. After that she would tally the day's receipts, teaching him how profits were made and invested. He had a quick mind, and soon he was doing more paperwork than counter work. Luis, who performed the most menial tasks for Doña Amparo, resented the intruder and began to show his hostility toward Guzmán in a number of unpleasant ways.

He referred to him as Amparo's boy in front of the customers. His intention was to bring to mind the scandal with La Cabra and to stir up the recent rumors that Guzmán had done more than steal jewelry at the Saturninos' the night he had been found under pieces of Rosario's window. When the patrona was not there, Luis ordered Guzmán around like an errand boy.

Guzmán kept silent only because he did not want to cause problems between Luis and Doña Amparo. She would not just fire the man, she would also ruin him. Guzmán had had occasion to look into Doña Amparo's business dealings, discovering in the process that she had custody of some of the juiciest secrets in Salud.

In the meantime he dreamed of the day the lottery would be held and he would hear his name called out in the public square. He felt certain that he would be chosen. It was his time to leave Salud, and Providence would not deny him this fervent wish.

At Mamá Cielo's everyone was busy planning Ramona's wedding. Ramona had had to assume all the household duties that would prepare her for marriage. She did everything automatically, dreaming of a different life for herself. Mamá had decided that the wedding should be shortly after Ramona's sixteenth birthday, some six months away. Papá Pepe kept Guzmán informed during his discreet visits to the store on his way home after work. He

147

tried to convince Guzmán to stay at least until after his sister and his best friend were married, but Guzmán knew he could not.

In growing anticipation Guzmán went through his days in work and daydreams. In his narrow army cot at night he thought about his life, and it seemed to him that he had opened his eyes to love and beauty only when he had met that much-maligned woman, Rosa. He regretted having left her house like a coward, and he determined to find her in New York—he was convinced that that was the only other place she knew to go. He imagined himself walking on a white carpet of snow in a city of light, his heart leading him to the place where she lived. Together they would explore that wonderful new world where everyone had television sets and drove big cars.

He would also meet Rafael and Ramona there. He and Rafael had discussed their plans a few days after Don Juan's funeral, when Rafael had signed his navy papers. He would be going to a place called Brooklyn Yard, a name neither of them could pronounce, but the man at the recruitment office in Mayagüez had said the place was right in New York. Rafael would go soon after the wedding, then send for Ramona after his training was completed. When Guzmán and Rafael shook hands after that conversation, they felt that they were finally men, discussing plans for a future that did not involve their parents or the town of Salud. They would come back someday as successful, maybe even rich men. They would point out to their children the humble place where their fathers had been born. What they did not consider were the years likely to pass between that day when they were standing on the dirt floor of the cockfighting pit, and the day when the long black car of their dream would pull up in front of Doña Amparo's little store, blocking almost all of the street.

Soon after, the newspaper carried the long-awaited advertisement, and the lottery came to Salud. The plaza began to fill up with people early on the big day. Vendors wheeled their carts to the corners, where they did a brisk business in codfish fritters and *mabi*, the cooling, sweet drink made from the bark of a tree. The artisans set up their tables, where they displayed their painted wooden saints and carved figures made to order in the form of any amulet the customer desired. There was a festival atmosphere, with the talk and the excitement building all morning as a stage was improvised and a microphone set up. All the men who had sent in their applications were there, of course, but also many women: wives, mothers, and girlfriends who would learn on that day whether their destiny called for a long separation from their men. There was an element of mystery and fear involved in the procedure. The men must have felt like the sailors who accompanied Columbus on his first voyage. Their destination was not certain, and though great adventures beyond their imagining might be part of it, there was also the uncertainty of not knowing exactly where you were going or what to expect when you got there.

The deal offered was that you would get transportation, food, and lodging paid for, to the U.S. Most men simply said Nueva York, because New York City was the only place most of them had heard of anyone from Puerto Rico going to. The size of the country they were heading for was beyond the grasp of men who had rarely gone farther even on their own tiny island than the city of Mayagüez, ten miles from Salud. The lottery had begun during President Truman's administration to help bring cheap labor to the growers on the mainland and to aid the Island's unemployment problem after the return of the soldiers from the Korean War. The population had exploded, and jobs other than those connected with the sugar refinery were very scarce. By this time, though, the lottery had slipped into

149

the hands of enterprising con men who made fortunes selling chances at the lottery to desperate men, then charging the growers per head for the men who were "recruited."

In the intense heat of midday the agent in a white shirt and tie took his place on the platform. He spoke into the microphone of the wonderful opportunity he was about to offer some of the lucky men gathered there that day. He said that he was recruiting laborers for a millionaire farmer in the state of New York whose farm was as large as the whole town of Salud. The men had been selected according to their skills for jobs varying from foreman, to picker, to cook. He told them anecdotes of how men just like them had spent one year on such a farm and had earned enough money to come back to the Island and buy land of their own, and how some had chosen to stay in the state of New York and had sent for their families. There was a gasp from the crowd when he told them that it was possible to make up to one dollar per hour if a man was a hard worker. Then he asked for questions from the men. A cutter raised his hand timidly. His leatherlike skin spoke of countless hours swinging a machete in the hot sun.

"Will we have to work in the snow?" he asked almost hopefully.

"You will be picking fruit, man. There are seasons for picking, but not in the winter. There will be other things to do in the winter. Any other questions?"

Guzmán, who had been making his way to the front, raised his hand. "When do we leave for Nueva York?"

Everyone laughed at the childlike anticipation in his voice.

"Well, young man, first you have to be chosen. Not everyone is qualified. It is very competitive. Thousands of men apply and only a few, the best, are selected." He looked at the crowd which had kept growing until the whole square was filled with expectant faces, many having walked in from the fields just to hear the names being called. "If everyone is ready I will begin calling out the names of the fortunate men who will be boarding a plane in ten days for a whole new life in America." There was applause, whistles, and shouts of approval.

With each name called out there was an outbreak of jubilation and embraces. There were about one hundred names called, and Guzmán was not among them. He was stunned. He had sent his five dollars in with his application. He had given his age as eighteen, and he had experience in the fields and in storekeeping. As the crowd began to thin out, Guzmán remained seated on the cement bench next to the stage. He wanted to talk to this agent man. There had to be a mistake.

After the plaza began to clear, Guzmán realized that there was a whole group of men waiting to talk to the agent. They were mainly cutters and farm workers, to judge by their clothes, and all were young. No one dared approach the stand, where the agent was taking his time gathering his papers into a briefcase. Guzmán rose from the bench and resolutely walked right up to the front of the little stage. The agent was directly above him, shuffling his papers importantly while ignoring Guzmán. Finally Guzmán spoke up: "Señor, my name is Guzmán Vivente. I sent in my application with the five-dollar fee on the first day the lottery was announced in the newspaper. Señor . . .?"

The man seemed not to have taken notice of Guzmán even after he spoke, but actually he was waiting for the other men to drift over to the stage area, which they were already beginning to do after someone had taken the initial step forward. He smiled ironically, thinking that there were always fifty sheep to one wolf.

"Señor . . ." Guzmán spoke up, irritated now at the

man's insulting indifference. Though his face flamed up with anger, he tried to control himself. He wanted to get in on this lottery. He had to keep that objective in mind.

"One moment, young man, can't you see I'm busy? I will answer all your questions. Yes, that's right, come closer so I can talk to you." He walked forward on the stage and stood at the edge, towering above the group of sun-aged young men wearing their *pavas,* peasant straw hats. Most of them were barefoot on the scorching cement of the plaza. "So you all want to go to the land of snow?"

They all answered *sí—la tierra de nieve* sounded like paradise. Their feet became aware of the hot cement just imagining the coolness of a substance they had only seen in pictures.

"I just got back from New York myself a few days ago, and can you believe it? Snow was falling like grated coconut from the sky. The children were running around making balls out of it and eating it like ice cream."

"You can eat snow?" One of the younger men spoke up, his round eyes describing wonder.

"Well, I have never tried it myself. I'm not one for sweets, but I hear it tastes like vanilla ice cream." There were ah's all through the crowd. The agent knew his business. Now that he had them riveted to his voice, he sat down on the edge of the stage; still he was above them by three feet, just enough so they had to look up to him like children to their teacher, or to their father.

"What about our applications?" It was that impertinent young man breaking the mood again. Guzmán pressed the issue: "Is there a reason why our application did not make the lottery? Will we get a refund of our five dollars?"

"One moment, one moment, dear boy. One question at a time. What is your name?"

"Guzmán."

"Guzmán. I seem to remember seeing your application." With deliberate slowness the agent opened his briefcase and brought out a sheaf of papers. Dramatically, he raised them above his head so that all the men could see.

"This is you," he said.

Questions were shouted by several men. The agent motioned with his hand for silence.

"All of you are qualified applicants."

"Then why . . ." Guzmán had placed himself in front of the stage.

Once again the agent waited for the men to fall silent before he spoke up.

"The lottery is conducted as a fair system. The men are selected from a large pool for their skills, their experience and their financial need. All you men are under twenty-one, most of you are not married. The quota was filled up before your names came up."

"Does this mean we have no chance of going?" A man in the back spoke up, taking his pava off to reveal a face like a wizened monkey. The sun and the endless hours of swinging a machete in the fields had taken him from child to old man with no stage in between.

"Well, it doesn't have to mean that. The growers in the north always need hands, but they can only afford, with the help of the federal government, to pay airfare for a certain number of workers."

"You mean that if we came up with our own airfare we would have jobs assured in Nueva York?" This was Guzmán, who had made his way to the very front of the crowd and was close enough to the agent to notice the man's expensive watch, his shiny patent-leather shoes and store-bought clothes. The agent in turn took a close look at Guzmán, noting his nervous energy and quick mind. He would remember him. The boy could turn out to be either

153

a leader or a troublemaker. Such men are useful in the business of recruiting.

"There are always jobs for honest, hard-working men."

"How much?" Guzmán had now assumed the role of spokesman for the group. The men followed the exchange between Guzmán and the agent with almost breathless silence. For some it was the last chance to escape the cycle of poverty of their lives.

"Well, let's see." The agent took out a pad from his briefcase and a gold pen. He wrote figures down for what seemed hours to the men sweating in the early afternoon sun. No one spoke a word.

"Fifty dollars will pay for the airfare and transportation to the farms."

As if they had been roughly awakened from a dream, several men shook their heads and walked away from the plaza. There were sounds of surprise and laments from others in the crowd. Fifty dollars! Two months' pay at the fields. Who could save that much when wages earned were already owed at the *bodega* or the butchershop.

The agent talked to the dozen or so men who were left of the money that was to be made in the north. He answered their questions about the farm where they would work. He said it was a large place with dormitories, like the army, except that the pay was better and you didn't have sergeants yelling commands at you all day long.

"How long do we have to bring you the fifty dollars?" Guzmán asked.

"I will be in Salud for three more days, until Sunday. I will be staying at Mr. Clement's house. The Big House. Sunday morning there will be a bus right here to pick up the men who are going with me. As I told the men chosen today, there will also be a meeting tonight in the field behind the Big House to go over the plans for the trip. You are

154

all invited to attend." With that the agent began to pack his papers in his briefcase. The men took this as a dismissal and dispersed excitedly in groups of two or three. Only Guzmán remained sitting on the cement bench thinking.

This was where Mamá Cielo saw him on her way out of the clinic where she had taken her child, Luz, for an injection. With the child clinging to her skirt, she stood at a distance and looked at her son. His head in his hands, leaning forward, he looked exactly as sad as when she had denied him permission to run wild around the neighborhood visiting crazy people and getting in everyone's way. She had then resisted the urge to comfort him because she thought that would make him soft and disobedient. Now he was getting farther away from her, more and more every day, and always leaning toward the protective arms of women: Rosa, Amparo. She felt a little surge of the familiar anger over her son's easy heart. He gave his days away to whoever wanted them, as if he did not have a future to work for. He now wanted to go to America, for the adventure, or to get away from the family. Maybe it was time for him to leave Salud and learn to suffer with no one to turn to. He would be back soon. Mamá Cielo resolved to ask Papá Pepe to find out what it was Guzmán needed.

And so it happened that Papá Pepe talked to his son that night. It was Papá Pepe who brought him the fifty dollars, much of it in old coins that had been saved in a glass jar buried in the garden. Mamá Cielo did not believe in banks and had always buried the money she wanted to save in special spots around the house. Guzmán's fifty dollars had been dug up at the base of the mango tree that shaded the house, where she had put it at the time of her wedding. Her funeral money she had called it. Papá Pepe did not explain this to Guzmán at that time. Mamá had let him

155

know that their son was not to know that she was financing his trip. For many years Guzmán believed that Papá Pepe had given him the money, and always he thought of himself as away from home without permission from Mamá, wandering in the world without her blessing.

Chapter Six

THEY SAY my mother, Ramona, was a beauty. Her bones were light and fine, and when nature began to clothe them in flesh she turned into an enchanting young woman, a combination of fragility and lushness that people, men in particular, remarked upon when she was only fourteen or fifteen. But she hardly had time for vanity in her childhood. While Mamá Cielo was bearing children, Ramona, as the oldest daughter, had to be nurse and babysitter. By the time she entered adolescence, she was tired of children and the endless drudgery of housework. She promised herself she would someday marry a man who would take her far away from Salud; the second thing she proposed to do was to convince whomever she married that one child was all she could or would bear.

Ramona grew up in a woman's world. The misadventures of her brothers, Carmelo and Guzmán, took place in the world of men. She was aware only of the repercussions of Mamá Cielo's anger, and the chaos the house could be thrown into when Guzmán, who was the acknowledged troublemaker, would get into scandals that made Mamá shut the front door, and sometimes even take to her bed for days, leaving Ramona to take care of everything.

Ramona became aware of her power over men the same year that Carmelo was killed in Korea. It was on Saturdays that Mamá Cielo would tell Ramona to walk to Las Fuentes out in the country and pick some herbs that grew wild around the springs. She used these to make home remedies for herself and the children. She made teas with yerba buena, chicory, and other weeds and plants that cured everything from constipation to menstrual cramps. She had taught Ramona how to identify the plants.

On this day Ramona was fourteen years old. She had already met Rafael at the church with her brother Guzmán and had begun to dream about him. In her mind she saw Rafael as an angel who lifted her from her bed at night and took her walking through the stars. There were vague sensations in her thighs and belly when she thought of the slender blond boy, but this part of the pleasure she had not yet named. She was thinking about Rafael when she reached the area where springs came out of the earth in burbling pools. There was a field just beyond the springs where cattle usually grazed, but today the field was spotted with green tents, and men in army uniforms were everywhere. She felt embarrassed to have come upon these men, some of whom were in their white undershirts shaving and washing themselves in the pools of spring water. But to get to the far end of the field to collect the herbs, Ramona had to cross the springs and walk through the pasture. It did not occur to her to return home without the plants. Mamá was home with a sick child waiting for her.

The men saw her. The ones who had been kneeling down to wash themselves stood up. Others also stopped what they were doing to stare at her. They were tall, most of them, and white-skinned, except for one man who was black, but not bronze, really black. She guessed they were American soldiers on a training expedition. One of them, a young blond one who reminded her of Rafael, approached her.

158

"Hello," he said in English. "Are you looking for someone?"

Ramona lowered her eyes and tried to walk past him. He blocked her path. Some of the men started cheering him on calling him "Sonny! Go on, Sonny. Ask her if she's got any sisters or cousins," one yelled out.

Ramona felt both frightened and excited. It was as if she were on stage. All these men were looking at her. In their eyes she saw both admiration and danger. She tried to wiggle out of Sonny's grasp, but he held her elbow, gently but with a firm grip.

"Just tell me your name. You're beautiful." He whispered so the others, already dispersing anyway, would not hear. Ramona understood the word "name" from her grammar-school English.

"Ramona," she answered him, her cheeks burning.

"Ramona." The young soldier pronounced the "r" too softly and she couldn't help but smile at how different it made her name sound. He seemed to think about it for a minute; then he said, "I'll call you Mona. Mona. Where are you going, beautiful Mona?" Ramona pointed to the far end of the field beyond the tents where there was a grove of trees and a single spring where medicinal plants grew in abundance.

"I'll go with you," Sonny said, then he called out to another soldier who was making coffee over an open fire. "Sam, hey, Sam." The other stood up and cupped one hand over an ear to indicate that he heard him. "I'll be back in a few minutes. Cover for me, will you?" The other soldier saluted mockingly and gave his friend a meaningful look.

"Sure thing," he said. Several men laughed.

In a trance of confusion, Ramona walked hand in hand with the young soldier to the other side of the pasture.

159

Cows followed them with their huge, moist eyes, moving against them with passive sensuousness so that Sonny had to slap them on the rumps to make them move out of the way. The air was thick with the pungent smell of manure and dew-wet hay.

When they reached the spring they found that it had become quite a large puddle of water. Ramona took off her sandals and attempted to jump across it, only to lose her balance and nearly fall in. Sonny caught her by the waist, and they both stood facing each other in the knee-deep, cold water hole.

"Be careful, little one," said Sonny, his face so close she could feel the blond down on his cheeks.

His eyes were such a transparent blue—Ramona had never seen any like them. To her he looked blind. How could anyone who had no depth in his pupils see the world the same as she did with her dark brown eyes? He was breathing quickly, his face close to hers. She felt his breath on her face. She felt suddenly afraid and broke away from the circle of his arms.

Hurriedly, she began to gather the plant she had come for into a kerchief she had been wearing as a belt. In her gray school skirt and white blouse she was at once both a little girl and a woman on the precipice of sexual ripeness. Her body was already developed, and it strained against the severe shapelessness of her clothes.

Sonny sat on a large boulder by the side of the springs watching Ramona. He was fascinated by the cascade of thick black hair that fell over her shoulders to her waist as she bent to gather her herbs. He didn't want to frighten her away. He was only nineteen himself and only a little more knowledgeable than Ramona about sex and its consequences. Not six months ago, on a farm in Georgia, he had sat through his preacher father's long sermon on "keeping

160

your mind and body clean, son." Then the endless indoctrination about soldiers and women at training camp. On this island he felt like a visitor from another planet. Everything was too lush, too green, too hot. Every rock's underside was creeping with life, and the people looked at him with intense unquestioning eyes. They knew what he was doing in their country but did not care who he was. The dark skin of the women, their voluptuous bodies, became the obsessive subject of his waking dreams. When he had seen Ramona walk directly into his line of vision that morning, his heart and stomach had somersaulted. Shyness, caution forgotten, he had decided to spend time with her. Hardly in control of his hands, which wanted to catch her by her slender waist, he sat and watched her bending to gather plants and roll them into a red square of material.

"What are they for?" Only when he spoke did she raise her long lashes to look at him. She looked directly into his eyes until, unable to help himself, he stretched out his hand to her, murmuring words that she did not have to understand to recognize in tone and intent. Frightened, she backed away from the intimate hoarseness of his voice as he said her name over and over, as he leaned closer to her. She tried to leap over the water hole, but with her hands full with the bundle of plants and her sandals, she lost her balance. She fell to her knees and the soldier pulled her gently toward him. He held her arms pinned at the wrists behind her with one of his large farmer's hands.

"Don't be afraid, don't be afraid, Mona. I just want to kiss you. I won't hurt you." Ramona wanted to scream, but even in her confusion of fear and desire she somehow knew that this boy would not harm her. And causing a scene would be devastating to her reputation. So she relaxed, wiggling her fingers to let him know that he could release his grip now. She turned to face him bringing her fragrant hands to his face. He took each of her fingers into his mouth licking them like candy. Ramona felt her body rising in a pleasurable wave that was taking her deeper and deeper into a delicious oblivion. She forgot about the hard, pebbly ground on which she lay, a man's weight pressing its hardness into her flesh. His mouth traveled up her arms to her neck where his tongue traced circles until it reached her parted, expectant lips. He told her with his tongue what he wanted, and when their faces parted, his hands caressed her hair in a questioning motion. He wanted to possess her but not to take her like a whore. He saw that tears were sliding down Ramona's flushed cheeks. He knew she was responding to his desire but was frightened and confused. He took her face, now fully a child's face with a mixture of want and anxiety written on it, into his hands and kissed her on the forehead. He got to his feet and raised her up. At that moment of renunciation Sonny probably felt more like a hero than he would ever feel during the rest of his life. After she had gathered her things, Sonny lifted her up in his arms and walked across the little pond. Holding hands like lovers, they walked across the pasture to the springs. There, in front of the idle men who watched them with lewd curiosity, Sonny kissed Ramona's hand. They never saw each other again.

AT MAMÁ CIELO'S HOUSE, Ramona took over more and more of the housekeeping work as Mamá recuperated from the birth of Luz and the death of Carmelo in Korea. She dreamed of escaping Salud. In school, which she had stopped attending after Carmelo's death, Ramona had seen pictures in books of the big cities of the United States. She

162

collected glossy magazines, imagining herself dressed in bright silk dresses with furs elegantly draped over her shoulders like the Mexican movie stars she had seen on the covers. She often had fantasies with Sonny playing her romantic lead in full-feature adventures that ended in him kissing her hand in public, an act she had taken as the ultimate tribute to her beauty. After her passionate encounter at the springs with the young soldier, Ramona had become aware of the power of her face and figure. She used it as a magic wand on her rare trips into town. While Mamá carried on her leisurely conversations, Ramona would concentrate on looking attractive. When a man passed by she would pose with eyes slightly downcast, her long black hair draped over her shoulders and her slender body held gracefully erect. Most men couldn't help looking at the child-madonna, for she usually had Luz in her arms. In their eyes she recognized the same look of desire and tenderness she had seen in Sonny's—Ramona had discovered the power of being a woman.

Ever since the young American soldier had kissed her into an awareness of possibilities, his physical image had become the subject of her daydreams, but blond Rafael, *El Angel Triste,* was the subject of her more practical dreams. In church, on the night when she had attended the novena to Our Lady of Salud with Doña Julia, their eyes had met. She had heard Guzmán speaking about Rafael's plans to join the navy and later to become a doctor. These items she also incorporated into her fantasy. She saw herself on the arm of a naval officer in a uniform of blinding white; she saw herself as the universally admired wife of a famous physician; but mainly she saw herself far away from the mountain of diapers, Mamá's constant vigilance, and her gentle father's sermons on virtue. After the exchange of a few words with Rafael when he had come over to help bring Guzmán back from the whore's house, Ramona knew that Rafael was to be hers. He had said, "I'll be back for you." And he had come back after Don Juan's death, though for several weeks during the old man's final collapse she had not seen him. He had written her once telling her that he would be asking Papá Pepe for her hand. He had apparently wasted no time about that, because the note had been delivered to her by Papá himself, though she knew Mamá had probably read it.

Finally, Rafael had just shown up one evening after his father's funeral looking pale and skinny. She herself was healthy and strong so that she felt like taking the exhausted Rafael into her arms and cradling him as she did little Luz, who was always ill. But their meetings were strictly chaperoned by Mamá Cielo, who sat in her rocking chair at one end of the room embroidering gloves out of a box that never seemed to empty.

Rafael and Ramona sat on an uncomfortable double seat of teakwood and straw weave, the typical furniture of the Island, where not many people had the leisure to sit for long periods of time. In hushed voices they talked about the future.

"I will be going to Mayagüez in a few days. To the navy recruitment office." Rafael kept his hands folded on his crossed knees. Ramona watched them as if they were white doves that would soon take flight and land on her shoulders.

"I wish I could go with you." They both looked up toward Mamá Cielo, who had raised one eyebrow. She had heard.

"It'll be boring, Ramona—just filling out forms. I'll bring you something from the city." Rafael, though only two and a half years older than Ramona, had soon discovered the secret of Ramona's charm. She looked like a woman, she showed maturity in her movements and in her abilities around the house and with children, but in reality she was still a little girl who liked to be complimented and surprised with gifts.

"What would you like?" Rafael always felt powerful when he could make Ramona smile.

"A belt."

"A belt? Why a belt?"

"I've never had a real store-bought belt to wear with my skirts." Now Ramona was visualizing her belt and Rafael listened attentively. He would go to the capital if necessary to get Ramona her belt. "It has to be black, wide, like this," she measured a hand's length for Rafael to see, "and shiny."

"Where can I find such a belt, Ramona? In a ladies' store?"

"I don't know. I have never been to the stores in Mayagüez." Ramona's voice was wistful, and at her end of the room Mamá Cielo dropped her needle on the floor. While she was bending down to find it, Rafael squeezed Ramona's hand, which lay between them like a kitten waiting to be stroked.

"I am going to take you shopping all over the United States. I am going to buy you belts in every color." Rafael whispered this silliness with passionate intensity. Ramona felt her blood turning into a running river. How she loved being spoiled and desired by a man and how little she had to do for it. With her eloquent eyes Ramona promised her sad angel paradise. By the time Mamá had resumed her embroidery they were both sitting apart again and discussing more practical matters, like the wedding which was to

165

take place in less than three months, when she would turn sixteen.

WHAT POSSESSED HER to cut her gorgeous hair? In the wedding photo, Ramona's little crown of flowers sits askew atop a thick crop of short curled hair. It was both her birthday and her wedding day. A cousin from the city had loaned her a satin wedding gown that was slightly too large for her. Though large-eyed and beautiful, the bride in the photograph looks like a little girl trying on her mama's wedding dress. She is not smiling, but looking a little annoyed past the camera. Rafael wears his high school graduation clothes: white jacket with wide lapels and padded shoulders, black pants, and white shoes. He is too thin. His blond, curly hair falls around his face like a halo of light in the black and white photo. He is holding Ramona lightly by the elbow. It is difficult to take this photograph as evidence of a real wedding. It could be a play they are putting on in their backyard. What does it have to do with passion, hardships in a strange land, and my future existence?

After a three-day honeymoon in a five-dollar-a-night hotel in Mayagüez—the gift of the groom's former employer, the American, Mr. Clement, who also sent baskets of fruit, a box full of linen that still looks new, and an envelope with twenty-five dollars (a month's pay for a cutter to the son of his best overseer, Don Juan Santacruz)—they returned to Mamá Cielo's house, where they lived for a few weeks until Rafael got his orders from the navy. His departure notice came quickly, and Ramona discovered in the second month of their marriage that she was pregnant. It was just as well that Rafael was preoccupied with making arrangements for his family. His mother was listed as his dependent after Ramona. It was just as well that he had so much to do these last few days before he took the ship in San Juan to go to New York, where he was to receive training at Brooklyn Yard.

Ramona was sullen. She could not bear the smell of Mamá Cielo's food, or of Rafael's cologne. She felt faint at all hours of the day and had become quiet and reclusive. Rafael tempted her with offers to go to the cinema, or to his mother's house for a visit. She claimed fatigue. He began to blame her pallor and listlessness on the pregnancy. He blamed himself for taking the blush from her cheeks. His father-in-law reassured him that Mamá Cielo had gone through the same moods during her pregnancies. Mamá Cielo would take care of Ramona while Rafael was away, until he could send for her.

At night, in the safe cocoon of their mosquito-netted bed, Ramona listened to her young husband talk about their future life in America.

"We will choose a name for our son that can be easily pronounced in English."

"I will never learn English, Rafael. It's too strange. I didn't do well in English in school."

"You'll learn." He kissed her on her warm cheek. She was always complaining of heat those days. She fanned herself constantly.

"We'll live in a skyscraper. Maybe on the twentieth floor."

"It makes me dizzy to think of a place that tall. I don't think they can be safe. People probably fall out of windows in Nueva York all the time." They giggled at the idea of people raining down from buildings. "The snow would keep them from breaking their bones when they land." They stifled their laughter out of respect for Mamá's presence just on the other side of the thin wall.

When they became conscious of their bodies' demands,

167

they made awkward love informed only by their imagination. Behind closed lids Ramona sometimes imagined that the arms that held her were the soldier Sonny's. And then she thought that Rafael was too timid in his lovemaking. Why wasn't her blood pounding in her ears as it did when the Americano had crushed her to the ground, his mouth drawing her breath and her tongue into himself, teaching her about desire?

Rafael treated Ramona like a porcelain doll, with a tenderness he never saw his father show for his mother. He would simply worship her from across the room if she indicated that was what she wanted from him. But what she wanted she did not have words for; it came to her in dreams, in images of flight.

Rafael left when Ramona's belly was beginning to look rounded and feel taut. She would stay at Mamá Cielo's house until he sent for her. Then she would take an airplane out of San Juan for New York, not to return to her birthplace for fifteen years.

I WAS BORN in my grandmother Cielo's house, and because of the slow fingers of an old midwife I nearly bled to death on my first day on earth. Mamá Cielo's vigils and her herbal teas kept my mother strong, and Ramona's warm body and plentiful milk convinced me I should stay. I was two years old before I saw my father.

Chapter Seven

RAMONA says Rafael was a stranger again to her when she arrived at the airport in New York on a bitter cold November day. Because she was unable to find an adequate coat in Mayagüez for either one of us, we were wrapped like gypsies in shawls and scarves. Ramona was beautiful, and people stared. Or perhaps we looked to them like two sisters, orphaned in a war. She was eighteen years old and in full bloom. Rafael in his dark navy uniform looked like an American sailor on leave. They were shy with each other, and Ramona says that I would not let him pick me up or even take my hand. He looked like no one I knew.

Though he was stationed at the Brooklyn Navy Yard, Rafael had decided that New York City was not a safe place for his young wife and daughter. He had looked up a cousin on his father's side who lived in Paterson, New Jersey—just across the Hudson River. His cousin, also distanced from the Santacruz family, had married his mother's maid, a woman older than he by ten years. He had finally left the Island with Severa, that was her name, and the two girls and a boy they had managed to conceive one after the other. There, in an apartment building inhabited mainly by Puerto Rican families, we lived the first few years.

It was in *El Building*, as it was called by the tenants, that

169

my brother was born three years after our arrival. As I became slowly aware of the world around me, my life became circumscribed by the sounds, smells, and barriolike population of the building and the street where we lived but were never fully assimilated. Though it was a Puerto Rican neighborhood with Jewish landlords, my father considered it only a place to land temporarily. He did not allow my mother to join the gossip circles of the women at the laundromat, or even to shop by herself at Cheo's bodega, a little general store just across the street from El Building where a little man named Cheo sold hard-to-find delicacies of Island cuisine such as green bananas, yuccas, and plantains. Instead, when Rafael came home on leave for the weekends we went shopping at the American supermarket. It was not snobbery on his part so much as fear for us. Two years in New York City had taught him that a street-tough Puerto Rican immigrant is not the same species as the usually gentle and hospitable Islander. He had escaped the brunt of racial prejudice only because of his fair skin and his textbook English, which sounded formal as a European's. His wife and daughter, both olive-skinned and black-haired, were a different matter altogether.

It was *la mancha*, that sign of the wetback, the stain that has little to do with the color of our skin, because some of us are as "white" as our American neighbors; and it was the frightened-rabbit look in our eyes and our unending awe of anything new or foreign that identified us as the newcomers.

It was easy for Ramona to become part of the ethnic beehive of El Building. It was a microcosm of Island life with its intrigues, its gossip groups, and even its own spiritist, Elba, who catered to the complex spiritual needs of the tenants. Coming in from shopping, my mother would close her eyes and breathe deeply; it was both a sigh of relief, for

170

the city streets made her anxious, and a taking in of familiar smells. In El Building, women cooked with their doors
open as a sign of hospitality. Hard-to-obtain items like
green bananas from the Island, plantains, and breadfruit
were shared. At the best of times, it was as closely knit a
community as any Little Italy or Chinatown; the bad times,
however, included free-for-all domestic quarrels in which
neighbors were called in to witness for a scorned wife:
"Estela, did you or did you not see my Antonio with that
whore Tita at the pool hall on Saturday?" Of course, after
the arguments were over, the third party would inevitably
be scorned by one or the other as an interfering fool. It was
difficult to hold grudges with other tenants because the
hallways were shared and there was one narrow staircase
for all, and it was impossible to avoid El Basement, where
the washing machines and dryers that several of the
women had bought collectively were kept. The basement
was a battleground where long-standing friendships could
be dissolved in a matter of minutes if anyone trespassed on
someone else's time to use the machines; or worse, if you
were one of the deprived ones who did not own interest in
the Sears *lavadoras* and you were caught sneaking in a
load—your fate would stop just short of public stoning. At
some point someone got the idea of hiring kids to patrol
the basement. This created a new hierarchy in the already
gang-oriented adolescents of El Building because it encouraged behind-the-scenes negotiations, bribes, and oc-
casional violence for control of El Basement.

Life was lived at a high pitch in El Building. The adults
conducted their lives in two worlds in blithe acceptance of
cultural schizophrenia, going to work or on errands in the
English-speaking segment, which they endured either
with the bravura of the Roman gladiator or with the down-
cast-eyed humility that passed for weakness on the

streets—a timidity that mothers inculcated into their children but that earned us not a few insults and even beatings from the black kids, who knew better. With them it was either get tough or die. Once inside the four walls of their railroad flats, though, everyone perched at his or her level. Fortified in their illusion that all could be kept the same within the family as it had been on the Island, women decorated their apartments with every artifact that enhanced the fantasy. Religious objects imported from the Island were favorite wall hangings. Over the kitchen table in many apartments hung the Sacred Heart, disturbing in its realistic depiction of the crimson organ bleeding in an open palm, like the grocer's catch-of-the-day. And Mary could always be found smiling serenely from walls.

Year after year Rafael, my father, would try unsuccessfully to convince Ramona to move away from El Building. We could have afforded it. With our assured monthly check from the navy, we were considered affluent by our neighbors, but Ramona harbored a fear of strange neighborhoods, with their vulnerable single-family homes sitting like eggs on their little plots of green lawn. Ramona had developed the garrison mentality of the tenement dweller that dictates that there is safety in numbers. When Father came home on leave he would complain of the lack of privacy in the place, the loud neighbors, the bad influences on my brother and me. Mother would point out that with him gone so much of the time she was safe there among others of her kind. He would take us for rides to Fairlawn, an affluent community where the doctors, lawyers, and other Paterson professionals lived. There was so much space, and you could even hear the birds. Mother glanced at the cold façades of the houses and shook her head, unable to imagine the lives within. To her the square homes of strangers were like a television set: you could see the people moving and talking, apparently alive and real, but when you looked inside it was nothing but wires and tubes.

Since Father's homecomings were of short duration—he was then on continuous tours of duty with a fleet of cargo ships delivering supplies to military bases in Europe—his arguments about moving from El Building were always left to be resolved next time. The one thing he was adamant about, however, was the school my brother and I attended. He was convinced that Public School Number 15, where all the other children in our block went, was a haven for winos and hoodlums. The hoodlums were the students; the winos slept on the benches of the so-called campus, a park that surrounded the gray prisonlike school building where drifters took naps on the benches and drugs were sold behind bushes. He enrolled us in Saint Jerome's, where the nuns were liberal and the academic standards high. We were the only Puerto Rican students. All the others were Irish and Italian kids several generations away from immigration, sons and daughters of established professional parents. At Saint Jerome's we were taught art appreciation, church history, and Latin. No home economics for the girls, no shop for the boys. And we wore uniforms with beanies. My brother and I walked the five blocks to and from Saint Jerome's in dread of the neighborhood children, who at the very least shouted imprecations at us "sissies," stole our beanies, or tried to push us into the dirty slush on the streets.

When we were very young, Ramona would walk us to school and pick us up in the afternoon. For her this was a risk and an adventure. She had been brought up to think of herself as sacred ground and of men as wolves circling her borders ready to pounce. She carried herself not humbly but like a woman who acknowledged her beauty. She

173

looked only straight ahead and walked fast, dragging us with her. I felt her fear and her anxiety through her hand, which held my own in a painfully tight grasp. On the streets of Paterson my mother seemed an alien and a refugee, and as I grew to identify with the elements she feared, I dreaded walking with her, a human billboard advertising her paranoia in a foreign language.

All her activities were done in groups of women. Though Rafael despised the gossip societies of El Building, he could do little to prevent Ramona from forming close bonds with the other women while he was away. The ones who did not work in factories formed shifting cliques based on their needs and rarely ventured out alone. They went shopping together, patronizing only certain stores; they attended the Spanish mass at ten o'clock on Sundays to hear the youthful Father Jones struggle through the service in heavily accented lisped Castilian; and they visited each other daily, discussing and analyzing their expatriate condition endlessly. They complained of the cold in the winter, their fights with the "super" for more heat or less, the stifling building in the summer, and their homesickness; but their main topic after husband and children was the Island. They would become misty and lyrical in describing their illusory Eden. The poverty was romanticized and relatives attained mythical proportions in their heroic efforts to survive in an unrelenting world.

RAMONA: "They say Mamá Cielo nearly died giving birth to Guzmán. She bled rivers, and the little devil came out kicking and screaming. She was never the same, never as strong after he was born. Some say a child in middle age can suck up your life's energy like a tumor. I got my womb sewed shut after my son . . ."

NEIGHBOR: "Me too, niña. One child was enough for me. In my town there was a woman who spewed one out every

174

year; after the fifth or seventh they looked more like frogs than children. My own mother dried up like a coconut from nursing kids. That's not for me."

RAMONA: "How Mamá Cielo managed to raise all of us on nothing is a wonder to me. We always had plenty of food. She had a garden and kept chickens in the backyard. Here, if you don't have this [she'd rub her thumb and index finger together to indicate money] you don't eat."

NEIGHBOR: "Here you even have to pay to stay warm and trust that son-of-a-great-white-whore super to fire the furnace."

Every month Ramona received a thin blue airmail envelope with a letter from Puerto Rico. It always opened with a blessing and a brief statement of Mamá Cielo's, Papá Pepe's, and my young Aunt Luz's health. Then, after some lines concerning people in Salud whose names meant nothing to my brother and me, there was usually something about Guzmán. This part we listened to carefully, for we had heard many stories about the black sheep of the family. How he had left the Island ten years ago and that it was six months before they heard from him. Mamá Cielo had nearly died of anxiety. Only Papá Pepe, who had had a vision in a dream of Guzmán in a cavern hiding from his enemies, was certain that his son was alive.

Because the old people had turned heaven and hell upside down trying to discover the fate of their son, the newspaper in Mayagüez had contacted the government office in charge of the lottery only to expose the fact that there was no record of the agent who had come to Salud, that the venture had been privately financed and was perhaps even a scam. The ensuing investigation took years, they say, and in the meantime hundreds of young men ended up in migrant worker camps such as the one in which Guzmán had been dumped after an arduous journey.

Though in his first letter to his parents Guzmán didn't go into details, it was clear that once in the camp he was forced to labor in the strawberry fields for ten hours a day under the supervision of armed guards. For weeks he did not even know that he was in the vicinity of Buffalo, New York, working for an absentee grower who took little interest in how his managers got a labor force. He got out only by getting to know the cook, a woman who commuted in from Buffalo to cook for the Ricans after the cook that had been drafted fell ill with a wet cough. The details of their relationship were apparently not brought up in Guzmán's letter home, just that he climbed in the trunk of her old Studebaker and rode out. Later, to escape from real or imagined pursuers, or maybe from her, Guzmán took a bus into New York City.

There he had somehow talked his way into a job as errand boy for the conductors in the subway system, buying cigarettes for them, catering to their needs in a way that he had learned from the cutters. It was strictly off the payroll. He depended on the tips. He slept on trains and ate from the vending machines. Guzmán feared that the people from the Buffalo farm were still after him, and rarely did he venture out into the city during the day, preferring to ride the line from one end to another. It was not a dull job, for on a subway he was able to observe and categorize the city's inhabitants and learn the language, but, most important, Guzmán acquired the skills necessary for street survival. He became a subway warrior, his senses attuned to the dark look in a pervert's eye, the nervous hands of the amateur mugger, and the deviousness of the pickpocket. It was his survival course.

All this, of course, we did not learn from letters. It had to be later inferred from *Guzmán's Adventures,* the ongoing narrative as told by my mother, enhanced and colored until Guzmán became in our imaginations the brown giant of

176

Island legend. There would be several versions of Guzmán's story, each one suited to its audience. And there would be gaps that would never be filled in, holes into which he would fall in silence.

As long as he lived strictly in our imaginations, Guzmán could be given any dimensions we wanted. When Ramona spoke of his rebellious childhood, I secretly thrilled at his defiance of the adults, whom I was just beginning to resent. At thirteen, I was being counseled in humble acceptance of a destiny I had not chosen for myself: exile or, worse, homelessness. I was already very much aware of the fact that I fit into neither the white middle-class world of my classmates at Saint Jerome's nor the exclusive club of El Building's "expatriates."

When Rafael had first visited Paterson, searching for a "safe" place to bring Ramona and their child, the city was in the midst of an internal flux that was invisible to a stranger. The white middle classes were moving out to the fringes, West Paterson, East Paterson; the Jewish businessmen were buying up inner-city property and renting apartments to blacks and Puerto Ricans. Thousands of immigrants overflowed from New York City, now in its final throes as an industrial center. But it was better than Brooklyn to my father, who witnessed the confusion of the streets while stationed in the Yard. In his white navy uniform he looked like an angel to me when he made his rare appearances at home. On those days we'd come home from school to an apartment smelling of pine cleaner and Ramona nervously wiping surfaces and picking up after us. The conversations with neighbor women were often giggly and whispered on the eves of his homecomings.

"Did you bring your papers home from school as I told you, Marisol?" she would demand as soon as I came in the door.

One of the first things that Rafael asked his children was

how they were doing in school. He would look through all the papers we were supposed to save for him, commenting on everything, including our handwriting, making pointed comments to make us see that the world judged by appearances and a sloppy hand meant a sloppy person.

Rafael's fastidiousness extended to everything in our lives. The apartment was painted so often the walls took on a three-dimensional look and feel, and when I leaned on a windowsill (and that was often) I could leave imprints of my fingers and nails on the soft enamel. He inspected everything, including our clothes, and if any item began to look frayed or worn, he would instruct Ramona to replace it immediately. We shopped in stores our neighbors couldn't afford or feared to enter, and my mother had a charge account at Penney's. The only thing he couldn't get her to do was move out of the crowded barrio of El Building. But within the four walls of our flat he did everything possible to separate us from the rabble. He managed to do that. By dressing better and having more than any of the children in El Building, we were kept out of their ranks; by having less than our classmates at Saint Jerome's, we never quite fitted in that society, either.

Unlike Ramona, Rafael almost never spoke of his childhood or the Island. In fact, his silences were more impressive than his speeches. When he came home on leave, the neighbor women would not just drop by as they usually did when Ramona was alone; we would prepare for his homecomings as if for a visiting dignitary. After Ramona received a telegram, for we had no telephone, she would begin cleaning the apartment and incessantly warning us about our behavior during his stay. Growing up, I knew only a few things about my father. Ramona's stories about Don Juan Santacruz, the cruel patriarch of a tragic family, could hardly be connected with the distant stranger Rafael had become. After nearly fourteen years in the navy he had risen only to the rank of noncommissioned officer, petty officer they called it. His job on an old World War II cargo ship was to watch the boilers. He spent ten to twelve hours a day below the water line, watching dials, alone. He learned silence there. He practiced it for hours, days, and months until he mastered it. When he came home to us, he found conversation difficult, and the normal noise of life disturbing.

During the Cuban missile crisis we did not hear from Rafael for months. Ramona still received a monthly check from the navy, but no letters, no sign of life from him. This was my initiation as her interpreter. For weeks we went from office to office at the Red Cross, where we were treated like victims of a natural disaster, given drinks in plastic cups, and asked to wait. Sometimes I would fill out forms for my mother. But there were never any real answers. Yes, he was on a ship. No, communication was not possible, please go home and wait, Mrs. Santacruz. I learned about waiting at that time, a woman's primary occupation. I watched my mother smoke cigarettes and drink coffee and wait. She never discussed her fears with me. She just told me what to do.

One day after we had watched President Kennedy make his speech on our grainy television screen, Rafael showed up with his duffel bag at our door. He had lost so much weight that he looked like a child wearing an oversized sailor suit. He was pale and feverish. Ramona took him into their bedroom, and when he came out the next day he was more a stranger to us than ever.

He stayed home longer than he ever had before, recuperating from the exhaustion of half a year at sea. Doing what? "Counting the days," I heard him say in a flat voice late one night to Ramona. The bedroom I shared with my brother, Gabriel, faced the tiny kitchen area, where Ramona sat with her cigarettes and coffee to talk to neighbors and wait for Rafael, to read her letters from the Island. Here Rafael and Ramona caught up with their individual lives. Their conversations were mainly questions softly phrased by him, answers emotionally delivered by her. Obviously concerned, this time Ramona pressed him for details of his absence.

"I was the captain's interpreter," he finally conceded, "the only one on board who knew Spanish, and I helped out." No more. Either he was under a military injunction to silence on the subject of the Cuban crisis, or he just did not want to talk about it; for whatever reason, he chose not to elaborate on his part in it. Ramona dropped the subject and fell back into the role of interviewee to his never-ending interrogation. It was as if, unable to share our lives, he needed a full report on all our activities, including the most trivial: to live our days vicariously, to make decisions, ex post facto. Listening from our bedroom I felt resentment at his intrusion into our lives and my sense of privacy violated as I had when I had to fill out all those questionnaires for strangers. One night, assuming that I was asleep, they discussed me.

"Marisol is a 'señorita' now, Rafael. I am sure she will begin menstruating soon."

"You were not much older than she when we got married, Ramona. We have to be very careful with her. Have you seen her with any boys? I don't want her mixing with the hoodlums in this place." This, of course, led to a familiar topic with my parents: moving out of El Building. But I was burning with shame under the sheets in my narrow bed. How dare she mention such private matters to him? Four feet away from me, my brother snored softly.

Rafael tried to show us he cared. He did this by taking

Gabriel for long walks in the city, excursions which my brother hated, for he was an overweight, studious little boy whose idea of a good time was reading his adventure books while consuming an entire double-row package of fig cookies. He was a favorite target for El Building's bullies, and so, once safely inside our little apartment, he preferred to stay there. School was another matter: there he had been identified by his fifth-grade teacher as possessing an amazingly high intelligence quotient and had been adopted by the well-meaning nun as her privileged guinea pig, the basis for her master's thesis. He had little to say to Rafael, so once again Rafael had to resort to the interrogation method. He always spoke in English to us: a perfect textbook English, heavily accented but not identifiable as Puerto Rican. Most of his shipmates, he once mentioned, thought he was German.

"Why does he have to follow me to school?" I asked Ramona. Rafael had begun this practice after he heard some black kids shouting threats at us one day. What he didn't know was that this was not unusual. Gabriel and I got it from both sides. In our Catholic school uniforms and beanies we were fair targets for all the public school kids. We had long since learned the usefulness of passive resistance. Unless they physically attacked us, we pretended not to hear. Rafael's shadowing us only added to our humiliation.

"He is just making sure you get to school safely." Ramona clearly understood my resentment, but she would never contradict her husband in our presence. "Do not cause problems, Marisol."

"I am almost fourteen years old, Mamá, I can walk to school by myself."

"I think you should go into your room and do your school work now."

We had both heard the unmistakable sound of Rafael's footsteps coming up the stairs. He always wore the heavy navy-issue shoes with the thick rubber soles which made a sound quite distinct from the street shoes of the other people in El Building.

"I don't have any homework. It's Christmas vacation time, remember? Today was the last day of classes." He was at the door, we heard the jingle of keys. It was obvious Ramona did not want a confrontation.

"There is a basket of laundry on the bathroom floor. Take it down to El Basement."

"It's almost dark." I was making it as difficult as possible for her to get rid of me. There was an agreement among El Building's housewives that women did not do their laundry in the basement after dark. It was known to all the tenants that some of the men used the place for gambling at night, and the teenage boys often met there to smoke and pass the time.

"There is still time. Just start the wash. I'll send your father after it later. Go!"

I waited until my parents went into their bedroom and started for the basement. Through the window at the end of the corridor I could see my brother's back. He was sitting on the fire escape, reading. Bundled up in his heavy winter coat, hat, and gloves, he looked more like a pile of clothes than a little boy, except that it moved as he turned the pages and adjusted his position. That was his private place. The stairwell was dim, lighted by a yellow bulb at each landing. I could hear the sounds of people in each apartment as I passed, getting ready for their evening meal; I smelled the thick aroma of fried sweet plantains, boiling beans, and the ever-present rice. I wondered if my mother's Island smelled the same as El Building at dinner time. But the thought that occupied my mind most of all was that of Frank, the high school boy I had a crush on. He was Italian. His father owned the supermarket near my school. He was entirely unaware of my existence. Why should he notice a skinny Puerto Rican freshman at Saint Jerome's, when he could choose any of the beautiful, well-developed girls from his own class?

Preoccupied with these thoughts, I entered the dank, ill-lit basement. At once I sensed that I was not alone, but the only sound I heard was the hissing of the steam pipes at first. I set down the basket and held my breath. I was not afraid—my mother's washer was near the exit and I could run toward the door if I saw anyone emerging from the shadowy maze of machines and cement columns. Then I heard a sound like that of a cat caught in a machine. It had happened before; the bad boys would sometimes put a stray in a washer to scare the women. It was probably the only thing that could have made me wander into the increasingly dark and dangerous far end of El Basement. As I tiptoed toward the sound, it became clearer that there was either a whole litter of cats, or it was no animal at all. It was definitely a human voice making little animal sounds in Spanish, a woman speaking:

"This floor is cold. Wait . . . wait . . ." Then some more moaning sounds.

I crouched down behind a dryer, which was warm as if recently used. I cautiously peeked around the corner. There were two people on the floor right in front of the machine. They were practically naked, though the man was still wearing his pants, only around his knees rather than his waist. I recognized him as the husband of one of my mother's coffee friends. I did not know the naked woman, but she was not the neighbor's wife. She had bright red hair. Her skin was dark but she was not black. Her breasts, the largest I had ever seen, hung down like two deflated balloons over her stomach. She kept complaining of the cold floor.

"This is not going to work, José."

He just kept saying "Sí, sí . . ." and trying to push himself on top of her. He was skinny, and I was sure she could have thrown him off her easily if she had wanted to. When he finally managed to climb on top of her, she wrapped her big legs around his skinny rump, and they both started rocking and moaning together. She seemed to have forgotten her initial discomfort and the cold floor. I watched fascinated until I heard Rafael's voice calling my name softly from the other end of the basement. The couple froze in the middle of one of their contortions, turning their faces toward the sound of my father's voice. The terror in their eyes was as exaggerated as the faces of the actors I had seen on the horror movies they showed on late night television. Eyes wide open and glossy, mouths twisted into a grimace. Not wanting Rafael to see this ridiculous scene, I crawled back toward the door.

"What were you doing back there, Marisol?" I could tell Rafael was practicing his self-control. His voice was low, and he kept his hands inside his navy coat, but a thick furrow divided his forehead. I had to think quickly.

"One of my gold earrings fell off." I brought my hand to my ear, which was luckily concealed by a layer of thick black hair. He had sent the earrings to me from somewhere in Europe for my last birthday. "It rolled away." I pointed into the dark. There were no sounds except the ominous hissing of the pipes.

"You should not come down here after dark. Ramona should know better." The last statement was made under his breath. There would be another late-night discussion about moving away from El Building tonight.

"You go upstairs, now."

184

"But what about the clothes and my earring?"

"I'll bring them up. You can wash them tomorrow. Forget the earring."

I raced up the stairs to lock myself in my bedroom and think about what I had seen by myself. Unfortunately, Gabriel had already claimed his side of the room and was busy constructing some heavy machinery with the expensive erector set Rafael had bought him on one of their walks. I lay down on my bed and put the pillow over my head for a little privacy. Ramona came in without knocking.

"Marisol, is something the matter? What happened down there?"

"Nothing happened, Mamá. Rafael came down to get me. You know why. I have a headache. Can I please just close my eyes for a few minutes?"

"Fine, but you are acting a little strange these days, young lady. We are going to have a talk very soon." She slammed the door as she left the room, and an intricate bridge Gabriel had just balanced between two shoe boxes came apart in the middle and collapsed. He frowned at the disaster in the exact manner Rafael had frowned at me. I hadn't noticed before how much they resembled each other—not in looks, for neither my brother nor I had turned out blond and fair like Rafael, but in the intensity of his brown eyes. My father always looked as if he were trying to figure out a very difficult mathematical problem. That was why he hardly ever smiled or talked. He was busy concentrating on solving that problem.

In the week following the episode in El Basement I saw José several times. He seemed to be watching me. It frightened me in an exciting way to feel his rat eyes on me when I walked down to the supermarket, but I was not worried that he would approach me. There was a sort of code of honor in El Building that I understood in a rudimentary way: it held that respectable wives and their daughters could be looked over and, if unescorted, even verbally complimented in the outrageous piropos, the poems invented on the spot and thrown at passing women like bouquets from open windows, doorways, streetcorners, anywhere where Latin men loitered. That was the price you paid for going out without a chaperone. But it was strictly hands off; if that unspoken rule was violated, revenge was usually swift. The offended husband or his representative could start a vendetta that often ended in the violator's having to leave El Building. He would certainly at the very least never be invited into a decent home again. This was part of the reason Ramona felt safe in El Building. I was just beginning to notice the effects of her beauty on men when we went anywhere together. The "uncivilized" way of the men of El Building was the main reason brought up when Rafael insisted that before I got any older we had to move out of the place. José, I knew, feared that I would tell on him. He couldn't know that I was not about to share my most terrible secret with my parents.

As Christmas Day approached, El Building began to fill up with relatives of the tenants up from the Island. Their voices filled the hallways with laughter, exclamations over the frigid temperature, the television sets, the children who had grown so much since the last time. It seemed all the women were cooking at once, saturating the place with the smells of coconut candy and pasteles the luckier ones had received from mothers and grandmothers on the other side, frozen and carefully wrapped in banana leaves and tin foil and hidden in the depths of shopping bags. The partying would last until Three Kings Day on January 6, when the children received their presents.

In our house we went shopping at Sears and Penney's.

186

We had a Christmas tree with presents under it that we would open on the twenty-fifth of December. I had been allowed to accept an invitation for a dinner party at my friend's house on Christmas Eve. She was the doctor's daughter, and Rafael approved. He gave Ramona money to buy me a dress. He called me a taxi. The driver looked nervous as he pulled up to El Building, and I noticed he had to reach over and unlock a door for me.

"At what time did you say you would be home?"

I looked at Rafael, annoyed. He had asked me the same question several times before. "All I know is that they eat at seven. Do you want me to come home right after I finish?"

"No. Stay a little while. Here is the number for the taxi."

"Hey, are you gonna tell me where you're going, or what?" This was the taxi driver.

My father gave him one of his furrowed-brow stares and waved goodbye to me. He stood on the dirty snow on the street in front of El Building the whole time we sat at a traffic light, and for as long as he could see the car and I could see him.

That night, Christmas Eve, while I was sitting in a dining room as large as half our apartment at a table that sat eight with an immense chandelier over it, hovering over a large turkey, my uncle Guzmán showed up at El Building.

THE EVENING at my friend's had begun almost perfectly. I had sat on her bed and talked with her while her parents received the dinner guests. Her room was done in eggshell colors: glossy white walls and matching drapes and bedspread of the softest pink hue. Everything in the room was hers. She didn't have to share the room with anyone. Her brother was eighteen, a freshman at Princeton. He had the same smooth Italian good looks as my love object, Frank.

Letitia's parents were carefully polite to me. Once, during dinner I noticed Mrs. Roselli staring at my hands. I had been eating a rice dish with a spoon: everyone else, I quickly surmised, was using a fork. She caught my eye and smiled quickly, but I was embarrassed enough to excuse myself from the table and run up to the bathroom. Foolish tears were in my eyes when I ran straight into the arms of the brother, who was coming out of his room. He had a date, I had been told, with the prettiest senior girl at Saint Jerome's. For whatever reason, we embraced. He pulled me into his darkened room and pressed his lips to mine. Instinctively I responded to his kiss up to the point when he tried to introduce his tongue into my mouth. Though I could have fainted with the warm sensations of pleasure mapping my body out in little currents, I suddenly panicked. I pushed him away and ran out of his room. In the bathroom mirror I saw my face streaked with tears, my cheeks red, and warm to the touch. My stomach hurt. Something had not agreed with me. And then—without warning—the dinner I had just enjoyed came back up in spasms. Mrs. Roselli knocked on the door and plied me with anxious questions.

I got through the dinner, managing even to raise my glass with the others in my first taste of wine. The doctor drove me home. It was beginning to snow, and Paterson seemed to me beautiful for the first time. The Christmas displays in the shop windows on Main Street looked less harsh and gaudy through the thin veil of snow. The names of the stores as we passed them blinked in and out of my vision like the words to a nonsense song: Franklin's, Woolworth's, Quackenbush.

"What?"

"Excuse me?"

"I thought you said something. Are you feeling all

right?" Doctor Roselli reached over with his hand and felt my forehead. "You're warm. Take aspirin as soon as you get home." His tone was very professional and I perceived that his concern was automatic, but I wanted more than anything to believe that people like the Rosellis could accept me as one of their own.

We were getting close to El Building. I wished I could just ask him to drop me off a block away. I could see there was a crowd of men and boys gathered on the front steps, probably drinking. One of them had a loud radio: it was blaring salsa music. The doctor pulled up to the curb. He came around to open my door and a snowball thrown from the alley next to El Building hit him square in the back of his head. He almost lost his balance and had to hold on to the car. I reached for his arm but he yanked it back angrily.

"Just go on in. Are your parents home?"

"Yes." I felt so humiliated. There was laughter coming from the group of men. There would be comments for me when I passed them. I hated them all. I started walking toward the door as Doctor Roselli's car pulled away from El Building, its wheels screeching in his haste to get away.

By the time I had climbed the five flights of stairs to our apartment I was feeling dizzy. When Ramona opened the door I saw her face as if from a carousel. She pulled me into our tiny living room. Her eyes were bright with excitement.

"Marisol, come in here. Look! Your uncle Guzmán is here."

A short, dark man stepped forward. He was dressed all in black. His face looked familiar in an oddly disturbing way, as if I were looking into a mirror in a darkened room.

"Marisol?" My mother's voice had taken on a concerned tone. Guzmán came forward, opened his arms as if for an embrace, and I fell into them in a dead faint.

189

Chapter Eight

THEY TALKED at the table in the kitchen, and I listened. I stayed in my bed, ill with adolescence for days. The midnight trip to the hospital emergency room on Christmas Eve had revealed nothing more than a few drops of blood on my underwear. The doctor, eyes glazed from celebration in the supply room, suggested in patronizing tones that the liquor be kept out of the reach of children and that my mother explain to me about babies. There was silence in the taxi coming home except for Guzmán, who hummed softly along with the Christmas carols playing on the car radio. Back at the apartment Ramona supplied me with the bulky paraphernalia of womanhood. I felt wounded and weak and was glad when she pulled the covers over me, holding me against her in a quick trembling hug before she went to join her brother at the kitchen table. Rafael had stepped out for cigarettes, or more likely for one of his solitary walks. He had only a few more days of leave left before an extended tour of duty in Europe. He had not recovered well: Ramona complained often about his lack of appetite. His silences were deeper. Starved for conversation, Ramona looked at her brother in happy anticipation. They had not seen each other for well over a decade, and the last time they had talked, it had been in a different world. Guzmán had been in her thoughts always. The roguish brother, the foolish and adventurous young man, Rafael's best friend, and here he was in front of her. A short man, bronze as a new penny, with the face of a wise harlequin.

I peeked through the slightly opened door. Ramona never shut doors completely inside her house, and it bothered her when anyone did. On the other bed my brother mumbled something about a lost book. He had resented being dragged out of bed for the trip to the hospital and had slept on Rafael's arm through most of it. I smelled the thick sweet aroma of café con leche. Ramona was getting ready for a late night. I could not make out her remark, but Guzmán's clear voice reached me through the thin mist of medication.

"The whole story? It will take days, Ramona." They spoke in Spanish for what seemed like hours. At some point I heard Rafael enter. He joined them but I did not hear his voice. Though I drifted in and out of sleep, I heard Guzmán's story, or I dreamed it.

"They said you were lost in New York, or dead. Mamá Cielo has been wearing black since the year you left the Island. What happened after you left the farm, Guzmán?" This is what Ramona would have asked Guzmán. And he would have answered:

"When we arrived it was dark and cold. We were all hungry and tired. We thought that once the plane landed we would be given food and a place to sleep, but there was a big yellow school bus waiting for us, and we barely had a chance to look around the airport. It seemed so huge to me, and so bright and full of people. It was as if a glass dome had been built around a baseball park. There were stores and places that sold food. I tried to get to the man in front who looked like he was in charge, but he ignored me. We were told to walk through the airport terminal in single file as if we were children. It seemed we rode all night and when we arrived everyone thought we had gotten lost. There was nothing around but a field, and in front of us what looked like a military camp. Army tents, dozens of them, and beyond them a cement building which we later found out was where the manager lived and where the kitchen was. It was cold, and the men began complaining. After a while the manager came out and talked to us in terrible Spanish. We could barely understand him. We did understand one thing immediately, at least I did. After the bus left, we were stranded in the middle of nowhere. For days I didn't even know that the nearest city was called Buffalo. We slept in tents. There was a wood-burning stove in the middle and many of us took our blankets and huddled around it. We couldn't believe it was so cold in the middle of the spring season. Many of the men thought we were just there temporarily, that we would be moved to the place they had all imagined, a place with real beds and televisions. But no one explained. Every morning we were awakened before the sun by a black man who spoke a little Spanish. We dressed as warmly as we could considering most of us did not own any winter clothes, and we headed for the tent where tables were set up for meals. The first few days this was the only thing we looked forward to since Marcelo—do you remember him?—had been brought into our group as a cook, but he was very sick. One day we just didn't see him anymore.

"Then an American woman started cooking. We all hated the half-raw vegetables she made and the meat that was always tough and overcooked. Though there were complaints about the long hours picking strawberries in the cold, it was the awful food that nearly caused a riot that first month. As for myself, I started exploring the place at night. I walked straight through those cold fields in the dark, and to the fence. It was twice the height of a man and strung with barbed-wire hoops all around. A guard stayed by the gate in a small lean-to. Most of the men thought this was something like a training place, even after the first week, when we found out that if we needed anything like soap or cigarettes we had to write it down and give it to the black man, who took the manager's truck into town every three or four days. We also gave him our letters to mail. I kept trying to talk to that man, to ask him why we were being kept like prisoners, but he ignored my questions. I even tried to get in to see the manager but there was always a man at the gate and he would always say the same thing: 'Mr. Rank is not here.' I thought he had a gun, so I didn't insist. I talked to the other men, but out of twenty of them only two or three were even willing to listen to me. We had been paid a check that first Saturday which we gave to the black man to cash for us. It wasn't the amount we expected, but it was better than any of the others had made for a week's work on the Island. Most of them sent it straight home. They were like zombies, slowly getting used to the routine of work, eat, sleep. I started planning my escape.

"Now I tell you, sister, you will not think that what I did was right, but I had to do it. The cook was a nice lady but she couldn't take the men's constant complaining about her food. I watched her throwing things around in the back of the tent and making things worse with the dirty looks she gave them. The more they complained the worse her food got. One day someone just plain refused to eat the meat loaf and boiled cabbage she had prepared—with good cause: it was as if she had used sawdust as the main ingredient for the loaf and had boiled the cabbage into a soup. A young one named Raymundo—do you remember him? He was a cutter along with about twelve of his brothers back in Salud—anyway, he just threw the tin plate down and walked out of the tent. Soon many of the others did the same. They were discussing a strike outside the food tent when the manager drove by in his Chevrolet truck. He got out followed by the man I told you I thought had a gun. They looked ready for big trouble. When they finally got the situation clear, the manager announced that the cook would be replaced. That's when I saw my chance. I worked my way up front. 'I can cook the kind of food these men like,' I yelled out. I knew I was exposing myself because some of the men had begun to look at me as a troublemaker, but they must have been hungry because they applauded me and shouted for the manager to make me the cook. He said, 'Come with me.' I got into the truck and we drove to the front gate of the manager's cement house.

"Rosalind, the cook, was not fired and my job was to assist her in the kitchen, but she resented me and did everything possible to run me out. She called the rice and chicken stew I made "orangutan soup." She made mistakes in the supplies I asked her to get. Worse, she drank from a flask all day long. One day when Joe, the black man I told you about, came in to pick her up and take her to the grocery store, she was passed out on an army cot she kept by the stove. We couldn't wake her. Finally Joe motioned for me to get in the pickup truck with him. My heart was pounding when the guard opened the front gate to let us through. I memorized every tree and rock on the way into the city. The city! I thought it was Nueva York. Buildings and streets and cars everywhere. We parked in front of the grocery store. I couldn't find many of the items I needed. (I was guessing at most of it anyway, but I had been in Mamá Cielo's kitchen enough to know a few things, and as you know she always made me go to the grocery store for her.) I wandered up and down the food aisles for hours, or what

194

must have seemed to Joe like a long time, because he finally grabbed me by the shirt collar and said, 'OK, José, no more sightseeing. Finish up.' 'OK, Joe,' I answered, and I saw the man smile for the first time. He thought my English was funny. He had a mouthful of gold teeth. When we got back to the farm, Rosalind was rolling around like a wounded animal. She had been vomiting. She explained she had an ulcer and took another swig out of that flask. Joe looked at me as if to say, 'She won't be around much longer.' I guess he thought I would be pleased to get promoted to full cook. But, Ramona, I tell you, I was beginning to feel sorry for that washed-out blond. She looked like a drowned rat—sick, lonely, and angry at the whole world."

"What did she really look like?" Ramona had gotten up from the table and was making coffee-making noises. From my bed I could tell Rafael had left the little circle again. He had not gone out of the apartment, though; I had not heard the door or his footsteps in the hall and down the stairs. This late at night it was possible to hear everything that went on in our apartment and sometimes in the one next door. I had learned a lot about my parents by staying awake late in my bed. Soon I saw where he had been. He came back into the brightly lit kitchen carrying our Christmas presents.

"I had almost forgotten about those." Ramona sounded sheepish. All three of them then went into the little area on the other side of the kitchen, the part designated for the living room, where the tree was. I heard their murmurs, but because there was the kitchen between us I couldn't make out the words. Fully awake now, I couldn't wait for Guzmán to resume his story. I must have made a sound because Ramona stuck her head into my room almost catching me with my eyes open. I had not heard her coming. I was grateful that she did not close the door. The smell of her sweet coffee drifted over to me and my mouth watered. I would have liked to have been old enough to sit at the table with them that night, but in a way, the delicious naughty feeling of listening in without their knowledge also appealed to me. When they returned to the kitchen, Ramona repeated her question. She was a storyteller herself, and the details were very important to her.

"She was nothing special to look at, Ramona," Guzmán settled into his narrative, "bleached blond hair, not always clean, thin. She was skinnier than your daughter, but her eyes were something else—big as lamps and bluer than sea water. But anyway, she had them shut more than open when I first met her. Man, how that woman could drink. She didn't talk much either. It took me a couple of weeks to find out that she was the boss's niece or something—not the manager's, but the owner's relative. Her family had sent her out to earn her living after the man she lived with took off with everything she owned. Or so she said. She hated her family, rich society people who wanted their children to go to college to learn how to make money and that was all. She had run away from home with an older man after graduating from high school. But it turned out that he was more interested in her family's money than in a vagabond's life with the restless girl. Then came the years on the streets and the alcohol. The last guy had been decent enough to send her parents an anonymous note giving her whereabouts—a bug-infested hotel room where they found her lost in an alcoholic fog and penniless, but still rebellious.

"All this I learned little by little, you understand, from days of listening to her drunken outbursts. It turns out that Rosalind also washed down pills with alcohol. The señorita was really in trouble. Though I pitied her, my own situation was unbearable. I was still picking half a day and working in the kitchen the other half. Two months had

196

passed, and we were still treated like prisoners. Some of the men were starting to get restless. I wanted to be out of there before the trouble started. It was in the air. I knew it, and the black man Joe knew it. He didn't say much, but when we rode into town to get groceries, he would say things like, 'June, July, always the worst months. Bad trouble coming.' So I decided to get out soon. Rosalind was my ticket.

"My chance came unexpectedly. Rosalind took an overdose of pills one day and I couldn't wake her. I ran to get Joe, and we drove at top speed to the hospital in Buffalo. There they pumped her stomach and told us she would have to stay overnight. Joe didn't like that one bit. He told me to stay in the waiting room, he'd be back for us in the morning. Well, I snuck into Rosalind's room that night. She was confused and hysterical. She didn't want her family to find out about it. Somehow I managed to ask her if she had a place. She said that she had the key to an apartment in New York City that she was supposed to be taking care of for a friend. We left that hospital at dawn. She paid for a taxi to the bus station. Rosalind was weak and slept most of the way there, but I kept my eyes wide open. When we arrived in New York City I felt completely confused. People seemed to be rushing everywhere. I kept wanting to ask them, 'Where's the fire?' After another taxi ride we arrived at a huge apartment building.

"Rosalind's friend's apartment was tiny. There was one window and it faced the wall of another building. It looked like a jail cell with one difference—I could come in and out whenever I wanted to. The first thing that Rosalind wanted was a drink.

"'Here, take this.' She thrust her wallet at me. There was money in it. More than I had ever seen all at once in my life.

"'Get some food,' she told me. I left her sleeping and

wandered into the street. I felt small surrounded by those buildings. I kept wondering how I was going to make myself understood at the store with my poor English. I avoided the large supermarkets and went into a little shop that advertised beer in Spanish. I was surprised to find that the owner was from the Island. We got into a conversation and it turned out he had visited Salud many times during the fiestas, you know. I told him I'd come back later. I was beginning to feel better about leaving the farm already.

"But I tell you, Rosalind wasn't easy to live with. She was a demanding woman used to getting everything she wanted. Regular as clockwork she got a check from her folks at a bank in the city. It seems all they wanted was for her to stay out of their way. But she kept talking about a man who had run off as if she expected him back.

" 'When he runs out of money,' she said once, 'he'll trace me to the farm. He'll show up one of these days and he'll see that I don't need him.'

"She was possessive too. She started buying clothes for me and dressing me up like a monkey. She had a flashy sense of style, you know. She kept drinking too. Even though I tried to hide the bottles, she always had money for more. At first I thought I could help Rosalind, but soon I realized that she wallowed in her misery like a pig in mud. Her favorite thing to do was to call her friends on the phone after drinking all day to complain about her life. She also boasted about me, as if I were a new servant or a dog she was training. I knew I had to leave there soon, or I would end up like her. Most days, while she slept, I wandered around the neighborhood and made friends. I couldn't believe how many Island people live in New York. But for someone like me, with little English and no connections, a job was hard to find. My friend at the bodega said he knew people and would try to help me out. His name was Gordo; you know, I have come to think that the best people in the world are little shop owners in New York City. They are like fleas on a dog. They just try to survive, you know, always willing to help out a *paisano.*

"Anyway, I continued to play nursemaid to this crazy Rosalind. Sometimes she'd sober up just long enough to go to a movie with me or shopping for clothes, but never for long. In the meantime I learned English, put away a little of the pocket money she gave me and waited for a sign. I always wait for the right time to move, you know, something always happens to let me know it is the right time. One day I was standing in front of the bodega with Gordo when I saw a familiar Chevrolet truck pull up in front of my building. Two men got out, the farm manager and another whose hair was down to his waist. The only reason I knew he was a man was because he had a beard that was almost down to his waist too. Immediately I thought, the former lover. I guess I was right. In a few minutes Rosalind came out of the building arm in arm with the hairy man and the three of them left in the truck. I told Gordo that this seemed like a good time to leave Rosalind and he agreed, but he warned me that sometimes these farm managers hired detectives to look for escaped migrant workers and that it might be a good idea if I stayed out of sight for a while. I don't mind telling you that I felt like an escaped convict when I got my things from the apartment and took them to the back of Gordo's shop. He said I could spend the night there but couldn't stay because the Board of Health would shut him down if they knew anyone was sleeping among the green bananas, sacks of rice, and salted codfish.

" 'Not that I haven't done it a couple of times myself to get away from the wife, you know, man?' Gordo laughed. He was the fattest man I had ever met, and the smelliest. I guess it was from handling the fish. But he had a big heart.

" 'I understand, Gordo, I'll get out of here first thing in

the morning,' I told him, though I did not have any idea where I would go. I had learned my way around a few blocks in the neighborhood, but I couldn't even pronounce the names of the streets in English. But Gordo laid his fat smelly arm on my shoulders and reassured me that he was not going to throw me out in the streets without a job.

" 'I have been talking to a customer of mine about you. He's a conductor on the subway. He said they needed someone to run errands, off the books, of course.' I must have looked puzzled because he sat me down for a lecture on how to survive in the city, all of which I don't remember but the message was clear. Take what you can get, and don't ask stupid questions.

" 'Now remember, Guzmán, you don't tell anyone that you are working for these men. They will get you keys and passes—if they take you, that is—and you will make yourself available to them. These guys work long shifts and they need someone young and fast on his feet like you to buy them coffee, cigarettes, that sort of thing. You interested?'

"Of course I said I was, although it seemed to me that I was back where I had started in Salud, running errands for the American. But I was in no position to refuse help. The next morning Gordo walked me to the subway entrance. It looked like the mouth of hell to me. His last words to me were: 'If I were you I would stay off these streets in daylight for a while. At night all cats and Puerto Ricans look black, hey?' He was still laughing at his own joke when I lost sight of him in the crowd."

Late, late into the night my uncle's voice lifted me in and out of consciousness. I heard him tell of dim and crowded tunnels where people were swallowed by the train in one place and vomited up in another. I dreamed of a train speeding through darkness while I, its only passenger, was thrown about like a weightless doll with the force of its starts and stops.

In the morning, Christmas Day, I heard my brother race out of our room. I heard his excited comments about each gift unwrapped, but I could not move. My back and legs felt heavy and my throat was so sore I could barely swallow. Ramona came into my room. Her shocked look as she sat on the side of my bed told me something must be very wrong with me. She called my father.

"Rafael, look at her throat. It looks like mumps."

I hated the way they were talking about me as if I were a child, or not there.

"Mother, will you please tell me what's going on? My throat hurts." As I spoke I noticed that my voice was coming out muffled. Fully awake now, I started up from bed and ran to the dresser mirror. Both sides of my throat were monstrously swollen. I looked deformed. I screamed. Ramona came over and led me back to bed.

"You have mumps, Marisol. The swelling will go down. We are going to call the doctor. But it is not serious. Everyone has mumps at some time in their lives."

"How long . . . how long will I look like this?"

Rafael spoke up now. His voice as always was calm and reassuring. But he did not touch me. Ramona, however, was squeezing my hand almost to the point of pain.

"It will take a week or ten days. I will have a doctor call medicine in to the drugstore. You will have to stay in bed."

"That's the whole Christmas vacation, Mother." I realized I was whining. About to cry, too. In my mind the arrival of menstruation and this horrible deformity were already connected.

"At least you will not miss school, niña. Think of it that way. I will bring your presents here. Lie back. I am going to bring you aspirin and a cup of café. There." Ramona was tucking me in, rearranging my pillows. I couldn't help but feel that she liked playing nurse. I thought she ought to be more worried.

My brother called Rafael out to help him decipher directions for a model warship. Ramona went into the kitchen. I heard her speaking in a low voice to Guzmán. To my embarrassment, he stuck his head in the door. I put mine under the covers.

"Niece, that is very impolite." He stood by my bed. I peeked out and saw his naked feet near my bed. His skin was copper red like an Indian's.

"Are you worried you will frighten me? I have seen fat girls before." He laughed. He waited a few moments then started to walk out.

"All right," I said pulling the blanket off my face. I was hot with a slight fever and almost beyond caring about my swollen neck. The cramps had moved to my stomach. I was miserable.

"What? Do I see tears? Maybe this will make you feel better." He handed me a tiny little box wrapped in silver paper. "Open it," he said.

It was a delicate gold chain with a crucifix pendant. My first adult gift. Until this year, until him, it had been dolls and clothes.

"Thank you." I muttered, my head was pounding.

"Want to try it on?" I nodded and leaned forward. Guzmán sat on the side of my bed. I could smell his cologne—a strange, heavy smell. Rafael did not wear fragrances any more; he always smelled like plain soap. My uncle lifted my heavy long mane of hair away from my neck and tried to fasten the necklace. It would not go around the swollen glands on my neck. I felt so embarrassed, I started to cry in great heaving sobs. Guzmán held me to him in a tight embrace that reminded me of Ramona's arms. In both affection and anger her hands always left a temporary mark on my skin.

If it had not been for Guzmán's company those miserable days of my illness would have been completely unbearable. Rafael's leave came to an end, and he began preparations for a long tour overseas. It surprised me to hear him ask Guzmán to stay with us for as long as he could. I had noticed an unusual animation, a liveliness about my father since Guzmán had arrived. The two men were as different physically as any two people I had ever seen. Rafael's paleness and his silence came into sharp contrast with my uncle's wild Indian look. Guzmán was unable to stay still for long, and the tiny apartment seemed suddenly overcrowded with this nervous man going from room to room, helping Ramona peel potatoes in the kitchen, throwing even my slow-moving little brother into a frenzy of activity by planning an impossible project with a building set, or involving him in some complicated card game. Ramona was obviously delighted. Even Rafael gave himself over to the spell Guzmán was casting.

After the first day, Guzmán did not stay in very much. But it was as if we were all in a state of suspended animation while he was out. "Getting to know the city," he called it. Except for Ramona, we were a quiet family, especially when Rafael was home. My father detested the well-earned reputation of our ethnic group for rowdiness. There was a party, fight, or spiritist meeting going on in El Building on any given night of the week.

My brother and I were great readers. We braved the worst section of town every Saturday to go to the public library—a Greek temple incongruously perched in the middle of the most decrepit section of the city. There actually were two life-sized cement lions at the entrance. Once I walked inside, the building changed for me, from the intimidation of its courthouse exterior to the warmth of a well-used library. I always headed straight for my favorite stack—fairy tales from all parts of the world. I had done

China, Spain, and Africa, in no particular order, discovering along the way that in every country there was always a poor but beautiful girl destined to be discovered by a prince. My brother chose books that showed how to do something, or how something worked. During the long seasons of our father's absence we read and read. Now Guzmán had instilled the worm of adventure into our brains. He had already promised my brother a bicycle, something Rafael had strictly forbidden us, for Paterson streets could barely hold the crowds, much less kids on bicycles.

A few days before Rafael was to take the bus to Brooklyn Yard, he and Guzmán talked at the kitchen table. Ramona was out with Gabriel, shopping downtown perhaps. I was supposed to be resting but I think the two men must have simply forgotten I was in the room a few feet away from them. Rafael offered Guzmán a beer and they sat at the kitchen table. Suddenly Rafael asked, "Did you ever find out what happened to your friend Rosa?"

"I looked for her, you know. I still think I see her sometimes, on the bus, or on the streets, but it's always someone else."

"She couldn't just have disappeared, man. Her daughter is still in Salud, you know. Your sister gets all the gossip in letters."

"Yes, I heard from someone just up from the Island that Sarita now lives in the house by the river." There was silence, as if they were remembering something. Then Guzmán continued.

"I have often wondered where Rosa went after she left Salud, after she was chased out by those jealous bitches in Salud. I mean, I understand my mistake now, and I know I put Mamá Cielo through hell. But I did love Rosa—I think I would have even married her if no one had interfered.

Don't look at me like that, brother, I know what she was, I know what she did for a living. But she was and still is the most interesting woman I have ever known. She was twice as smart as all the others. All those months I spent in hiding, riding those trains to nowhere, eating on my feet, sleeping on benches, I dreamed that one day I'd look up and there would be Rosa. That kept me going for a long while, you know. It sounds foolish now, but I was young and stupid then. Now I know that both the hiding and the dreams were a waste of time. No one was looking for me. Who cares if one more laborer is missing? Again, the only thing I regret was making the family on the Island suffer. I didn't write home for months fearing that they—the people in Buffalo—would contact Mamá and Papá and force them to reveal my whereabouts. Stupid, stupid. But the subway was my school. Though I lived like an escaped convict for months, that is where I learned what it takes to survive in this place. It wasn't always bad; I met people."

"But all these years, man," Rafael said, "why didn't you look us up? Most of the time we knew you were alive, but only because your father wrote that he had heard from you by letter."

"The years go by fast when you don't count days. I was busy, brother, trying to do something with my life. I didn't want to go back to the Island or come see you and Ramona with empty pockets. Sometimes I almost did come home, but something always happened. Remember the last time we saw each other how we swore we'd go back rich men? And you were going to be a doctor."

There was silence for a few minutes. The two men were perhaps remembering the other life they had lived, in a place so far from their present lives that they could have just imagined it.

"A doctor." Rafael's chuckle had a lifetime of bitterness

in it. I heard the refrigerator door open and more beer cans set on the table. The talk turned to Rafael's imminent departure for Brooklyn Yard and then for Europe for six months. To my delight I heard Guzmán agree to stay with us for a while. The other thing Rafael asked Guzmán to do was to help him convince Ramona that we should move out of El Building when he came back. Rafael was sure his wife would listen to her brother. Guzmán seemed reluctant to promise this, saying only that he'd see what he could do. I had already noticed that El Building, with its constant activity, was Guzmán's natural environment. The beehive nature of life in this vertical pueblo suited him well.

When the day arrived for Rafael to leave I was already feeling well enough to jump at the chance of walking him to the bus stop. We made quite a parade: Rafael looking like a visiting dignitary in his winter blues, and us, his entourage, following behind, Guzmán carrying the duffel bag. Ramona looked, as always, like the gypsy queen with her colorful winter scarf and red coat. Gabriel bounced along looking into every storefront as if he were shopping for something in particular and were having trouble finding it. I tried to keep up with Guzmán. People stared at us, especially as we left El Building, and I noticed that Rafael took Ramona's hand and practically dragged her to the other side of the street away from the men who were already congregating on the corner. The year was promising to be a bad one for jobs, from what everyone was saying. When laborers and factory workers were to be laid off, the first ones were usually from our neighborhood.

We were attuned to the rhythms of life based on Rafael's long absences and sporadic visits, so that all of us took up our activities where we had left off, with a feeling of having passed inspection one more time. Ramona's women friends, who had kept their distance during Rafael's stay (behind our backs they called him the Gringo), came back with their usual stories. There had been fights, separations, reconciliations; someone's dead husband was haunting her apartment, and a spiritist meeting was being arranged with the enthusiasm and noise usual for large wedding preparations. Guzmán naturally became the focal point for female attention. Here was an unattached man, attractive and related to the Gringo, who had money. He relished talk and was at his best in the middle of a group of admiring women, though he rarely spent more than a few hours in the apartment. He used to come in to have coffee with Ramona in the afternoons and sometimes to cook meals that delighted all of us. He was creative in the kitchen, seasoning food with abandon—his chili could have started a car's engine in the middle of a snowstorm. Where he went we didn't know, but he seemed to have money, and his presence in our dreary little apartment was a gift.

One bitter cold afternoon I was walking home from school alone, since Gabriel was staying late to be tested. It was the first Friday of the month, when the Saint Jerome students always attended mass as a group, and according to school rules I was wearing my "dress uniform": a blue skirt hemmed below my knees, a starched blouse, and a ridiculous blue-and-white beanie on my head. As I came to the last street I had to cross before reaching home, I felt a brutal shove on my back and fell in the dirty slush, scattering my books all over the sidewalk. I recognized the laughter as I slid into the puddle of frigid water: it was Lorraine and her friends who had ambushed me. Lorraine was a black girl who had been my playmate in grammar school but had become, in the "normal" course of development for black and Puerto Rican kids in Paterson, my adversary. The hostility was not personal; even the children seemed to know this on an instinctive level. It was a reflection of the adults' sense of territorial and economic competition. The conversations we heard at home told us that jobs and places to live in were scarce for people like us, and if we didn't fight for them, blacks would get them. The kids carried this resentment to the streets. Usually Gabriel would be by my side, craning his little neck like a periscope on the lookout for trouble, and we could usually avoid it by ducking into a store or walking behind the bigger kids. That day I was distracted, thinking of other things, and I failed to notice the knot of tough girls looking for easy prey. Humiliated, soaked to the bone, I began to gather my things when I saw the pointy black shoes of my *tío* Guzmán approaching. He looked concerned and angry. He lifted me by the armpits as if I were a soggy parcel and deposited me on my feet. Then he retrieved my books.

"Do you know them?" He was pointing in the direction where Lorraine and her gang had disappeared, running. I nodded. "Why don't you tell me what's going on, Marisol? Here, let me help you with those. You need to get into dry clothes; then we're going for a walk."

I was too surprised to protest, and I guess he must have said something to convince Ramona to let me go out with him—either that or she was too involved with her planning of spiritist meetings to object. In any case, I was delighted to find myself wandering around Paterson in the company of my uncle, who had apparently gotten to know more people in the few days he had been with us than we had in all the years we had lived in El Building. He asked me many questions about Rafael and Ramona and school. He asked me some strange ones too, like was Rafael always as quiet and sad as he had been over Christmas. I

208

told him all I could think of to tell him, with only a little fine embroidery to make my life seem less dull to this man whose adventures I had been hearing all my life in tantalizing installments.

I also told him I was considering entering a convent when I graduated from high school. Of course, until the moment I spoke of it, the thought had only been a vague option the nuns had taught us to believe was open for each of us; if we had a *vocation,* it would become clear as we got older. As a shy girl with a culturally ingrained air of humility, I had been given the privilege every year of attending a retreat with other similarly inclined girls. The sisters took us out in the suburbs, an ideal location for vocation to become clear to a city girl, because the place was in a great expanse of wooded land where real birds perched on real trees, and God's creation was at its best in April, when the retreat was always scheduled.

My uncle looked into my face closely. "You don't look like a nun to me, Marisol," he said as we came near the convent. "What do you suppose the good sisters are doing at this hour?"

I just giggled in response to Guzmán's question. What nuns did after hours had never been something I speculated on. They prayed, I supposed, and they prepared their lessons. But Guzmán meant to follow through. The next thing I knew he was lifting me up onto a trash bin to look over the convent wall. It was beginning to get dark, and this end of the property was hidden by a corner of the church building—I suspect he had taken all this into consideration before placing me on my perch. I had a perfect view of the kitchen and laundry areas, but I nearly fell off when I saw what was hanging on the clothesline strung between the back porch and a utility pole: underwear! Brassieres and underpants of all sizes. Instinctively I covered my eyes with my hands, as if I expected to be struck blind for my blasphemy. My uncle pulled on the end of my coat.

"What do you see, girl, tell me." So I described to him how one nun wearing a white apron was kneading dough on a kitchen counter. I could see that her lips were moving, but no one else was in there with her, and several others were having coffee or tea at the dining room table. One of them was my young biology teacher, and she was not wearing her coif. She had hair—curly yellow hair.

I described their activity to him, enjoying the sense of theater it gave me. I was watching a play called "A Nun's Life" with a blind friend, I pretended, and my own ability to drink in detail and tell a story delighted me. My uncle was an appreciative audience, but when we heard footsteps approaching the alley, he lifted me easily down to the ground like a ballet dancer. We discussed the nuns for a while.

Guzmán seemed interested in everything I was saying, but he did not miss anything that went on around him, either. He said we were going downtown to eat at the pizza place under the Erie Lackawanna railroad overpass. I was thrilled. We first went into Cheo's bodega to buy him a pack of cigarettes. The woman I had seen in the basement was there. She was dressed as if for a dance in a tight black dress and high heels; red costume jewelry adorned her neck and wrists. She was putting on her dyed pink rabbit-fur coat when we came in but seemed to think of something else she wanted at the back of the store when Guzmán walked back there to get us two bottles of Coke.

"Wait here," he said to me. Feeling my ears burn, I leaned against the counter, pretending to be very interested in the different brands of chewing gum and candy bars set up in their display boxes. I recited their names in my old game, "Juicy Fruit, Chiclets, Dentyne, Bazooka, Twinkies, Baby Ruth, O'Joy, M&M's with peanuts, M&M's plain, Three Musketeers." I felt the cold wind on my back, and the heavy smell of perfume I was familiar with from the hallways of El Building wafted by as the woman left the store. Guzmán handed me a Coke.

"Are you feeling OK, Marisol?" He touched my forehead with a cool hand. "Maybe it is not a good idea to have you out for so long after you have been so sick."

I did not say anything; I just looked down at the grimy floor in the mock modesty I had been taught by the nuns. Lowered eyes hid anger, disappointment, rebellion.

"Tomorrow we will have pizza downtown. There is something I want to show you." He took my chin in his fingertips and made me look up into his smiling eyes. "There are many things I want to show you, Marisol, but you must learn to wait for what each day brings. Smile for me, pretty girl." And I did.

Our apartment was now always full of women. They came to visit Ramona morning, noon, and night, to ask her advice, to gossip, to borrow things, but really to see Guzmán. This was evident in the way their behavior changed when he was in the room. Their voices got higher and softer, they laughed more, and their perfume thickened the air I breathed so that I had to join my brother at his fire-escape retreat in the afternoons. It was not unpleasant there, though the freezing breeze he had apparently gotten used to still cut through me, bringing hot tears to my eyes. The feeling of being suspended in midair was exciting, and we could look through the bars and see people's heads on the sidewalk below like a moving connect-the-dots game. His adventure and invention books were not as boring as I had imagined, and I began to read about a world in which boys were as smart as Sherlock Holmes and as intrepid as any of the knights in the fairy tales I favored.

Sometimes Gabriel would ask me questions about our father in his shy way and I would try to answer. He wanted to know if Rafael would ever come live with us all the time like other dads did, and whether we were really going to move to a real house with a yard and a basement for him to play in. He showed me a letter Rafael had written in English just for him. He called Gabriel "My Dearest Son," and told him he was proud of his report card. Rafael had never written to me, though the letters Ramona read us always said things like "tell Marisol I will send her a doll from Spain," or Italy, or Greece. I had dolls dressed in national costumes from every country he had visited. He also sent me souvenir picture books. My favorite was one that folded out like an accordion: *Ricordo di Napoli.* The place looked like the towns I imagined for my princesses and their loyal champions with beautiful houses, cobblestone streets, gardens tended by little old ladies, and marble lions guarding every public building. But never did my father send me a letter that said "To My Dearest Daughter," even though I made all A's in school too.

Sometimes Guzmán would come and find us. I could sense his coming down the hall by the nervous step I perceived rather than heard; it was as if he were holding back from running. When he walked down the street, the black raincoat he always wore flapped like wings at his back.

"Let's go for a walk while your mother makes dinner," he would say, sticking his head out the fire-escape window. I would smell the cologne he splashed on his neck, and I had noticed that it smelled different in the bottle than on him. On his skin it turned into a heavy scent like what I imagined as the smell of a greenhouse of tropical plants. Ramona complained of his extravagant clothes and said that she could not smell her own cooking when Guzmán was in the kitchen, but her complaints were at this point good-natured. She was enjoying his company and the relief of having a man around the house.

One Saturday afternoon when the sun had managed to burst through the gray clouds that stuck to the Paterson sky like a dirty blanket most of the time in winter, Guzmán came home in high spirits. He told Ramona he had just won some money in a card game.

"Look." He emptied the pockets of his black raincoat on the kitchen table. There were crumpled twenty- and ten-dollar bills, and a stack of quarters. Gabriel and I, just on our way out to the library, came close to look at the little fortune. Even Ramona was impressed.

"What are you going to do with it?" she asked, adding with a smile, "Spend it on a girlfriend?"

"Maybe, maybe. But first I'm going to take a boy and a girl I know out for a pizza."

My brother and I hugged our generous uncle and, putting our books down on the kitchen table, helped him gather his money. He gave us each a couple of dollars in quarters and Ramona two twenties. "I'll send one of these to Mamá Cielo," she said. Guzmán winked at her, dragging us by the hand out of our apartment.

As soon as we were out of the front door of El Building, the man José approached us. He reeked of rum and sweat. His clothes were dirty and looked as if he had slept in them.

"You, hombre, I wanna talk to you." He pointed his grimy finger at Guzmán.

"Not now, man, I'm in a hurry."

"Now, we'll talk *now*. I have been waiting for you." He staggered closer. Guzmán pushed us back into the door and stood in front of us.

"I'll meet you at Cheo's tonight, man, and we can talk then. Can't you see I have my sister's children with me?"

"Maybe it's time they knew what their uncle is really like, you bastard." José lunged forward suddenly, and Gabriel started screaming as he clung to me. He had seen the knife in the man's hand. I stood frozen, recalling the image of this animal and his woman in El Basement, when he was throwing himself on top of her with the same maniacal look on his face as when he stabbed my uncle.

Chapter Nine

AFTER THE AMBULANCE and the panic, Ramona nursed her brother back to his feet, but the tension in our apartment was as real and perceptible as the bloody bandages she changed and the smells of alcohol, both the kind she used to disinfect his wound and the kind he drank to help him get through the weeks of convalescence.

The man José had plunged his knife deep into Guzmán's side, barely missing a kidney. There had been a lot of blood lost and enough damage to make my uncle lean to one side from then on, a little lopsided, like a badly tailored garment. Ramona tended Guzmán's needs ably but with the hard hands and sharp voice I knew so well. Those fingers were like silk threads that could caress my hair until all anxiety and pain disappeared, or, in anger, dig angrily into the soft flesh of my arm, as if they wanted it to be my neck.

The shock of the attack affected my brother severely. Gabriel's nightmares filled some of our nights with the re-enactment of bloody sidewalk, sirens, and screaming women—the scene that had impressed itself so thoroughly in the boy's imagination that he stayed away from Guzmán's room, and out of his way whenever possible. This meant that our little apartment was divided by anger, fear, and pain.

I took Guzmán's meals in to him and sat by his bed watching him smoke cigarettes, wincing slightly with each breath. Bare-chested, his thick black hair grown over his ears, my uncle looked like a wild man. It was the look in his eyes too that startled me when he looked straight at me, not seeing me. I brought him the Spanish newspaper, and after a while he began to talk—not really to me, but at me. I knew the things he said were not directed to his four-teen-year-old niece but were only meant to fill the silence of those long afternoons in bed. He read the articles about the rising unemployment in Paterson, about the layoffs of Puerto Ricans that were creating more welfare dependents in our community. This angered him. He called them par-asites and beggars. The women and the children, he said, were the victims. He spat the words out in anger.

"You know how I have money?" he asked me suddenly one day.

I shook my head no.

"I saved everything I made in those holes I worked in. For the past couple of years I've slept in rats' nests and shopped at the Salvation Army store for my clothes. I put all my money in a bank where the woman at the desk looked at me like I was going to hold up the place every time. She never remembered my name even though I went in every first of the month with my money."

His eyes had glazed over, with pain, I guessed. He reached over for another cigarette, and I noticed his ban-dage was soaked with blood again. I couldn't take my eyes off that bright square of red.

"I saved my money. You know why I saved my money?" It really wasn't a question he asked, not really directed at me. I just sat quietly and waited.

"I dreamed of going back to the Island in style. You know, send a car first. A big black car. Have it delivered to

Mamá Cielo's house in Salud. Then I would arrive in a new suit, a wallet thick with dollars in my pocket. Stupid, isn't it? Every bastard in this building is dreaming that same dream right now. But I thought I was smarter than the rest of them, and I was. I have money, girl. Not a fortune, but enough to buy that car, enough to have it shipped. What I don't have anymore is . . ." The pain had apparently grown too sharp, because he turned on his left side away from me and fell silent. His breathing was harsh as if something were stuck in his throat.

"Do you need anything?" I waited a long time, but there was no answer.

It was a bitter winter in Paterson. The snow fell white and dry as coconut shavings, but as soon as it touched the dirty pavement it turned into a muddy soup. Though we wore rubber boots, our feet stayed wet and cold all day. The bitter wind brought hot tears to our eyes, but it was so cold that we never felt them streaking our cheeks.

During Lent the nuns counted attendance at the seven o'clock mass and gave demerits if we did not take into our dry mouths Christ's warm body in the form of a wafer the priest held in his palm. The church was dark at that hour of the morning, and thick with the steaming garments of children dropped off by anxious mothers or, like us, numb from a seven-block walk.

In the hour of the mass, I thawed in the sweet unctuousness of the young Italian priest's voice chanting his prayers for the souls of these young children and their teachers, for their parents, for the dead and the living, for our deprived brothers and sisters, some of whom had not found comfort in Christ and were now in mortal danger of damning their souls to the raging fire of hell. He didn't really say hell, a word carefully avoided in our liturgy: it was all innuendo and Latin words that sounded like expletives. *Kyrie Eleison,* he would challenge; *Christe Eleison,* we would respond heartily, led by the strong voice of Sister Mary Beata, our beautiful homeroom teacher, whose slender body and perfect features were evident in spite of the layers of clothing she wore and the coif that surrounded her face. She was the envy of our freshman-class girls. In the classroom I sat in the back watching her graceful movements, admiring the translucent quality of her unblemished skin, wondering whether both her calm and her beauty were a gift from God, imagining myself in the medieval clothes of her nun's habit.

I sat in the last desk of the last row of the girl's side of the room, the smallest, darkest member of a class full of the strapping offspring of Irish immigrants with a few upstart Italians recently added to the roll. The blazing red hair of Jackie O'Connell drew my eyes like a flame to the center of the room, and the pattern of freckles on her nose fascinated me. She was a popular girl with the sisters; her father was a big-shot lawyer with political ambitions. Donna Finney was well developed for her age, her woman's body restrained within the angular lines of the green-and-white plaid uniform we would wear until our junior year, when we would be allowed to dress like young ladies in a pleated green skirt and white blouse. Donna sat in the row closest to the boys' side of the room.

The boys were taller and heavier than my friends at El Building; they wore their blue ties and opened doors for girls naturally, as if they did it at home too. At school we were segregated by sex: every classroom was divided into girlside and boyside, and even the playground had an imaginary line right down the middle, where the assigned nun of the day would stand guard at recess and lunchtime. There were some couples in the school, of course. Every-

218

one knew Donna went with a junior boy, a basketball player named Mickey Salvatore, an Italian playing on our Fighting Irish team—and it was a known fact that they went out in his car. After school some girls met their boyfriends at Schulze's drugstore for a soda. I saw them go in on my way home. My mother, following Rafael's instructions, gave us thirty minutes to get home before she put on her coat and high heels and came looking for us. I had just enough time to round up my brother at the grammar-school building across the street and walk briskly the seven blocks home. No soda for me with friends at Schulze's.

Ramona had come looking for us one day when an afternoon assembly had held me up, and that episode had taught me a lesson. Her long black hair loose and wild from the wind, she was wearing black spiked shoes and was wrapped in a red coat and black shawl when she showed up outside the school building. The kids stared at her as if she were a circus freak, and the nuns looked doubtful, thinking perhaps they should ask the gypsy to leave the school grounds. One boy said something about her that made a hot blush of shame creep up my neck and burn my cheeks. They didn't know—couldn't know—that she was my mother, since Rafael made all our school arrangements every year, explaining that his wife could not speak English and therefore would not be attending PTA meetings and so forth. My mother looked like no other mother at the school, and I was glad she did not participate in school activities. Even on Sunday she went to the Spanish mass while we attended our separate service for children. My gypsy mother embarrassed me with her wild beauty. I wanted her to cut and spray her hair into a sculptured hairdo like the other ladies; I wanted her to wear tailored skirts and jackets like Jackie Kennedy; I even resented her youth, which made her look like my older sister. She was what I would have looked like if I hadn't worn my hair in a tight braid, if I had allowed myself to sway when I walked, and if I had worn loud colors and had spoken only Spanish.

I was beginning to understand why Rafael wanted to move us away from El Building. The older I got, the more embarrassed I felt about living in this crowded, noisy tenement, which the residents seemed intent on turning into a bizarre facsimile of an Island barrio. But for a while my fascination with Guzmán overpowered all other feelings, and when I came home from the organized, sanitized world of school, I felt drawn into his sickroom like an opium addict. I looked forward to the air thick with the smells of many cigarettes and of alcohol. More and more I took over the nursing duties which Ramona, with her impatient hands, relished little. She was used to fast-healing children and an absent husband. Guzmán's bleeding wound and his careful movements tried her patience.

And so it happened that my uncle and I began talking. Guzmán told me about his childhood on the Island in general terms, leaving out things he did not think I would understand, but his silences and omissions were fuel to my imagination and I filled in the details. I questioned him about his friend Rosa, whose name came up whenever he began to describe the Island. It was as if she were the embodiment of all that was beautiful, strange, and tempting about his homeland. He told me about her amazing knowledge of plants and herbs, how she knew what people needed just by talking to them. Once I asked him to describe her to me. His eyes had been closed as he spoke, seeing her, I suppose; but he opened them like one who slowly rises from a dream and looked at me, sitting by the side of his bed in my blue-and-white first Friday uniform, my hair pulled back in a tightly wound bun.

"Let your hair down," he said.

I reached back and pulled the long black pins out of my thick hair, letting it fall over my shoulders. It was quite long, and I never wore it loose.

"She had long black hair like yours," he said rising on his elbows to look intently into my face as if seeing me for the first time. I noticed his knuckles going white from the effort. "And she was light-complexioned like you." He fell back on the pillow, groaning a little. Ramona came in at that moment with fresh bandages and looked strangely at me sitting there with my hair undone, but did not say anything. Ordering Guzmán to shift to his side, she changed his bandage briskly.

"I need you to go to the bodega for me, Marisol," she said, not looking at me. I hated going into the gloomy little Spanish grocery store with its fishy smell and loiterers who always had something smart to say to women.

"Why can't you send Gabriel?" I asked petulantly, feeling once again that strain developing between my mother and me which kept getting more in the way of all our attempts at communication. She refused to acknowledge the fact that I was fast becoming too old to order around.

"He is doing his homework." Tucking the sheet around her brother as if he were another child, she turned to me. "Just do what I tell you, niña, without arguments or back talk. It looks like we are going to have a serious discussion with your father when he comes home." She looked at me meaningfully.

When she left the room I braided my hair slowly. It was the new impasse we had reached. I would obey her but I would take my time doing so, pushing her to a steady burning anger which could no longer be relieved by the familiar routine of spanking, tears, reconciliation. It was a contest of wills that I knew no one could win, but Ramona was still hoping Rafael would know how to mediate. He was the absent disciplinarian—Solomon, the wise judge, the threat and the promise that hung over us day after day in her constant "when your father comes home."

I couldn't understand how she continued to treat me like a child when she had not been much older than I when she married Rafael. If I were on the Island I would be respected as a young woman of marriageable age. I had heard Ramona talking with her friends about a girl's fifteenth year, the *Quinceañera,* when everything changes for her. She no longer plays with children; she dresses like a woman and joins the women at coffee in the afternoon; she is no longer required to attend school if there is more pressing need for her at home, or if she is engaged. I was almost fifteen now—still in my silly uniform, bobby socks and all; still not allowed to socialize with my friends, living in a state of limbo, halfway between cultures. No one at school asked why I didn't participate in the myriad parish activities. They all understood that Marisol was *different.*

Talking with my uncle, listening to stories about his life on the Island, and hearing Ramona's constant rhapsodizing about that tropical paradise—all conspired to make me feel deprived. I should have grown up there. I should have been able to play in emerald-green pastures, to eat sweet bananas right off the trees, to learn about life from the women who were strong and wise like the fabled Mamá Cielo. How could she be Ramona's mother? Ramona, who could not make a decision without invoking the name of our father, whose judgment we awaited like the Second Coming.

As I reached for the door to leave Guzmán's room, he stirred.

"Rosa," he said, groggy from medication.

"Do you need anything?" I was trembling.

Alert now, he pointed to the dresser against the wall. "Take my wallet from the top drawer and get me a carton of L&M's when you go to the bodega." He closed his eyes again, whispering, "Thanks, niña."

I took his wallet, unwilling to make more noise by looking through it for money. In the kitchen Ramona was washing dishes at the sink, her back to me, but she was aware of my presence, and her anger showed in the set of her shoulders. I suddenly remembered how much she used to laugh, and still did when she was around her women friends.

"The list and the money are on the table, Marisol. Don't take long. I need to start dinner soon."

I put my coat on and left the apartment. The smells of beans boiling in a dozen kitchens assailed my nostrils. Rice and beans, the unimaginative staple food of all these people who re-created every day the same routines they had followed in their mamá's houses so long ago. Except that here in Paterson, in the cold rooms stories above the frozen ground, the smells and sounds of a lost way of life could only be a parody.

Instead of heading out the front door and to the street, an impulse carried my feet down an extra flight of stairs to El Basement. It was usually deserted at this hour when everyone was preparing to eat. I sat on the bottom step and looked around me at the cavernous room. A yellow light hung over my head. I took Guzmán's wallet from my coat pocket. Bringing it close to my face, I smelled the old leather. Carefully I unfolded it flat on my lap. There were several photos in the plastic. On top was a dark Indian-looking woman whose features looked familiar. Her dark, almond-shaped eyes were just like Ramona's, but her dark skin and high cheekbones were Guzmán's. I guessed this was an early picture of my grandmother, Mamá Cielo. Behind that there was one of two teenage boys, one dark, one blond. They were smiling broadly, arms on each other's shoulders. There was a fake moon in the background like the ones they use in carnival photo booths. Though the picture was bent, cutting the boys at the neck, and of poor quality, I recognized them: it was Guzmán and Rafael. I looked at it for a long time, especially at my father's face, almost unrecognizable to me with its unfamiliar look of innocent joy. Perhaps they had been drinking that night. I had often heard Ramona talking about the festivals dedicated to Our Lady of Salud, the famous smiling Virgin. Maybe they had the photo taken then. Was this the night that Guzmán had seen Rosa dressed like a gypsy at the fair? I had heard that story told late at night in my mother's kitchen, eavesdropping while I pretended to sleep. Did Rafael know Ramona then—was he happy because he was in love with the beautiful fourteen-year-old sister of his best friend?

In one of the plastic windows there was a newspaper clipping, yellow and torn, of a Spanish actress, wild black hair falling like a violent storm around a face made up to look glamorous, eyelashes thickened black, glossy lips parted in an open invitation. She was beautiful. I had seen her face often in the magazines my mother bought at the bodega, but why did Guzmán carry this woman's picture around? Was this what Rosa had looked like, or was she just his fantasy?

Deeply engrossed in my secret activity of going through my uncle's wallet, I was startled to hear men's voices approaching the top of the landing. I sat still waiting for them to go up the stairs, but they came down instead. There were four or five whose faces I recognized in the dim light as the working men of El Building, young husbands whose wives were Ramona's friends. I was not afraid, but I hid the wallet in my coat pocket and quickly got to my feet. My mind raced to come up with an excuse, though it was *their* presence in El Basement that was odd. The laundry room was used legitimately by women and otherwise by kids. The only other users, as I very well knew from my encounter with José and the woman, were people who wanted to hide what they were doing.

The voice I heard most clearly was that of Santiago, the only man from El Building ever to have been invited by Rafael into our apartment. After a severe winter week several years before, we had been left without heat until this man went down to city hall and got a judge to force the building superintendent to do something about the frozen heater pipes. Rafael had been in Europe at the time, but he obviously respected Santiago.

Coming down the steps, Santiago's voice directed the others. One man was to stand at the top and wait for the others, the rest were to follow him into the basement. He nearly stumbled over me in the dim light, not seeing me wrapped in my gray coat.

"Niña, *por Dios*, what are you doing here at this hour?" His voice was gentle but I detected irritation.

"My mother lost something here earlier and sent me down to try to find it." I explained rather rapidly in my awkward formal Spanish.

He took my elbow in a fatherly way: "Marisol, I don't believe your mother would be so careless as to send you down here to this dark place at the dinner hour alone. But I won't mention that I saw you here, and you must do the same for me, for us. These men and I want to have a private conversation. Do you understand?

"Yes," I said quickly, wanting to be released from his firm grasp, "I won't say anything." He let go of my arm and I ran up the stairs. Several other men had arrived and were talking in hushed tones at the top of the steps. I managed to catch a few sentences as I slipped by their surprised faces and into the streets. It was the factory they were discussing. Someone had said *huelga,* a strike. They were planning a strike.

Outside it was cold, but not bitter; a hint of spring in the breeze cooled my cheeks without biting into my skin. For once I felt a sense of pride in my father, who had managed to escape the horrible trap of factory work, though he was paying a high price for it. Tonight I'd have something to talk about with Guzmán. He would be interested in the secret basement meeting and the strike.

Chapter Ten

OST DAYS were for me a gray blur of school, church, and the afternoon shock of El Building. During Lent, many of the men were out of jobs and hanging around at the bodega, a place I had to visit daily for my mother, who believed in day-by-day grocery shopping. I heard the men talking about the bosses and the factories, how they hired and fired at will, giving the jobs to blacks moving up from the South or out from New York City—or worse, to newly arrived paisanos, who were desperate for work and would accept low pay and demeaning work conditions. Their words didn't interest me except for the fact that Guzmán wanted to know what was going on in the streets. My expeditions to the bodega had become like secret missions to gather information for him. Even Ramona did not know why my attitude about running her errands had suddenly improved.

I felt detached from the troubles brewing in El Building, though I knew that the tension was mounting from listening to my mother's friends discussing their money problems endlessly in our kitchen. The loudest complaint was that tempers were out of control in homes where the wife was still working and the man unemployed. The men, they said, did nothing around the apartment except mess it up, then expected dinner to be done instantly. The women's freedom to come and go into each other's kitchens was curtailed for the ones who were at home, since the men always wanted a reason for these visits, when the women themselves knew (this I surmised) that no reason was necessary. Ramona, knowing that Rafael's navy check would arrive every month on schedule, took on the role of adviser and confidante in these matters. I couldn't help but think that some of these women whom my mother considered her close friends resented her and even used her. They never left our place empty-handed, my mother being compulsively generous.

Guzmán asked me questions interminably about what I had heard the men discussing, especially about the huelga—that word, strike, which was beginning to be used like a forecast of a storm. His interest seemed to revive him. Though his wound was healing very slowly, and he seemed to be leaning more and more toward the side where the stitches looked like a puckered mouth, at least he was sitting up to read the newspapers I brought him. The first time he got up from bed, I was shocked to see how much he had shrunk in the few weeks of his convalescence. He seemed almost my size, a skinny adolescent with a wizened monkey face.

The pain he had gone through had left its mark. It was evident in the way he winced from time to time, as if he were remembering something painful. His movements were, of course, no longer rabbit-quick, and he often fell into long silences. When he got up from bed, I began to lose him. Though he was still unable to leave the apartment and thus still depended on me for news of the world, he and Ramona sat at the kitchen table now and talked in hushed tones. Their conversations went on late into the night, and I had to strain to hear.

Guzmán was trying to convince Ramona that trouble was coming to El Building.

"You should take the children and move in with Rafael's relatives for a while." He really sounded serious, but Ramona's voice told me that she no longer considered Guzmán reliable.

"Guzmán, you've been lying in bed imagining all these dangers. Sure there are men out of work, but they'll find other jobs, they always do. Besides, it would take more than the threat of a strike to make me move in with those snobbish Santacruz in-laws. Not that they'd let us in the front door with suitcases in the first place. How about you, brother, what are you going to do with your life after you're all well?"

It was obvious that Ramona wanted Guzmán out of the apartment, and I really resented her for her obvious maneuverings. He knew it too, but like a veteran survivor he was determined to heal himself before he moved on. One night in response to Ramona's questions about his future plans, my uncle said something surprising:

"I am thinking of going back to the Island." Even Ramona found this incredible. She, like all the other voluntary exiles in El Building, *talked* about returning to the homeland, but the implicit understanding was that one could not go back empty-handed, except for the funeral of parents, unless you were trash to begin with and didn't mind admitting failure. This was the conviction that justified fifteen years without seeing her parents. When she went back, it would be in style.

"You must have a little fortune hidden away then, eh? Tell me, do you have enough to buy some land? Will you live in Salud? Mamá Cielo will want you to stay at home until you build a house . . ."

Ramona's fantasy-making embarrassed even me, wide-eyed under my blankets in the next room. Guzmán let her go on for a while, then he spoke in his new slow way.

"I have a little money put away, but not enough to buy much more than a ticket there, Ramona."

Her voice was the beginning of a reprimand when she said, "And what do you think you're going to do when you get there, move in with the old people?"

"I just want to see them." He sounded tired. "I don't know what else to say. I have no other plans."

Never at a loss for topics, Ramona began to tell Guzmán about the spiritist meeting that was being planned at El Building. It would be an important affair revolving around the factory strike that the men were planning. She had been asked to organize the women. Her voice was almost childish in its enthusiasm. Sometimes I got a glimpse of my mother's loneliness in this way. How silly all that talk of spiritist meetings would seem if Rafael were there to talk to her about important things.

"Don't do it, Ramona." Guzmán's warning caught her by surprise. I could tell by the way she set her coffee cup on the table, hard enough for me to hear in my room.

"What do you mean, Guzmán?"

"It's dangerous to have meetings of any kind right now in this place. I have heard that the police are watching certain people here. They know a strike is being planned. It's no good to do anything that looks suspicious right now. Do you understand?" His voice was almost a whisper and I had to strain to hear him. It was pain that was making him slow in his movements, but his mind was quick. He knew everything that was going on without leaving the apartment, and I was his helper, his secret spy.

"I think you have been in your sick bed for too long, Guzmán. The newspapers exaggerate everything."

Ramona was now clearing the table. She was dismissing her brother as she did my brother and me, by simply turning her back.

I heard Guzmán whisper *buenas noches* to her. I did not hear her answer. His steps went past my room. Did he pause outside the door? I allowed sleep to fall over me like the extra blanket Ramona sometimes brought in on cold nights, tucking it around me with her strong nervous hands.

WE GOT LETTERS from Rafael postmarked Palermo, Naples, Athens, and a big box from Capri containing two dolls for me in typical Greek costumes, the man doll wearing a little pleated skirt, and a music box for Ramona with a photograph of a sea cave in moonlight decoupaged on the lid. It played an exotic little tune when you opened it. Gabriel got picture books. The note from Rafael said that he'd be home in June and we would then start looking for a house to buy. Ramona read us the letter full of plans as if it were a fairy tale, smiling at its more imaginative parts. She delighted in gifts like a child, and Rafael never came home without something special for her. She owned silk pajamas from Korea, hand-painted, lace-bordered fans from Spain, and jewelry from everywhere. But she hardly ever wore any of this in public. She said it would embarrass her friends in El Building.

That winter more and more men were laid off from Paterson factories, and El Building, being the spot with the biggest concentration of unemployed men, became their meeting place. There were never so many fist fights and domestic disputes, and Paterson police cars circled our block incessantly.

I went to school enveloped in the light of another world. There I was petted and praised by the nuns for my good grades and my humble demeanor, which was nothing more than fear of being exposed for the total alien I felt myself to be in that environment of discipline and order. I became completely involved in El Building, gathering news for Guzmán and helping Ramona with her endless preparations for her spiritist meeting, which, as the days went by, became obsessively important to the women, almost a countercampaign to the one the men were planning on the street corners and in the basement. *Huelga*, I heard, *huelga, meeting, huelga, meeting,* until my head rang from the words. Everyone, it seemed, was always whispering, planning, hiding behind everyone else's back: the women hid from the men to plan their spiritist meeting, the men hid from the police to plan their huelga, and I sneaked around, an unlikely double spy in my Catholic-school uniform, running errands for the women, keeping my word to Santiago about not telling anyone (except Guzmán, who had to know everything) about the meetings in El Basement, and pretending at school that I came from a normal home. I did this easily in my mask of humility. When you are shy and obedient no one asks you questions, and your company is not sought after. She's *different*, I imagined they said, and they were right.

Guzmán was now able to get up from bed and walk around the apartment, though the wound was healing badly. After weeks, it still seeped blood through the light bandages he now wore, and the skin had been pulled around it so that Guzmán leaned noticeably to accommodate his pain. His movements and speech were slow, and Ramona's nervous activity, her constant chatter, contrasted sharply with his new silence. It seemed to me that he was restless within it, though, for wasn't he the same man of my mother's stories, the man who had scandalized a whole town and come to the U.S. only to find himself a prisoner in a labor camp, and hadn't he escaped into the New York City subway system? Wasn't he the black sheep of the family whom I had imagined as Zorro leaping from adventure to adventure? Though my uncle did not look the part I had assigned him in all those years of listening to adult storytelling, he was still Guzmán, at the center of my imagination, capable of anything. Until he regained his strength, I would be his assistant, learning the tricks of the trade from him: how to rebel, how to prepare for escape, how not to fear anything or anyone.

While Ramona and Guzmán argued at the kitchen table of our apartment in El Building, neither one of them venturing out much, things were coming to a boiling point in the streets. In one afternoon alone there were two fights that the police were called to the scene for. One was a setup, as anyone could see, or at least that's what I heard the men say at the bodega. The leader of the men who wanted to organize a strike at the factory, Santiago, had been insulted by the man José in public. José, who was a junkie, had obviously sold out. The point was to get Santiago booked so that it would be easy to arrest him when the time was right. The other fight was between a black teenager and a Puerto Rican boy. It was really a spectacle in which the adult men formed a circle around the boys taking bets and encouraging them to beat their brains out on the pavement, and they very nearly did so. I duly reported these things to Guzmán, who seemed to get very nervous about it, especially the news about Santiago, which he said was the beginning of something big. That night at the dinner table he made an announcement that shocked all of us.

"Ramona, there is going to be trouble here soon. You have to get out with the children."

Ramona swallowed her spoonful of chicken soup calmly

and raised her blazing dark eyes to her brother. "We've had this discussion before, Guzmán. I am not going anywhere, especially with Rafael on the verge of coming home. He said in his last letter that it would be a matter of weeks before the ship returns to New York. I'll let him decide then about this *trouble* you are always talking about. Besides, the meeting is this Saturday. Only three days and so much to do."

"Listen to me, Ramona, there is no time to wait for Rafael, or for meetings. This spiritist thing is a big mistake. Don't you understand? The police are watching this place, waiting for anything suspicious to happen so they can move in and break up the plans for the huelga."

Gabriel, who had been following the conversation with wide-eyed interest, chimed in: "My teacher said that this building is like a ghetto. We were doing a lesson on riots. Will there be a riot here?"

"No, Gabriel. There is not going to be any riot. What a ridiculous idea." Ramona was now heading for the stove so she could turn her back on the table. "Do you see what all this talk about trouble is doing to us? It's making us imagine stupid things." This last was obviously intended to end the argument, but Guzmán had one more important bit of news to give us:

"Ramona, I wrote to Rafael."

She turned around so abruptly that a dish fell from the counter and broke on the floor. I scrambled to pick up the pieces at her feet.

"You did what?" She stood in front of him trembling with anger. "Did you just say that you wrote to my husband without telling me first?"

"I had to, don't you see? You won't listen to me." He stood at the table shaking—from pain or anger, I couldn't tell. He had her attention now, though, and he was prepared to press his argument. My brother and I sat at opposite ends of the green formica table, our eyes on Guzmán and Ramona, who faced each other like boxers in a ring. "This place is going to explode, Ramona, listen to me. I have seen it happen before, in other places. In New York that's how they clean slums. The newspapers always report riots in the barrios, and it always starts like this— people having secret meetings and getting busted."

Ramona interrupted, "How do you know so much, anyway? You have done nothing but *cause* trouble all your life, and now you're an expert on riots. I suppose you think of yourself as the man of the house, just because Rafael is away. Well, Rafael has always been gone more than he's been at home, and I have always managed. It is time for you to move on, Guzmán. I hate to say it, but Mamá Cielo is right about you. You are cursed. The only trouble in this place is you."

"No, Mamá . . ." I got up and ran to my uncle's side, but my mother grabbed my arm hard. I felt her long nails digging into the soft flesh above my elbow.

"You stay away from him, Marisol. I don't know what ideas he has put into your head, but you are not to run any more errands for him, or anyone else for that matter. Both of you"—she yanked Gabriel up from his chair and gave us both a shove in the direction of the room we shared— "stay in there until I call you out."

For a while longer I heard them arguing, though they were keeping their voices low to keep us from hearing. At some point I fell asleep, exhausted from crying and from the anger I felt at Ramona's unfairness. Gabriel tried asking me questions, but I ignored him, and soon he turned to his book in his own twin bed, which was pushed as far away from mine as was possible in the tiny room. For a moment I felt sorry for this little boy trapped in this crazy

235

house. He was so serious and intelligent, and usually in the clouds. I understood then why, more often than not, Gabriel could be found in his hiding place outside the window, reading or staring down to the street on the fire escape. It terrified Ramona, and I used to tell on him to get on her good side. Gabriel would be spanked; he would cry for a little while, then go right back out. I learned that this place was important enough for the child to risk our mother's anger and her spankings, so I started protecting his privacy by lying to Ramona. I even came up with a secret code to get him back in the apartment without her knowing. I would go into the utility closet and knock on the far wall. The way the building was constructed, the wall of this closet was right next to the window with the fire escape. Gabriel sat with his back to it. He told me he could actually feel the tapping, the wall was so thin. This should have frightened me, for it meant that not much was supporting that rusted contraption that hung from the side of the decrepit husk of our tenement. But in some ways I was not much past childhood myself, and in my growing resentment of Ramona, any deception played on her was a small victory for me.

When I awoke, it was almost noon and there were new voices in the kitchen, all female. They were speaking loudly, making plans like excited girls for the spiritist meeting. I got up and began walking like a somnambulist toward Guzmán's room. When I got to the door, I saw that it had become the living room again. There was no trace of him anywhere. It smelled like roses and incense. I felt sick and curled up around a cushion he had used to prop himself up during his long convalescence. It still held his musky scent. Ramona came into the room on silent bare feet, and I did not hear her until she sat next to me and put my head on her lap. Her fingers were trembling as she ran them through my long, tangled hair. I tried to get up, but she held me down gently. Smelling agua florida on her fingers and noticing her bare feet, I knew she had been consulting her spiritist friends. She always did that during a crisis. They would get together in someone's apartment, and then one of them would go into a trance after much praying and chanting and advise the troubled one about which "untranquil" spirit was bothering her home, and how best to appease it.

"Niña, niña," she said softly, caressing my head, "when your father is away, we have only each other. You have to understand that it is just the three of us: your brother, you, and me. No one else. Guzmán is my brother and I love him . . ." I tried again to release myself from her hands, but she turned me around to face her. Though I was already several inches taller than she, she was stronger. She looked into my eyes. I could hear the women talking in the kitchen. I worried that one of them would walk in and see me being handled like a baby by Ramona. ". . . But he is and has always been a troublemaker. It is good that he has gone his own way. But we will hear from him. Guzmán is like a bad penny; he always turns up." She bent down and kissed me on the forehead, smiling brightly. She was so beautiful and young that I could not forgive her. Perhaps if she had been like other mothers, wrinkled and wise, I would have believed in her sincerity. "Now go wash your face, and come to the kitchen for a cup of café. I have a job for you."

Reluctantly I obeyed, thinking all the while of schemes to get out of the apartment to look for Guzmán. Without knowing it, Ramona provided me with the best opportunity for doing so. My mother's plan was to keep me so busy that I would forget about Guzmán. My plan was to do whatever she asked, especially if it involved getting out of El Building.

In the kitchen that day were two women who were

237

important members of Ramona's society. They were both spiritist mediums, but of different persuasions. One, Elba La Negra, was a *Santera*, that is, she belonged to the sect of spiritists who combined Catholic symbols and ritual with ancient African rites to call forth spirits and to predict and heal. The other woman, whom everyone called Blanquita because she was so pale and emaciated, was a *Mesa Blanca* medium, like Ramona's father, Papá Pepe. The Mesa Blancas did not have the elaborate paraphernalia of the Santeros but followed the precepts of the European spiritists of the nineteenth century, who needed only a table and a few volunteers to summon spirits. Actually, the rites and philosophy of spiritism were much more complicated than I cared to know. To me it was all an embarrassing activity my mother spent too much of her time on. She was a novice who had been told by several well-respected mediums in Paterson that she needed to develop her faculties. Each of these women was trying to discover where Ramona belonged in the spiritual hierarchy.

My favorite of the two was Elba, a statuesque black woman with a voice that rebounded off walls, who liked to crush people in an overwhelming embrace whenever she felt they needed it. She had a sense of humor and instinctively understood my patronizing attitude toward spiritism. Her conspiratorial winks had often saved me from getting into pointless arguments. Her eyes took it all in: my resentment, my mother's loneliness, the pride that separated us—and she dispensed her uncritical affection to both of us in equal amounts, as she did with everyone in El Building, where her apartment was the refuge for the emotionally distraught, always full of neglected children and abused wives. After the fights, the contrite husband or father knew where to look. The price for getting a loved one back was to accept counseling by Elba, who lectured in self-righteous tones and a voice loud enough to be heard on several floors, and who had been known to threaten a full-grown man with a whipping for crimes she was not unwilling to publicize. Even the Paterson police knew whom to ask if they needed to find a child-support evader or runaway teenager.

As I entered the kitchen, steered by Ramona, I avoided Blanquita's gaze by lowering my head. This woman looked like a week-old corpse: yellow skin, protruding teeth, bones sticking out everywhere, and a raspy voice that told the story of her miserable life at the least instigation. She had been abandoned by two men—for her childlessness, she claimed, begging with her moist, bulbous eyes for pity as she said it, and for her ability to foretell future infidelities and her willingness to punish the transgressions before they happened. She did not have many close friends, but she did have a lot of followers. Her record at predicting marital discord was uncanny. No sooner did she identify a philandering husband than the couple would undergo a prueba, a trial by fire that would either strengthen or destroy the marriage. Blanquita's services were then sought again, for only her intense prayer meetings could summon the spirit guides that would lead the distraught couple back onto the road of reconciliation. Her fees were modest and her success rate respectable. She was one of the women Ramona could not see when Rafael was home. He despised her for her deviousness. He often said that Blanquita was a bitter woman, full of hatred for men and any woman who had what she had always wanted—a husband and children. Of course, this only made Ramona more anxious to be Blanquita's associate. She understood that Rafael was a skeptic about spiritism, and she felt that Blanquita's powers were the real reason her husband did not like her. Surprisingly, Rafael had no real objections to Ramona's friendship with Elba, whom he considered a "good soul." He did draw the line, however, at any of us visiting her apartment when there was any spiritist hocus-pocus going on. Unfortunately, this was most of the time, since Elba La Negra liked both company and a good time, and her Centro was filled with people most of the week, especially during her sessions on Tuesdays and Fridays, when she dressed in the vestments of her *orisha,* Chango, an African deity who likes rum and the color red. Elba would don her red gown and satin cape and dance into the room barefoot, stomping to a record of African drums. As Chango, she would pour red wine into the cups of her followers, chanting prayers in a language she made up as she got deeper into her trance. Chango is an aggressive soul; he is said to have been a hermaphrodite when he ruled on earth. And Elba became by turn imperious and seductive like a huge black African queen, or despotic and rough, commanding grown men to kneel at her feet or crawl about the room like babies. All this was done in utmost seriousness, for at some point in the evening there would be a mass *despojo,* a group exorcism led by Elba as Chango. She would exhort the devotees, who were by then in various stages of self-induced trances, to speak out their troubles. All at once these people would begin speaking in Spanish, English, or a new tongue about their sorrows. Some would cry and cling to their neighbors; others just faced the front of the room, where on a high table there was always a red candle or a bowl where lighter fluid had been set aflame because Chango liked fire. Some would fix their eyes on the flame and talk until they fell exhausted to the floor. Though Ramona usually sent me upstairs after the initial ceremony to stay with Gabriel while she participated in the mass confession, at least twice I had slipped into Elba's apartment late at night to witness the amazing spectacle of adults reduced to weak infants as Elba walked through their ranks like a big-breasted pope dispensing her blessings, hugging and kissing her flock while they wept away a week's misery.

Sitting at my mother's table, Elba looked even fatter than I remembered, as if she were absorbing everyone's problems. She was writing something on a yellow pad but motioned to me with one huge arm to come to her side. Her hug was overwhelming. She folded me into her chest where I inhaled the sweetness of this woman who needed to make the whole world her nursling, perhaps because many years before her only child had disappeared in New York City while playing on the sidewalk one day, never to be seen again. This was when she had become a Santera spiritist, immersing herself in a way of life that permitted her to give to others what she had been deprived of when her baby had been stolen. Ramona had cried telling me this story. Elba handed me the list she had been composing.

"Niña, do you know where Arcadio's *botánica* is?" Her voice was deep as a man's, but the hand that lifted my chin in order to look into my eyes was softer even than Ramona's— Ramona, who was the most feminine woman I knew.

"The store that sells herbs on Market Street?" I had been there several times with Ramona. It was the place where we bought the incense and the candles she burned every Saturday. Ramona pulled me toward her. I recoiled slightly from the nails that never failed to scratch me whether she was hugging or hitting.

"She knows where it is, Elba. Just give her the list and the money and she'll go shopping for us. Won't you, Mari? Either Don Arcadio or his wife, Doña Lola, will help her find the items."

I read the list quickly. Some of the names were familiar

241

to me; others weren't. I knew what agua florida was: scented alcohol used in my house for everything from deodorizer to bath cologne; holy water we had also bought before, though not by the gallon, as the list specified; and candles—there was an order for two dozen in red, blue, white, and yellow. I knew, or could guess, the uses of these common items, but the lengths of ribbon in the same colors as the candles, the lodestones, and the two boxes of cigars really baffled me. I asked Elba to explain.

All she said was: "If you can't carry it all, have Arcadio deliver it. For the amount of money we're spending in his store, he should be able to do this little thing. And, niña, can you remember to tell Lola that they are both expected to be at my apartment for the meeting on Saturday? Tell her it is the big one. You want me to write that down?"

"No." I felt somewhat insulted that she had ignored my question, but as I put my shoes on, Elba rose from her chair and, announcing to Ramona that she was leaving to prepare her place, managed to walk out with me. On the landing she took my elbow and leaned down to whisper in my ear.

"You too will be at my meeting, *mi amor*. There you will find what you seek." Placing a noisy kiss on my cheek she plodded down the narrow stairs of El Building before me, blocking my path so that I had to follow her at her slow pace. I did not dare ask her what she meant. At her door, she turned to look at me with a broad smile on her fat face, which was like a new moon suddenly illuminated by a shooting star. As she went in I smelled a familiar musky smell, but since I had a lot of shopping to do and intended to spend as little time as possible doing it so that I could look for Guzmán in a few places I had in mind, I rushed down the stairs and into the street. Spring had arrived in Paterson as it always did, with a sudden melting of old, dirty snow, making the sidewalks an obstacle course of

242

slushy puddles that sometimes looked like concrete until you stepped into freezing water up to your ankles. I kept my eyes down and walked fast.

On my way to the botánica I thought about places where Guzmán could be. He was street-smart and could talk his way into any place for the night. He wasn't broke, but he would not go to a hotel, since in Paterson hotels, the good ones that is, were not for blacks and Hispanics. The flophouses were regularly busted by Paterson's police force, which received orders straight from city hall, from a mayor who believed in cleaning house. I learned all this from the newspapers I had read to Guzmán while he was recuperating from his knife wound. The Spanish newspaper called the mayor the New Hitler, claiming that he hated nonwhites and permitted his policemen to persecute them.

I was convinced that Guzmán would not leave the city while he thought we were in any danger. Where could he be? I looked into the bodega. Santiago, the huelga leader, was there, talking excitedly to Cheo, the owner of the bodega, and to one other man, an American with a crewcut and thick-soled shoes. Guzmán had told me this was how you could always recognize a cop in disguise. They were speaking in English, but when Santiago saw me come in, he signaled to the others to stop talking. I felt their eyes on me as I selected a candy bar. Defiantly, I took my time fingering each row of candy on the tiered display case—top: M&M's, O'Joys, Ring Ding Juniors; middle: Dolly Madison cupcakes (chocolate or coconut), Baby Ruth, Ju Ju lemon and cherry drops; third row: gum (Juicy Fruit, spearmint), Bazooka bubble gum, Lifesavers. I chose a roll of Lifesavers and handed it to Cheo while I dug in my purse for change. (My wallet was thick with spiritist shopping money, but I did not pull it out.)

I heard Santiago say to the American policeman that it

was time for him to go back home, adding in a sarcastic tone, "Since I don't have a job any more, I get to eat three meals at home—when there is money for groceries, that is."

The American walked to the door as Santiago spoke. In the doorway, he turned back to face the men, hands deep in the pockets of his black trenchcoat, collar turned up. He was very tall and had a deep voice. He seemed to be imitating a TV cop—the sergeant from Dragnet perhaps—for when he spoke his words were clipped and sounded rehearsed: "Just remember what I said, boys. And tell your friends not to try anything foolish. Big Hermano is watching." He turned swiftly, making his trenchcoat fly like a cape behind him.

All three of us watched him cross the street toward El Building. I gave Cheo my dime, and he took it but, distracted, forgot to give me the Lifesavers. Then he remembered.

"Perdón, niña," he said, "the gringo made me forget what I was doing."

Santiago followed me out. I didn't want to talk to him. I just wanted to get the shopping done and start looking for Guzmán. But though I walked fast, trying to let him know that I did not want his company, he kept up with me. He didn't say anything until we were on the corner of Straight Street and Market, where I had to make a decision since the botánica was just a block away. I didn't want Santiago to know where I was going. The habit of secrecy that I had acquired in recent weeks had made me very paranoid. I decided to face him.

"I don't have permission to be walking with you, señor," I said, putting on my humblest Catholic schoolgirl face for him. The last thing I wanted was a confrontation with the leader of the huelga.

244

"I want to talk to you, Marisol. I did not speak because I wanted to be sure we were not being followed, you understand? Where are you going?"

"To the store for my mother." He looked around. We were nowhere near a grocery store, nor were we heading for the downtown shopping district. In fact, the only store I could be going to in this direction, as any Hispanic in Paterson would know, was the botánica.

"I see. You are being sent by the *espiritistas* of El Building for party supplies." He smiled wrily. "I am surprised that you are participating in this voodoo stuff, niña, a nice Catholic girl like you."

I did not answer but started walking fast. Santiago took my elbow. "I did not mean to insult you, señorita. I will accompany you to Don Arcadio's store."

"I don't need a chaperone, señor." I yanked my arm out of his grasp.

"But you do need someone to tell you that what you are doing, what your mother is doing, is dangerous. Do you remember that night in El Basement when I asked you not to tell anyone about the meeting we had?" I nodded. "Well that bastard José, the same one who hurt your uncle, sold us out. He told on us, and now we are being watched. El Building is a target. The police are just waiting for something suspicious to happen to pounce on us like a cat on a bunch of cornered rats."

"Are you saying that they are going to use this spiritist meeting as an excuse for trouble?" That was what Guzmán had been telling Ramona all along! I felt frightened for the first time. This was no longer just a game. Santiago was a serious man with a reputation for honesty in our neighborhood. I had to warn Ramona.

"I do not know what it means except that everyone is angry at everyone else. The mayor is scared of a labor strike, the police have been instructed to watch for any signs of activity in the black and Puerto Rican neighborhoods, and the men who are out of work do nothing but plan trouble. We are sitting on a time bomb, niña, that is all I know."

"But what about this meeting on Saturday? Shouldn't we warn the women, shouldn't we try to stop it?" We were in front of the botánica now. My feet were cold from stepping in puddles of slush. I was shivering, and I felt like crying. Santiago looked at me, saw the tear making its way down my cheek, and wiped it with a calloused finger.

"Could we stop it even if we wanted to, Marisol? Would your mother listen to you, would my wife pay attention to me?" He shook his head sadly, "No, you should know this about Island women, not little *Americanitas* like you," he smiled to soften his words, "but women who are brought up to believe that we are not alone in this vale of tears and misery that is a human life. They believe that we have invisible friends, these spirits of theirs, who are supposed to be like loyal dogs, summoned with a whistle, to come help us and defend us from our enemies. They mean well, but here in America their hocus-pocus only complicates things. Can you imagine trying to explain to our crewcut *policía*, the one giving us the third degree at Cheo's, that the meeting Saturday is to ask for assistance from the dead?" Santiago laughed, but it was only a sound like laughter, his eyes were sad. He too was shivering. The afternoon was turning cold. I had a lot to do.

"Should I buy this stuff for the meeting?"

"Buy it. Maybe nothing will happen. Maybe this is what we all need—a little party to help us forget our troubles. Just in case, I'll be there. My friends will be stationed in different parts of El Building, too. Just to be on the safe side, eh? Take care of yourself, Marisol. You are getting to be quite a pretty young lady, and there are bad men around every corner." He patted me on the shoulder and started to say good-bye, but I had one more question for him:

"Don Santiago, have you seen my Uncle Guzmán around today?"

Santiago looked surprised. "Doesn't he live with you, Marisol? I saw him this morning where I always see him, smoking a cigarette on the fire escape of El Building, the one where your little brother usually sits. By the way, you should tell him that's a dangerous place. Tell your mother to keep them both out of there. *Adios.*"

My heart leapt up from the dark place it had fallen. Guzmán was still in our building! I rushed into the botánica and read my list out to the startled Don Arcadio, a little old man with hands gnarled by arthritis. He pointed with a crooked finger to where every item was on a shelf, and I placed it all before him on the counter. "It's for the big meeting on Saturday," I explained. "Elba says you and your wife are invited."

"Sí, señorita, I am grateful for the invitation and for your business, but my wife is sick with the flu. We will not be able to attend. But here," he went over to where the large candles were arranged by color on a shelf and selected a blue one. "Please tell Doña Elba to dedicate this one to La Milagrosa for my wife's health."

"Thank you, señor. I will tell her."

"God bless you, niña."

I hardly felt the weight of the shopping bag full of exotic paraphernalia that I carried home that day. My mind was on another mystery: Where in El Building was Guzmán hiding?

Chapter Eleven

I TOOK GABRIEL to the library the Saturday morning of
the big meeting because Ramona wanted us out of
the way. Walking there, I noticed that even the few
scraggly trees that had clawed their way up from little
clumps of earth between buildings were sprouting a few
green leaves. Soon it would be the Easter season. At Saint
Jerome's the nuns had been in a frenzy of activity preparing us for a pageant. Though I had kept up my grades, I
had neglected my friendships, turning down invitations
from Letitia, who had managed to talk her parents into
accepting me back into their house after Dr. Roselli's encounter with the hoodlums at El Building on Christmas
Eve. Even the boy I had a crush on, Frank, seemed pale
and uninteresting to me those days. In spite of myself I was
completely immersed in the life of El Building. I rushed
home after school to drink café with my mother and her
friends, though it was news of Guzmán I listened for, having little interest in their domestic problems and in the ongoing feuds between them. By that morning I had a pretty
clear idea of where Guzmán was spending his time,
though the women did not talk about him directly, especially in front of Ramona, who would never admit she
was as anxious as I to know if Guzmán was all right.

"When is father coming home?" Gabriel asked again for
the umpteenth time that week. He was tired, I could tell, of

being around Ramona and me all the time. With Guzmán gone, he had no one to play with. He was a quiet little boy who did not at all fit in with the rowdy, street-wise urchins of El Building, and we lived too far away from most of our classmates for him to have any other friends.

"Soon, Gabriel. Rafael—that is, Father—will be back from Europe in a few weeks."

"Before Easter?" He wanted to know.

"I don't know exactly when. Why does it matter?"

"I'm in a play at school. I want him to come to it. Mamá won't, you know."

I knew. Ramona took care of all our physical needs, but unless it was an emergency, she avoided knowing any-thing about our other lives away from El Building. She made sure we made good grades because she was an-swerable to Rafael. She bought our uniforms, and she signed excuses I wrote myself when we were sick. Other than that, nothing. PTA meetings and bake sales were not part of her reality. Rafael understood her timidity and made it easy for her by taking care of tuition and other matters ahead of time while he was home on leave. I sometimes wondered what would happen to us if Rafael died or was lost at sea. But even then I knew our options. Either I would replace Rafael as mediator with the world for Ramona, or we would go back to the Island. At least once I had heard Ramona say that Mamá Cielo always had a place for us under her roof. She said this to Rafael during an argument once, and he had softly reminded her that Mamá Cielo was getting old and would not always be there for her children. Ramona had cried all day, and Rafael never said anything else about the legendary old lady whose memory seemed to keep Ramona hopeful.

When we got back to El Building, there were more peo-ple in the hallways than I had ever seen before. Many apartments had their doors thrown wide open, and women were coming in and out carrying dishes of steaming food back and forth and talking loudly. Someone was playing a *salsa* record at full volume, and several men were standing on the landing singing along. They all had cans of Corona beer in their hands. One made a comment under his breath as I walked past, another blew me a kiss. My brother ran up the stairs ahead of me, yelling back that he was going to read his books "you know where."

"But what if Mother wants to know where you are?"

"She won't."

He was right about Ramona again. Smart kid. She was at her control post in her kitchen giving directions to the women who came in and out with their offerings for the big meeting. The kitchen was full of flowers. There were red roses for the adherents of Santa Barbara, whose favorite color is red; white and blue carnations for the mild-mannered La Mercedes; greenery in glasses filled with water colored according to the saint or orisha whose favor they sought. The women also came to buy ribbons in their special color and left a donation in a cigar box. A new aluminum pail and several cans of lighter fluid sat conspicuously on the kitchen table. I recalled Elba La Negra's dance around the flames, hoping Ramona would skip this part of the ceremony. She saw me trying to sneak into my room and motioned for me to come over to where she was pouring out the contents of vials marked "holy water" into a ceramic bowl. Her long black hair fell over her shoulders as she worked. She was a tiny woman, not quite five feet tall, and though she appeared voluptuous, she had the slim hips and legs of a teenager. At my age she had been engaged to Rafael, though, and she became a married woman and a mother not long after. She had not been a child

250

for long, or perhaps had never come out of her childhood. I felt pity for her, so involved in this silly game of spiritism.

"I need you to help me and Blanquita carry these things to Elba's apartment in a few minutes. Where's your brother?"

"Reading. Is that where the meeting is tonight? At Elba's?" I said with feeling some relief that our place was not going to be invaded by the living and the dead in a few hours.

"Of course. Her place is bigger, or at least it seems bigger since she lives alone, and she's got it set up for meetings. You know that, Marisol, what's wrong with you? You seem so distracted these days. Are you in love or something?"

Blanquita heard the last comment and pulled up a chair next to me. "Let me see your hand. I can tell you your future. She's old enough to know things now, isn't she Ramona." Though irritated at her intrusion, I was curious to know what this skeletal woman saw on the palm of my hand.

Blanquita placed my hand palm up on the table and spread my fingers down flat holding them down with her own. "A long life," she said, "and many loves. But look, Ramona, see that deep line that cuts her palm in two? You know what that is?" Without waiting for an answer she said, "It's the Line of the Sun."

Both my mother and Blanquita looked intently at my open palm. My mother traced the line across my hand with her long fingernail, making me close my hand involuntarily. This was getting on my nerves, but I was still curious. "What does it mean? What is the line of the sun?"

With an almost comical look of concentration on her cadaverous face, Blanquita bent over my open hand. She

251

traced several lines on it including the three running across my wrist like razor cuts. She spoke across me to Ramona. "Her Line of the Sun is deep and clear. See how it starts just inside her Lifeline straight across the Mounts of Venus and the Moon? What's interesting is that it crosses over her Fate Line just at this point." She stabbed the soft swelling of my palm she had called the Mount of Venus with her red nail. I jerked my hand back, tired of the game. "Don't you want an interpretation of the reading, young lady?" Blanquita's tone was mocking. "It's not every day I do this for free, but you have an interesting hand."

Ramona rose abruptly from the table. "Marisol does not believe in any of this, Blanquita. She's done enough for us today. Let's let her go back to her schoolbooks." My mother seemed anxious to get me out of the room, which piqued my curiosity. I offered my palm to Blanquita across the kitchen table.

"What does it mean?" Ramona turned to the sink where there were flowers in water glasses that needed to be arranged.

Blanquita smiled mysteriously, sucking in a deep breath, and grabbed my hand, rather roughly, I thought. "You see how plump your Mount of Venus is? This part right here. That means you are a passionate woman . . ."

"Blanquita, we don't have much time before the meeting tonight, and I can't do everything by myself." Ramona's activity at the sink was getting louder as she slammed down things and opened and closed cabinet doors.

Blanquita ignored my mother while continuing to run her fingernail up and around the fleshy part of my hand. "You will have many loves in your life. Look at the stars that come out when I squeeze your hand. Each represents a great passion in your future. But there will also be heartbreak. When there is a line that cuts through your Mount

252

of Venus, that means interference, usually from your family. Are you in love with someone your parents don't approve of, Marisol?" I was caught up in her game now, and though I knew Ramona would soon break it up, I wanted to hear more.

"Blanquita, don't you think this has gone far enough?" Ramona came to stand behind me, placing her cool hands on my shoulders. She was trying to force me to leave the kitchen by making me uncomfortable with her proximity, sending me urgent messages in the morse code of her hard fingers. But I wanted my fortune told now. I opened my hand wide for Blanquita.

She smiled her sarcastic smile and continued speaking in a mock-serious tone, like a doctor explaining a diagnosis to an ignorant patient. "Your Line of Fate starts here at the base of your third finger, do you see it? If it's smooth and deep, running right across your palm, it means a good life, no tragedies, no heartbreak, no misfortune—yours isn't like that, though when it finally takes off, right here at the Line of Life, it gets clearer and stronger; up to then it's just a mess. What this means is that you will be hindered by those closest to you from attaining what you want in life. You have natural gifts, this is indicated by your Line of the Sun. Here, see where it springs from Life? That means you have an artist's soul. That may be why you like books so much. Eh, niña? But you will have to struggle to succeed in that area. There are many lines of interference there; you may even fail because you will have affairs of the heart to distract you."

"That's enough of that, Blanquita. It's late and we have to take all these things down to Elba's apartment." This was Ramona who was now pulling my chair back. "Marisol, you will stay here with Gabriel tonight while I am at the meeting."

253

"That's not fair. I helped with all the work for this thing, so why can't I go with you?" I was furious. This was typical behavior for my mother, who involved me in her activities until the fun part. Then she excluded me, always claiming I was too young, or that Rafael wouldn't like it.

"Marisol, be reasonable. You have never liked these meetings; you have said so many times yourself. And besides, somebody has to watch Gabriel tonight."

"If you hadn't thrown your own brother out of the house, you'd have more people here to serve you." I shouted this into her face, seeing with the periphery of my vision Blanquita smile with demonic glee at our argument. Ramona slapped me with the full force of her anger. Her thin hand cracked like a whip on my face. Stunned, I ran to my room and locked the door. Gabriel ran to me. He had obviously sneaked in during the palm reading. He grabbed me by the waist, burying his head on my chest. Our mother's violence had frightened my gentle brother more than it had hurt me. We stood like that, holding on to each other for a while, then I composed myself for his sake, though still trembling from the pure hatred of a mother only a teenager can feel. I read to Gabriel and practiced his lines for the Easter play with him, showing him how to wash his hands of guilt convincingly, since he was playing Pontius Pilate.

As EVENING FELL, El Building was buzzing with activity. News of the spiritist meeting had made its way to relatives and friends in New York City, and cars began to pull up early, spewing out women dressed in the incendiary colors of their patron saints and men carrying bags of food and liquor for the socializing that would precede and follow Elba La Negra's spectacular show. Throughout all this Ramona remained at the control center, our apartment, di-

254

recting the flow of traffic and sorting the stream of supplies that had turned her kitchen into a botánica, with candles of all colors and sizes lining the counters, flowers in the sink, gallons of agua florida, as well as several cans of lighter fluid for the flame that would give all the untranquil spirits light that night.

I stayed in my room with Gabriel, who was very restless because of all the unusual activity in our house. He wanted to go read on his fire escape, but I kept him from doing so because there was too much going on in the hallways of El Building. I promised him that I would take him out myself that evening, a rare treat since he had never had the opportunity to look at the city from his vantage point at night.

Ramona brought us a tray with two bowls of Franco-American spaghetti. It was what we ate for lunch when she didn't have time to cook the rice dishes that made up our regular meals. She was dressed in a fire-engine red dress that was tight around her breasts and waist and flared like a dancer's costume over her legs. Her long black hair was loose over her shoulders. She looked radiant and beautiful. We both stared at our mother who could transform herself with color this way. Around the house she usually wore a baggy housedress and her hair was usually severely pinned back in a bun. The only time she dressed like this was when we were expecting Rafael. Of course, Gabriel brightened up immediately.

"Will Father be home tonight?" He wanted to know.

The question took Ramona by surprise. She sat on the edge of Gabriel's bed where she had set up a tray for us. She ran her long nails gently through my brother's hair. "Your papí will be home in a few days, mi amor. Didn't he say so in the last letter he wrote to you?" She kissed him on the forehead, and as if to avoid more questions from him, turned her eyes to me, sitting across the room, cross-legged on my

255

bed. I was pretending to read one of Gabriel's books. "Marisol, you know where I'll be tonight. I probably will not be home until early morning since I have to help clean up after the meeting. If there are any problems . . ." She saw that I heard her, though I did not lift my eyes from the book. My cheek still burned from her hand. I knew she was ready for some sort of reconciliatory gesture, but I wasn't. She looked at me for a few more moments, giving me a chance to speak, but I kept my eyes on the illustrated catechism I had hastily picked up when she came in the room. *Thou shalt not* do this, and *Thou shalt not* do that. I wondered if Mamá Cielo had ever gotten Guzmán to memorize all the rules we had had to learn by heart. Ramona finally gave up trying to will me to respond to her and kissed Gabriel on the cheek. "You get in your pajamas soon. If you need anything, tell your sister." She swung out of our room on her black high heels leaving a trail of Tabú, the perfume Guzmán had given her at Christmas. When she left, Gabriel and I went to the kitchen to make ourselves ice cream sodas. All the flowers, incense, candles, and assorted "magic stuff," as Gabriel called it, had disappeared, leaving only the odd mixture of smells that I imagined were like the odors of a funeral parlor. I lifted open a window for fresh air. There were people talking loudly on the sidewalk below. In fact, they were shouting at a passing police car. Hearing the obscenities clearly, Gabriel rushed to my side at the window.

"Is it a fight?" he asked in an almost hopeful tone.

"Not yet," I answered, remembering Santiago's warning and Guzmán's words. I enticed Gabriel back to our room with the promise of reading to him from Rafael's collection of *Popular Mechanics*. Knowing what would happen if Gabriel got his enthusiastic hands on them, Rafael kept them high up on a shelf in the closet he shared with Ramona.

"But when will we go outside?" he insisted.

"When the meeting gets going, Gabriel. I'll take you then. You don't want anyone to find us out there, do you? You know what she would do." I was hoping he'd forget about going to the fire escape. There were a lot of strangers going up and down the stairs of El Building tonight. I figured I could get him to fall asleep after I read to him for a while.

"Yeah." He yawned. He was already curled next to me, though there was hardly any room in my twin bed for both of us. He chose a magazine with a picture of a man and a boy, obviously his son, building a play area in a backyard. From the kitchen window a pretty woman in a pink dress and white apron waved to them with a big smile on her face.

"Read about this." My brother closed his eyes and stretched out beside me, ready to dream, as I read the lists of materials necessary for a Stanley Backyard Gym Set Project. It wasn't long before we both fell asleep. The last words I remember reading were a warning that if you were going to allow a child to assist you in building the Stanley Backyard Gym Set, you should make sure he did not handle any power tools. I awakened to the sound of a key turning in the front-door lock. Ramona must have forgotten something, I thought, but the footsteps I heard enter the apartment were not the sharp little tap of her high heels. I had a moment of panic, followed almost immediately by joy as I recognized the familiar sound of a raincoat thrown over a chair, the heavy man's shoes on the linoleum floor, and the aroma of a lighted cigarette, a different brand from the mentholated kind Ramona smoked.

I got up gently so as not to awaken Gabriel. Turning off the light in my room, I walked into the kitchen, where Guzmán sat at the table, smoking. I rushed to embrace him, and he returned my kiss on the cheek with a light kiss on the forehead. He pulled a chair close to his for me. He had lost more weight, and the circles under his eyes were deep and purple.

"I'm alone with Gabriel," I said, not knowing what else to say.

"I know," he said and smiled. It was the grin of complicity I had seen often in the past months as I played spy for him. "I've been staying at Elba's, but it got a little crowded there tonight."

"I know," I said, and we both laughed. But we fell silent again as we heard people talking in the hallway. Suddenly loud music with the insistent beat of African drums drowned out everything else. Stomping and clapping followed. Elba's apartment must have been wall-to-wall people, judging from the level of noise drifting up the staircase and through the vibrating heater pipes.

"I was going to find you tomorrow," I said to Guzmán, who was now on his second cigarette in five minutes. He seemed nervous.

"I knew you'd figure it out, Marisol. But I have a place now. Today I looked at a room in a boarding house. Come here, I'll show you where it is."

We stepped up to the kitchen window, and he pointed to a building on Market Street, just visible because there were two lampposts in front of it.

"You see them?"

I nodded. Blue and red flashing lights had suddenly filled the street.

"They're expecting trouble," Guzmán said.

"You mean here, tonight?" I asked, even as we saw two

258

police cars stopping in front of our building. The men got out of the cars to talk. They were gesturing and pointing up at El Building. The boys who had yelled at them earlier were still loitering at the front door. I could hear whistles and catcalls. Instead of answering my question, Guzmán abruptly grabbed his black raincoat from the chair and put it on.

"I'm going down to Elba's. I'll check on you later."

"I'm going with you."

"That is not a good idea, niña. You stay here with your brother. I'm going to try to convince your mother to get out of here while there is still time. You stay in your clothes and make sure Gabriel is ready too."

"Guzmán." This was the first time I had called him by his name instead of uncle, but I was angry. "I am not a niña, *not* a little girl, and I am tired of everyone telling me what to do. Gabriel is safe here. Elba's is just down one flight of stairs. I am going to that meeting, either with you or by myself."

At that moment there was a commotion on the street, the sound of running and then shouts. We both rushed to the window. One of the policemen we had seen earlier had grabbed a young man by the arm and was dragging him to the squad car still parked in the middle of the street. His partner was talking into his car's radio microphone while keeping an eye on the other men. Guzmán raised the window all the way up and we could hear the obscenities they were yelling out in Spanish. Their friend was spreadeagled on the police car and was being frisked not too gently by the officer. We heard sirens in the distance. Guzmán pulled the window shut again and said:

"Let's go get your mother; we'll come back over here for now. Is Gabriel sleeping?"

We looked into the bedroom and Gabriel had not moved.

259

Fully clothed, he was curled up around the pillow on my bed, Rafael's magazines by his side.

EVEN AT THE TOP of the landing we smelled the smoke, heavily perfumed with incense, coming from Elba La Negra's apartment. When we got to her door we saw the smoke actually seeping through the sides of the door. There was a loud murmuring as of many people praying quietly together. We tried the door, and it was unlocked though people were packed around it. The smoke in the place was so thick we nearly tripped over the many pairs of shoes in the hallway. I had forgotten that upon entering a Santero meeting people remove their shoes since they believe that spiritual influences enter the body through the head and leave through the feet. Shoes hinder the flow of *flúido,* the beneficial spiritual force, as it goes through the faithful, absorbing all that is not good. Guzmán told me in a whisper to keep mine on.

I could barely see him through the thick smoke though he was right beside me. The smell of cigar smoke was overpowering. All of the participants of the session who were not just observing or accompanying someone had lit cigars and were puffing away even as they chanted the invocations to good spirits. Elba was sitting like an African queen in their midst. I made out her large figure dressed in a brilliant red gown and cape, a purple scarf knotted together around her head. She was in a mild trance already for her eyes were closed, and her lips moved in the prayer she was reciting. Her hands were fluttering on her thighs, like brown birds. Soon she started fanning herself. This was her way of calling the spirits she was going to work with into her mind. We were able to observe Elba in the packed room because her chair had been raised on a platform above the level of the crowd. The oxygen in the room was thinning out as people puffed madly on their cigars. I was feeling dizzy and slightly disoriented.

Guzmán was craning his neck trying to find Ramona among the many dark-haired women wearing red that night. Santa Bárbara was a favorite guide among young women, who liked the saint's aggressive nature. While in trance under the influence of Santa Bárbara, Elba had given many a straying husband a good tongue-lashing. But there were many other saints and orishas represented in the vestments of the congregation: the mild La Mercedes in the virgin's colors of blue and white; and San Carlos, also called by his African name, Candelo, in a cardinal's crimson vestments. Along with his colors, during a session the saint's protégé takes on the behavior of his spirit guide. I had once been to a meeting that had been taken over by the followers of San Espedito, patron of drunkards and gamblers, who had led the congregation in uproarious games of chance (Ramona had dragged me out of that one). I had also witnessed another meeting led by the pious cripple San Lázaro, whose faithful walk on crutches and chant prayers for the ill. My favorites were the occasions when one of the women would become Santa Bárbara, who in her African manifestation is Chango, the spirit of fire. Even if her earthly host was a timid woman, Santa Bárbara would make her strut across a room puffing on a cigar, often demanding a shot of rum which she gulped down. That session ended up as a dance with everyone prancing around the room on her orders.

They were all here in their costumes, ready to be led in games and in prayer by their priestess, Elba. I remember thinking that this was not so different from the plays Gabriel and I acted out from our books, except that these people took all this so seriously. Did they really believe there were spirits and demons out there in the dark who

261

helped or hindered them? Or was this all just fantasy-making, an escape from the dreary cycle of factory work, tenement living, second-class citizenship? Perhaps I had these thoughts as Guzmán led me by the hand through the closely packed throng of people in Elba's apartment. Already drunk or hypnotized, they were like cattle, all pressed together in a smoky room.

Elba rose from her dais and called out in a strange wail for a man named Pito to come forth. Her assistants, one of whom was Blanquita, again relegated to a secondary role, led him forward. He seemed reticent. He was a known troublemaker in El Building, one of the first to have lost his job. He had taken out his misfortune on his wife and children, who had finally gone back to the Island, escaping through Elba's intercession, as everyone knew. Pito drank too much and was mistrusted even by the other men, for he liked to instigate trouble with the police, taunting them as they made their slow patrols around El Building. He had been standing against a wall in the back of the room and it took many hands to pull him forward into Elba's arms. He was a small man, unhealthy looking and thin. He had the look of an orphan or a neglected child, Ramona always said—especially since his family had left and he had to depend on the charity of his neighbors to live.

We had inched our way toward the front, where people stood elbow to elbow, murmuring their prayers and swaying as if they were drunk. I was nearly smothered among them. The smoke was thick as fog. Guzmán put his arm around my shoulders, and I leaned on him. He whispered in my ear:

"We'd better wait until this *despojo* is over before we get Ramona. I see her on the other side." He pointed to the pail next to Elba on the dais. Behind it sat my mother. She would be the one to strike the match at the right moment. I felt I would get sick any minute.

Elba shook the man Pito like a doll. Her eyes were closed in a trance. Then she let go of him and began to move her arms back and forth in a fanning motion between his head and hers. She was taking on his spirits, *despojándolo*, exorcising him of evil influences. Some people in the audience shook violently and cried out as if they were physically involved in the process. Others just swayed in a wave that put the entire room into movement. I was afraid I'd be swallowed by this snake with many heads. I hung on to Guzmán and watched as Elba prayed over the man, who was unabashedly crying and begging for God's mercy. Elba cradled him in her arms like a baby. Finally opening her eyes, she gently sat Pito on her chair, faced the crowd, and pronounced him free of evil. She said his protective guide had revealed herself to Elba during the trance as La Mercedes, the gentle Obatalá, father of the African gods, who would make him a new man. He was weak as a newborn baby now. "Help him grow," she shouted out, "Help him grow in goodness." The chant was taken up by the crowd as Pito was helped down off the dais by many arms. He went through the crowd in a daze. Many embraced him speaking words of encouragement to him.

Guzmán said "Now," and we began our slow progress through the crowd toward the other side of the room. Elba had mounted her dais and asked for silence. When she had everyone's attention she gave my mother a sign and the lights went out. The pail of lighter fluid burst into flames as if on its own in the darkness. Standing before the flame, Elba raised her arms and blessed the crowd. Then she lifted her long skirt above her knees and with amazing agility for such a large woman, she jumped over the flaming pail four times, each time invoking the name of a saint. Back and forth she went in one direction, then back and forth in the opposite direction, making with her movements, I finally discerned through the haze that was thickening in the room and in my head, the sign of the cross. The smoke in the room was really getting unbearable, so as we passed a window in the rear of the room I signaled Guzmán to stop for a minute.

"What is it, Marisol, are you sick?" he asked, bringing his face very close to mine in the darkness. I pulled him to the window. The street lights cast a yellow glow on his face. It frightened me. He looked like a death's head.

"I feel dizzy, but I'll be all right as soon as I get some air," I said. "Can you help me open this window?"

"If we open a window all the smoke is going to get sucked out of this place." He seemed to be considering what to do. "But it might be one way to get all these people out of here. Look!" He pointed to the street below. There were several squad cars parked almost directly in front of El Building.

"What are they looking for?" I asked, beginning to feel really scared now.

"Trouble," he answered.

"Let's get Mother and get out of here, now, please," I said, tears streaming down my face from the smoke, now intensified by the fact that Elba was bringing people one at a time to the fire, where she fanned the flame and prayed over them. Some were so emotionally wrought up that they fell before her, shaking violently. For each she said a special prayer which was answered by the crowd before they received the purified person back in their midst as if each were the Prodigal Son just returning home. My mother, I saw, was in line with the sinners. She looked radiant in the glow of the fire. Guzmán also saw her.

264

"Marisol, listen. This is what we'll do. You go get Ramona while I open this window. Tell her anything to get her out of here."

"Like what?" I asked desperately, knowing how angry Ramona would be at the mere sight of me here at this hour of the night.

"Tell her Gabriel is sick and needs her," he said. "I'll meet you back at your apartment, and I'll explain everything to her. Now go."

I started pushing through the bodies of people as if they were a herd of passive cows, unable to see them clearly in the thick smoke. I kept my eyes on the illuminated figure of my mother moving closer to Elba's pyre. The scene was becoming distorted as if in a dream. There was a golden halo around Ramona's head. Her lips were parted in a be-atific smile I recognized from a cheap print of Our Lady of Salud that hung above my parents' bed. Elba seemed to be swelling like a balloon, getting larger and larger every time she went over the fire. She hovered above the crowd, her gown billowing. I shook my head to clear it and tried breathing deeply, but that made my condition worse since the air by now had very little oxygen. All around me people swayed in concentric circles, each chanting his or her own prayer. In the background African music played in a rising crescendo of drums. Elba called each person up by name, her eyes closed in a trance. I was close enough to touch my mother when I heard a crash in the back of the room where I had left Guzmán trying to pry open the window. It was the sound of glass shattering, so I figured he had re-sorted to a drastic method of getting some air into the room. What followed was chaos.

Startled out of their smoke-induced lethargy, people screamed. I grabbed my mother's arm and began dragging her toward the door. As I passed in front of the dais, I saw an old woman swaying in the light of the flaming pail, her face distorted by fear and confusion, trying to grasp Blanquita's arm. She had obviously been next in line for the despojo and now didn't know where to turn, for as the smoke was sucked out of the room through the broken window in the back, people were pushing in every direction like a herd of cattle frightened by a shotgun blast. I saw Blanquita shove the old woman toward Elba, who was calling for everyone to calm down.

What ensued was not clear, but Ramona, dazed as she was, managed to reverse the situation so that it was she dragging me out of the room. I thought I saw Elba tripping over the pail of flames as the old lady fell into her arms. There were screams as the lighter fluid spread around the plywood platform, which caught on fire immediately. The last thing I saw as Ramona literally pushed and clawed her way through the hysterical mob with me in tow was Elba rising from the flames like a great black bird, her dress on fire, her arms raised as if still trying to bless the people. Her face was a mask of agony.

I screamed hysterically. What came from my throat as we reached the hallway was my uncle's name. Ramona was telling me something I couldn't hear over my own screams. She slapped my face hard and shook me by the shoulders. She was telling me to run outside and call the fire department. That she was going to get Gabriel. At that moment what seemed like an army of policemen began trooping up the stairs and forcefully dragging people out of the apartment. Everyone in the hallway went first. I saw my tiny mother fighting like a wild animal as a burly black man picked her up in his arms like a child. She screamed my brother's name with such anguish that her voice went right through my heart like a knife. I calmed myself enough to get the attention of the man who was shoving me down the stairs:

"Officer, please, listen to me." He pushed me hard and I fell two or three steps. I could still hear my mother's screams. The heat was becoming unbearable. I flattened myself against the wall and yelled out to the man standing like a blue giant over me, getting ready to pick me up in his arms.

"My brother is sleeping in the apartment upstairs. Five-B, he's in five-B! Go get him please!"

The policeman—I remember him clearly, a middle-aged man with thinning red hair and very light blue eyes—looked at me kindly before he gently lifted me up in his arms. He spoke into my ear, for the screams of the people plunging headlong down the stairwell were deafening:

"There are many people still up in those apartments, girl. The fire department is on its way. They'll get your brother out." I went limp in his arms. I must have passed out. When I came to I was lying on the sidewalk across the street from El Building. Ramona was standing over me, her dress was torn in several places, and she was barefoot. She was screaming at a man in a suit. She was saying in Spanish that she was going into the building for her little son. He was yelling back that the building was being barricaded so the firemen could get to it. I saw the badge on his lapel. I pulled myself up calling out to my mother. She ran to me and hugged me fiercely.

"Tell this man to let me get my boy, Marisol, tell this man to let us get Gabriel, *por Dios, por Dios.*" I held her trembling body for a minute, but when we turned the detective was gone and a circle of uniformed policemen were protecting a barricade around El Building, which by this time was spewing flames from several open windows.

Ramona fell to her knees and looked up in the direction of our apartment, which was on the floor above Elba's.

I sat on the sidewalk next to her. I thought of my brother asleep on my bed, not knowing that flames were licking the floor and would soon plunge him into a hell like the kind we heard about in catechism class: "the other place," as the nuns called it. And Guzmán, where was he? Had he gotten caught in the back of Elba's living room doing what I had asked him to do?

The hysteria around us was rising. People were screaming out the names of children, wives, husbands, neighbors, still inside El Building. Many were trying to break through the police barricade. Fire trucks screamed up to our block, caped men clinging to their sides. They set up their long ladders and began pulling people out of windows. They were like rag dolls being dragged out of a dusty toy bin in their colorful costumes now torn and smudged. These were the lucky ones who had gotten to a fire escape in a hallway. From where we were, I could see that the fire had spread to other apartments on Elba's floor.

Though I surveyed the whole scene in my daze, my eyes kept turning to the floor above Elba's and to the right—our apartment. What did I expect? For Superman to fly up to our kitchen window and rescue Gabriel? I don't know, but I prayed. I held my mother's head to my knees feeling the vibration of her screams on my skin, keeping her from collapsing on the concrete pavement, and I prayed every prayer the nuns of Saint Jerome's had taught us.

Out of the front door of El Building, out of its windows, down rusty fire escapes, came forth the people who not long ago were pretending they had guardian spirits, who thought they had some control over their lives, now vanquished, doleful as children caught in a forbidden game— pathetic in their absurd costumes. They held on to one another and wailed. *Ay Bendito, Ay Bendito,* they said over and over, as if reduced to this half-whine, half-blessing, invoking and blaming the Savior all at once. I saw José, the man who had stabbed Guzmán, carried out in the arms of a fireman like a skinny child. Guzmán had not pressed charges after the knifing. Why? I guessed it involved the red-headed woman. I saw Blanquita walking calmly down a fire escape, refusing to be assisted. I saw her walk away from El Building like a ghost in her white dress, not looking back. I saw Santiago, his arms and face blackened by soot, yelling out directions to his men, working side by side with the policemen who had been his persecutors and enemies. I ran to the barricade and called out to him at the top of my voice. I thought if I could let him know that Gabriel was trapped in our place, he would try to get to him. Ramona got to her feet and joined me there, but the noise of the crowd, the sirens, the men shouting orders, drowned us out. Santiago did not hear us.

Both Ramona and I looked up at the same time and saw that the flames had reached our floor. There were shouts of "Move back, move back!" as the firemen brought their ladders and hoses away from the left side of the structure which was being lost as the fire consumed one floor and then another. Ramona and I held each other. Ambulances were arriving and the injured were loaded in. For the first time that evening I thought of my father. Nothing and no one would have been able to stop him from going in for Gabriel—I knew this with a terrible certainty. I felt rage at our helplessness. At that moment there was a loud crashing sound and through the smoke I saw a scene that left me stunned. I shook my head and rubbed my eyes, hoping that I was not just conjuring this up out of desperation. The noise had been the ancient fire escape at the window in our floor's hallway sliding down to the pavement. Immediately men ran to it with hoses, for the iron steps were red hot. I shook my mother:

"Look! Look! Oh God, look!"

Coming down the steps with Gabriel bundled up in a black cape in his arms was Guzmán. In order to keep his balance he was miraculously holding on to the red-hot rails. I could see the steam rising as the water hit the metal. How could he stand the pain? A fireman made his way slowly up to them, reaching them one level above the street. He took Gabriel from Guzmán's arms. Guzmán collapsed where he was. Both Ramona and I screamed his name, frantically crawling under the barricade but unable to get past the policeman who guarded it. He held us back each by an arm. We saw the fireman holding Gabriel hand him down to Santiago, and go back for my uncle.

Somehow Ramona pried herself loose from the policeman's grasp and ran to get Gabriel from Santiago. He seemed shaken but stood on his own as Ramona held him to her. He even waved at me behind her back with a patient look on his smudged face. When she removed the black raincoat that he was wrapped in, books and papers fell out. Gabriel had managed to save his homework and Rafael's *Popular Mechanics* magazines. I noted all this in the brief moment before my eyes returned to the fire escape. Two men were carefully holding Guzmán's limp figure between them. To my horror I saw the growing red stain on his shirt. As calmly as I could, I explained to the man holding my arm that I needed to join my family. He spoke in his walkie-talkie, then escorted me to my mother's side. Convinced that Gabriel was all right, she too was watching as Guzmán was handed down like a corpse into the waiting arms of medics who placed him on a stretcher. Santiago came over to us.

"Are you all right?" he asked in a weary voice. He had

actually gone back into El Building several times before the firemen took over, and I could see that his hair was singed. His face was red and raw looking, and though he was now wearing a fireman's asbestos suit I could see that underneath, his clothes had holes where sparks had burned through. We assured him that we were fine.

"You'd better take this boy in to the emergency room anyway. Get them to check him for smoke inhalation." Then he pointed to where Guzmán was being strapped into a stretcher. "He is in bad shape. It looks like his knife wound opened up. Somebody better ride with him to the hospital."

"I'll go," I said immediately.

"He's my brother," Ramona's voice was just this side of hysteria, "I'll go. We'll all go," and she held us to her so tightly that Gabriel moaned. For once, I felt only comfort in the pain of her strong fingers digging into my flesh.

Chapter Twelve

I F THE PLACE you live in is destroyed in a fire, your priorities arrange themselves before you as a checklist, with the corresponding emotional reaction like a dictionary definition following. The lives of your loved ones come first, with hysteria or terror prescribed by your brain now functioning under stress; once they are safe, then comes concern for possessions, accompanied by regret for their loss and anxiety over the need to replace them—the need for survival leads to the immediate desire to find a substitute shelter. The aftermath of all this activity seems to be a morbid dwelling on the idea that you were singled out for punishment. All this I realized while watching Ramona go through her paces during the first few days after the fire at El Building.

The first few days after the three of us had ridden in the ambulance with Guzmán to the hospital, we stayed in a shelter provided by the Red Cross. We had used the same phone number that I had memorized during the Cuban crisis in trying to locate my father, and the nice lady with the gentle voice and persistently patronizing manner came to our rescue. We were first taken to the basement of their headquarters, where cots had been set up for providing temporary shelter. But when it became evident that it would take days to fly Rafael home, since he was somewhere in the middle of the Atlantic ocean on a ship heading for England, they moved us to a hotel in downtown Paterson. From there we could walk to Saint Joseph's Hospital, where Guzmán was being treated for smoke inhalation, minor burns, and an infected wound that would have to be cut open and sewn back together again like a ragged tear on a garment.

Once again I found myself in the role of interpreter of the world for my mother who, after all these years, still believed that it operated like an extended family: in times of need or tragedy people naturally came to your rescue. She never quite understood why I had to make ten phone calls before we got an appointment with the man from the navy office; she shook her head in disbelief when she was told it would be days before the paperwork was completed and Rafael could come home. I told her where to sign and answered most questions without consulting her. I learned something during those days: though I would always carry my Island heritage on my back like a snail, I belonged in the world of phones, offices, concrete buildings, and the English language. I felt truly victorious when I understood the hidden motives in my conversations with adults, when they suddenly saw that I understood. Their acknowledgment of my insight was usually accompanied by either irritation at my presumptuousness or a new tone of respect in their voices.

The lady from the Red Cross office was very curious about the fire at El Building, and on the day when we were to move out of the Red Cross shelter to the hotel she asked me to come to her office alone.

"Honey, how did this happen? Every time we ask one of the residents, we get a different answer." She smiled her volunteer smile at me, the one that said *I am here out of the goodness of my heart to help the unfortunate and inferior.* I had learned to recognize this smile earlier in my life when

273

for weeks we had tried desperately to get news of Rafael. It was a pleasant smile that also warned: *Don't ask for too much, or you'll get nothing.*

"Sit down, please, María."

"It's Marisol," I said politely.

"Pardon?" Still smiling, she pointed to a chair in front of her desk. Her name was Mrs. Pink, and there were objects in her office that paid tribute to her favorite color, such as the oil painting of pink roses that hung behind her desk. The walls were a pale rose, and there was a paddle hanging from a hook on the wall that had been painted pink and there was a pink bow wrapped around its handle. Mrs. Pink saw me looking at the paddle. "I am a retired teacher," she said with apparent pride. "Won't you sit down, María?" Her smile was fading as I continued to stand in front of her desk as if I had not heard her. She looked at me sternly. "Do you know what caused the fire? I understand there was a wild party going on in the tenement building where you and your family resided. Is it true?"

"I know nothing about it, ma'am. I think it was an accident that caused the fire." I spoke with my eyes lowered, my arms at my side, my feet together, in the posture of respectful attention taught to us by the nuns at Saint Jerome's.

"There were dozens of people drinking and carrying on like they do in a tenement building where the walls are thin as paper, and you didn't hear anything? You didn't know there was a party going on right next door? You look like a smart girl to me. You know there is going to be a big investigation. Is there something you are hiding? Remember we are here to help you."

Through my lowered lids I saw that she had put on the smile again. Her tone of voice, which had turned hard when I had refused to acknowledge her order to sit down,

274

was once again condescending. I knew that her questions were nothing but curiosity about us and El Building. She was just a woman with time on her hands and had no right to insult me with her questions.

"I'm sorry, Mrs. Pink, but I have told you what I know. We are very grateful for your help, and when my father comes home I will tell him to come to see you. I'm certain he will be able to answer your questions after he speaks with my mother. I will tell him that you are investigating the fire."

Mrs. Pink got up from her chair so abruptly that a little stack of pink memo papers fell off, scattering all over the floor. She ignored it. I kept my eyes down.

"There is no need to tell anyone about our conversation. I just wanted to know a little more about your case so I can help you better. Here is the address of the hotel where you will stay until further notice." Flustered, she looked on her desk for the slip of paper, but apparently it had gotten mixed up with the mess on the floor.

Her face flushed an angry red, Mrs. Pink got down on her knees and gathered the wildly strewn notepaper, throwing it on her desk with an angry slap. "The truth will come out, that is all I've got to say," she mumbled as she dug through the pile. "One big eyesore removed in one fell swoop." She continued to mumble as if she had forgotten my presence while involved in her frantic little search. I had noticed teachers did that to children. It was as if they could shut us completely out of their perceptions for minutes at a time.

Finally, she looked up at me. "Don't you have some packing to do?" she said, as if offended that I was still there. "I know where to find you when I'm ready."

I don't know if she saw how my face struggled to remain impassive. I felt like laughing hysterically at this foolish woman. Pack? No, we didn't have much packing to do unless you counted the magazines Gabriel had salvaged in his terror and to which he clung these days as if they were his torn, smelly security blanket. He wanted to give them back to Rafael himself. And the nuns of Saint Jerome's had come through with clothing and coats straight from the homes of my tall classmates. Ramona and I looked more than ever like gypsies in our long skirts.

From the hotel we walked the few blocks to the hospital to see Guzmán. He was in a ward with five or six other men, and I could see that this made Ramona very uncomfortable. I encouraged her to sit in the waiting room and to read her Spanish romance novels or crochet while I visited with her brother. Gabriel had chosen to go back to school, though his teachers had volunteered to help us make up the work we missed. They understood that my mother needed my services as interpreter until Rafael arrived.

Guzmán had lost a lot of weight and looked like one of those South American children who appear in posters advertising their hunger and their need. At the Red Cross shelter, I had awakened in the night to look into those famished eyes staring down from the wall above my cot. I felt I had joined their club. Not a large man to begin with, Guzmán had now shrunk to the size of a twelve-year-old— either that or I had grown. Standing next to his bed, I felt that if necessary I could lift him and carry him. His dark eyes seemed immense in his cadaverous face. Pity overwhelmed me. He forced a smile pointing to the chair next to his bed.

"Is there anything I can get you? Anything you need?" I heard my new efficient voice with some surprise. But I felt that I could do anything he asked.

276

Very slowly Guzmán reached his hand to the night table next to his bed, but could not manage to pull the drawer out. I quickly laid my hand over his and pulled with him. He sighed deeply as he fell back on the pillows. He pointed to the drawer. "There is a wallet in there, and a bank book. Get them out for me."

"Anything else?" I did as he told me, laying the two items gently by his hand on the bed.

"That is all I need for now. Come closer, Marisol, I'm going to ask you to do something important for me."

I pulled my chair as close to the head of his bed as possible, and, leaning down to hear his weak voice better, I listened while Guzmán explained to me that he wanted to withdraw all his money from a bank in Paterson. He was going to call them and tell them that they were to give me or Ramona the money. As proof that I was his representative he provided me with all his identifying documents and a note (which I wrote in English, and he copied). Once I got the money I was to buy money orders with it and bring them to Guzmán. He did not explain what it was all about, and I did not want to ask, thinking that it was a sign of maturity not to question people when they asked you to do a favor. But I couldn't help saying something that I knew would lead to some kind of clarification:

"Your money will be safer in the bank, Guzmán. Are you sure you want it lying around while you're in the hospital?"

He turned to look at me. On his lips there was the hint of an amused smile. Even in his suffering he could read me better than anyone.

"I will tell you my plan after you finish this part of your mission." He touched my fingers with his. He was obviously exhausted. He allowed me to smooth the bed cov-

277

ers around him. I felt like bursting into tears when I saw the outline of his thin body with the thick bandage on his side.

"I'll be back tomorrow morning with the money." He didn't hear me. His eyes were closed.

ARRIVING BACK at the hotel Ramona and I were surprised to find Gabriel's schoolbooks thrown all over the floor. It wasn't time for him to be back; in fact, his bus was not due for another hour. Ramona, whose emotions were barely under control since the fire, burst into hysterical tears. Something had surely gone wrong. What would she tell Rafael? Her self-recriminations and tears made me feel resolute. I was about to dial the school's number to begin the process that I had by now mastered: putting into practice what I had learned about dealing with the world through words, persuasions, politely phrased threats.

Then the door burst open and Gabriel ran in shouting excitedly. His grin told us it was good news, whatever it was, though his words came out confused in his excitement. Rafael walked calmly in after my brother. He was wearing his white navy uniform and cap. For the first time in my life I felt a sense of relief at the sight of my father. His serious face, his immaculate appearance, brought light into the dim room that was our refuge. His voice was low and his words measured as he greeted Ramona, who threw her arms around him, still weeping. Gabriel held on to his hand as if glued to it. I stood by the phone waiting for my turn, but I meant it when I said to him as he kissed my cheek:

"I'm glad you're home, Father."

IT WAS OBVIOUS by the new humble posture Ramona had fallen into, her easy tears and long silences, that there were many matters to be resolved between my parents. Rafael treated all three of us delicately, as if he feared we would break into pieces before his eyes. He and Ramona whispered to each other late into the night in the bed just a few feet from the one I shared with Gabriel. What I could hear from their intense conversations told me that our lives would never be the same. Rafael cursed El Building and its inhabitants, and Ramona wept quietly on and on for the friends she had lost: Elba was dead, the last to be taken out of the blazing shell that El Building had so quickly become; Santiago was fighting for his life in the hospital after rushing in to bring out a child whose mother had left him sleeping alone in their apartment while she went out. No one had known he was there until she came home screaming for her boy during the last stages of the fire. So many others were hurt, left out in the cold streets of Paterson with nothing but the silly costumes they had been wearing that night. What Ramona felt, what she wanted to be forgiven for, was her part in planning the meeting that led to the horrible disaster. Patiently, Rafael explained that she could not have known what would happen that night, but he also reminded her that she should never have left us alone. At the thought of what could have happened to Gabriel she sobbed so pitifully that in my bed, under my blankets, I also cried for the ones who had not been as lucky as we.

The day after he arrived, Rafael met alone with Guzmán for a long while. Then he told us what my uncle had decided. He wanted to go back to the Island as soon as he was discharged from the hospital. He had asked if Ramona could accompany him there. Rafael thought that this was a good idea. Easter vacation was coming up and he had decided to spend his month's leave looking for a house to buy. Ramona did not say anything. She seemed too sad for

279

words these days. Not even the thought of seeing Mamá Cielo and Papá Pepe after all these years seemed to excite her. Knowing how she had resisted the idea of a house in the suburbs, I felt sorry for her.

"Guzmán asked me to take all his money out of the bank," I volunteered.

"I will take care of that now, Marisol." Rafael looked at Ramona kindly. "Part of that money is for Ramona. Your uncle wants her to buy herself some clothes and presents for the family." He looked at her expectantly, but she had nothing to say.

RAFAEL was like a golden angel whose presence assuaged our fears and brought hope for our future. Though his silences were as deep as ever, we fell into their rhythm in the enforced closeness of that hotel room, where even our breathing was audible. Ramona's grief had now settled into a quiet state of melancholy. It was a *tristeza* that she would hold barely at bay for the rest of her life. The destruction of El Building had been her initiation, her rite of passage, and she was slowly accepting the fact that life would never be the same.

After the Easter holiday, I went back to Saint Jerome's, where I was treated with kindness by the nuns and my classmates. The parish raised money to help those left homeless by the fire, and since Gabriel and I were the only students to have been directly affected, we were the beneficiaries of Catholic hospitality, which left us perhaps richer in necessities such as clothing and household items than we had been before. The nuns collected and stored every contribution, while one of the priests advised Rafael about real estate. In the meantime, Guzmán recovered from his ailments and wounds as much as he ever would and was discharged from the hospital. We all went to pick him up in a rented car.

I had to stifle a gasp when I first saw him out of bed. He was dressed in his favorite black, but he looked lost in his garments—a little boy, or a wizened old man in pants that were two inches too long, and a shirt whose winged collar swallowed his neck. He visibly leaned toward the side of his knife wound. It was this posture and all the weight he had lost that made him look so small. I saw Ramona's eyes mist over when she looked at him, and I prayed that she would not cry in front of him.

Rafael put his arm around Guzmán's shoulders and they walked slowly down the hall. The dark and the light. Their heads close together, they talked. I couldn't hear what they were saying, but I could imagine them together as boys, planning to sneak up to the American's Big House. I could see them whispering like this on the banks of the Red River where La Cabra lived. I saw them holding up old dying Don Juan Santacruz between them, and saying goodbye early that morning when Guzmán took the bus to the airport, when they had parted, not to see each other for the next fifteen years—my lifetime.

GUZMÁN had insisted on taking a plane to Puerto Rico with Ramona on the same day he was discharged from the hospital. We drove to New York on that bright early spring day. The two men sat in front, and Ramona sat between Gabriel and me in the back seat. Surprisingly, she did not give us endless instructions and warnings, though she would be away for almost a month. She drew Gabriel tightly to her, and held my hand in hers. I felt her trembling. When we neared the terminal she turned to me and said simply, "Take care of your brother as if he were your child." I assured her that I would.

Watching Guzmán climb the steps into the Pan Am jet with Ramona close behind him, I felt a strange sense of nostalgia. It wasn't sadness really—I was still young enough to be excited by the prospect of moving into a real house, of starting a whole new life, but I think I would have liked to have been the one to take Guzmán back to the Island. In my mind I had made his life story mine. I had kept track of him through my mother's stories, Mamá Cielo's letters, and all those late-night conversations I had stolen from my parents when they thought I was sleeping in my room. I had filled the gaps with my imagination until Guzmán had shown up at our door; then I had become his secret biographer, drawing excitement from all he represented to me.

This broken man taking one step at a time into the belly of the airplane had little to do with the wild boy I had created in my imagination, but I loved him too. He was a good man and brave, even if finally not the hero of my myth. In a way I was glad that he would no longer be around to confuse me. He and El Building would be gone but not forgotten.

We waved to them from the terminal as they turned to look back before they entered the plane. They waved too, but I don't think they could see us from that distance.

IN THE NEXT FEW WEEKS our world changed completely. Rafael, Gabriel and I entered the land of suburbia, first as tourists guided from house to house by cautious real estate agents who were obviously concerned about introducing the first Puerto Rican family into the middle-class Italian neighborhoods which they seemed to think were the best compromise. Rafael's navy uniform and his credit references calmed their fears, though, and soon we found ourselves committed to buy a little house in West Paterson. It was surrounded by a yard already turning green. It had an attic set up as a child's bedroom that I fell in love with for its privacy and for the desk built into the wall where a window faced an oak tree that would also belong to us. At present the tree was still mostly bare, its gnarled branches scraping the window panes like the hands of an old woman.

The day we decided on the house, I went up to this room I had already decided was mine, only to find Gabriel surveying it for his own purposes. It was late in the afternoon, and since there was no electricity, the room was soon in shadows. I pointed out the tree to my brother, showing him how the bony fingers of the witch came into the room as shadows. I dug into my memory for all the fairy tales I had consumed and made up for him the ultimate tale of darkness, and concluded with a rhetorical question: "Why do you think the previous owners of this house were trying so hard to get rid of it?"

By the time Rafael came up the stairs to tell us that we would be in this house before Ramona got back from the Island, Gabriel was more than eager to announce that he had chosen the little room across from the master bedroom as his. I was, of course, a little ashamed of what I had contrived to do, but in the years that followed, as I sat at the desk facing that window, watching the long arms of the witch change from brown to green to gold with the seasons, I knew that I had only done what I was destined to do all my life—I would always trade my stories for what I wanted out of life.

WHEN RAMONA CAME HOME, it was really spring. Rafael had used all of his leave time to set up the house for her. He had bought furniture and appliances on the installment plan, and he had given me the job of paying the bills so that Ramona could enjoy her new life in the suburbs without worry. With the help of a Sears catalogue, we had color-coordinated everything: curtains, sheets, throw rugs, and cushions matched in the best middle-class American taste. Though it was a pleasure for me to set up this house in the soothing hues that appealed to my father and to me, I had a feeling that Ramona would feel like a stranger in it. Where were her plaster saints, the ones who got her through the lonely, difficult times when Rafael was at sea? What about the brilliant reds and greens and yellows that reminded her of her lost Island paradise?

So it was with mixed feelings that I dusted and polished everything and opened windows and yelled unnecessarily at Gabriel to keep himself clean on the day Mother came home. Rafael pulled up in the driveway in the rented car, and when she stepped out, I could see that she was darker, her cinnamon skin several shades deeper. The white embroidered dress she wore accentuated her brown arms. I knew before she told me that it was Mamá Cielo's handiwork—I had heard about the old lady's magic touch with a needle all of my life. Ramona's long black hair gleamed in the cool white sunlight of the spring day. She wore sandals and carried a shopping bag. To our neighbors (and all of the years we lived there I always felt that their eyes were upon us) she must have looked like a new immigrant. Though she was lovelier than ever, it hurt me to see how easily Ramona had given herself back to the Island.

Though she smiled during the tour of the house, holding Gabriel's hand tightly as he chattered nonstop about his plans for a treehouse he would build in the summer and about his new friends in the neighborhood, there were no loud exclamations of joy like I had heard at the slightest provocation when we lived in El Building. She smiled and smiled, but she did not make plans with the rest of us. Since then I have confirmed this fact about human nature: that to live fully in the present your mind has to be always focused on tomorrow; happiness is the ability to imagine something better for yourself. Ramona's dreams of going back in style to her homeland had been her way of dealing with the drab reality of everyday life in a foreign land. Instead, she had lost what little she had and had come back from her real home to a place that threatened to imprison her. In this pretty little house, surrounded by silence, she would be the proverbial bird in a gilded cage.

IT WAS after Rafael left us again that my mother allowed me to approach her. She was lonely and fearful of life in a place where each house was an island, no sounds of life seeping through the walls, no sense of community. Even to go to the grocery store, you had to take a bus. I assured her that in a year I would be able to drive and that Rafael had promised me a car. I would take her anywhere she wanted to go.

"Across the ocean too?" She smiled at my confusion. "I mean, do you think there will ever be a bridge across the water to my Island?"

This was the opportunity I had been waiting for, a break in the ice wall she had surrounded herself with since her return.

"Mother, will you tell me what happened with Guzmán and Mamá Cielo when you got there?" We were in our little kitchen, which gleamed with a new range, a new table and chairs, new pots and pans. It was a Saturday, and Gabriel was in the backyard, planning his next project. Hammer, nails, and wood lay all around him—Rafael's last gift to him before he left for Brooklyn Navy Yard. Ramona poured us both a cup of coffee and sat down across from me. She took a deep breath and began her story.

Epilogue

Guzmán's story took a long time to tell; in fact, it is not, nor will it ever be, finished. My mother told me her story throughout the long, lonely first season of our newest exile. She told it leisurely through the summer when the fingers of the witch, scratching at my bedroom window, awakened me to the full moon, and I would hear Ramona walking around this house that she could never make hers. We would sit in the kitchen and drink coffee and talk about her Island and Guzmán. As if to encourage us to continue with our thousand and one nights, the letters from Mamá Cielo started coming in like installments in a biography. Ramona bequeathed all these letters to me years later when Rafael lost control of the car he was not used to driving, and by his death allowed her to return to her beloved Island.

In the years we lived in that house, though, Ramona became Penelope, weaving her stories into a rich tapestry while she waited for her sailor to come home. I held the threads for her. When she left—still the gypsy queen, though she had cut her hair and learned to dress in the more subtle colors of our life away from El Building—her grief over Rafael's death weighed her shoulders down like a heavy shawl, and she promised me that she would write her life for me in letters. I was a senior at the city college then, and Gabriel had just earned a scholarship to MIT after having exempted his senior year at Saint Jerome's High School. Our lives were decided.

In a trunk I kept at the foot of my bed I stored Guzmán's life—all the letters, the childish journals I had kept in the years after the fire at El Building; the pages written under the gaze of the witch at my bedroom window in our house in the suburbs. One day I would have the courage to put it all together, I thought: a puzzle that would reveal many things about my own life. Perhaps I would start the story in the present and go back, giving myself more and more freedom to invent ways of telling it. I would tell how Mamá Cielo took Guzmán back into her nest—her broken sparrow—and how she and Ramona had nursed him back to his feet. I would tell how soon Guzmán became a character in Salud, with his sideways gait and famous knife wound; how he spent his money at old Doña Amparo's bodega, now owned by the adulterer Luis, an old man still working on his bad reputation.

And I would tell what Ramona said, about the do-gooder, Sarita, who came to Mamá Cielo's house to pray for Guzmán, and left him in a trance. How he went crazy with desire for the woman who is said to look just like her mother, La Cabra, from whom no one had heard since she was run out of Salud by Doña Tina and her Rosary Society ladies. How Sarita was raised by nuns, under Doña Tina's guardianship, and now surpassed even Doña Tina herself in religious zealousness, having appointed herself the new guardian of Salud's morals. Ramona said that she had met Sarita, and that she was really as beautiful as everyone claimed but such a shrew and moralizer the town had never seen. When she was known to be in a neighborhood distributing catechisms to the children, Bibles to the old, and free advice to everyone else, people suddenly felt the need to lock their doors, something that was formerly

287

done in Salud only at night, and during times of sickness or tragedy. She was that unpopular. They say even the new priest—a young intellectual from Madrid who had finally replaced the senile Padre Gonzalo when the old priest could no longer remember what day of the week it was and said Sunday mass on Tuesday, failed to show up in church for confessions, or worse, fell asleep while listening to lists of sins—tried to regulate Sarita's missionary activities, but her tongue and her pious fire were too much for the timid, studious young man. After a while, he simply followed the town's example, leaving the rectory by the back door whenever he heard the young woman's sharp voice quoting Holy Scripture to the housekeeper at the front door.

They say Guzmán's arrival set off all of Sarita's missionary instincts like a fire alarm. Here was a man to save. Here was a man who was a legend in Salud for his past sins (though no one spoke of it in her presence, all assumed she knew about her mother, La Cabra, who had sent money to the nuns for Sarita without fail for the past fifteen years but whose whereabouts were a mystery). Here was the Prodigal Son come home broken in body and in soul, and she knew that it was at his weakest point that a sinner was likeliest to see the Truth.

They say that no sooner had Mamá Cielo, an old woman now but still strong, settled her son in her own four-poster bed, moving herself to a cot in the parlor so she could be near when he needed her, than Sarita appeared at the door armed with her Bible. Ramona claims that Guzmán was struck by the thunderbolt when he saw her, for no doubt about it, Sarita had her infamous mother's beauty, though not a speck of makeup enhanced anything the good Lord had given her, and the long-sleeved, severe blouses she

288

wore and the shapeless skirts and clunky shoes would have cancelled out a lesser body. But Sarita's voluptuous flesh could not be subordinated by mere cloth. Her radiant beauty was a burden to her. Her flashing dark eyes distracted the faithful from her holy words, the temple of her body drawing sinners to it for its awe-inspiring façade, like a heathen mosque. Guzmán's feverish gaze rested on the feminine form that he knew so well from his memories and his dreams. To him it was Rosa looking young and fresh, sitting next to his bed, talking and talking as she had when he lived with her in the enchanted valley. Mamá Cielo and Ramona attempted to put an end to his fantasy, but love is deaf as well as blind, and Guzmán's passion put him back on his feet faster than any medicine. His mother's pleas went unheeded once more.

They say that the zealot and the sinner made quite a strange pair in Salud. The whore's daughter, radiant in her conquest, and Guzmán, the wild boy who had come home from his world-wanderings, broken in body, the seventy-five-degree angle of his body reminding everybody of Franco El Loco, who had been laid to rest a few years ago in a pauper's grave. They say that Guzmán followed her in her missionary wanderings around Salud like a dog on an invisible leash, that he did not speak but was content to be near enough to Sarita to look at her. And as for her, many think that she saw him as sin personified, and like a good missionary she wanted to transform him. Of course, their mutual attraction being based on such precarious ground, the only thing they could do was to get married.

They say no one had seen Mamá Cielo get as angry as she did about anything since Guzmán left Salud so many years ago. Her curses shook the tin roofs in her neighborhood, driving the infirm Papá Pepe to Luis's bodega, where it was still possible for a man to find refuge. Mamá Cielo recalled La Cabra's specter from the grave of her memory, swore on it that she would never set foot in the town's church again (for it had engendered a different monster in Sarita), and once again banished her son from her house.

The wedding took place without Mamá's blessing, though the timid Papá Pepe was seen in the back of the crowded church invoking his own peculiar blessing on the strange couple. It was curiosity seekers who filled the church. Many people had known Guzmán as a child and wanted to see what the demon boy had become; others had heard of the scandal with La Cabra and were amused to see the story wrapped up so neatly. Some young girls had come to see the beautiful bride in her modest white dress and plain mantilla looking lovelier than any ordinary woman in satin and lace. The groom in his black suit standing crookedly at the altar stared at his bride throughout the ceremony. They say he looked *perdido,* so lost in his desire for this woman that it would be a long time before he awakened from his dream.

IN THE YEARS that followed I concluded that the only way to understand a life is to write it as a story, to fill in the blanks left by circumstance, lapses of memory, and failed communication. Guzmán's story did not end happily at the altar as all good fairy tales and love stories should. It continued through my mother's letters and in my imagination until one day I started writing it for him. And when I reached the part where he arrives with his beautiful new wife at La Cabra's valley, where a small white boat awaits them at the banks of the Red River to take them to the house that will be their love nest, when she makes him kneel down right there in the mud and swear to her that he will never sin again before she will go one step further into their new life, and when he actually kneels and swears for the hunger he feels in his heart—right at that point, when he and I tell our best lie, I say, this is the end.